Eight Vagabond Eight Vagabond Eight Vagabond

Can the Gods Cry?

by Allan Cameron

Vagabond Voices
Glasgow

First published in April 2011 by
Vagabond Voices Publishing Ltd.,
Glasgow,
Scotland

ISBN 978-1-908251-00-8

Printed and bound by Thomson Litho, East Kilbride

Cover design by Freight Design, Glasgow

The author and publisher acknowledge Creative Scotland's subsidy towards the writing of this work

For further information on Vagabond Voices, see the website, www.vagabondvoices.co.uk

For Margaret

And in memory of Desmond Walker, a veteran of the "unforgiving years" whose wife and children were killed in the Blitz but whose humanity was never extinguished

Contents

Can the Gods Cry?

The Narrative Voice, Litter, Dog Turds and Sundry Other Things Most Base and Foul

A young man, neat in his person and slender of build, closed the door of his parents' home behind him and set off for the late shift at a factory making garden sheds, one of the few things still manufactured in the post-industrial city. No doubt garden sheds are bulky and relatively low-cost, so even the exploited labour of a distant, supposedly communist state cannot provide, in this restricted market, for our consumer needs.

He picked his way across the crumpled crisp packets, dog turds, fag ends flattened underfoot and newspapers turned to papier-mâché by rainwater sticky with city dirt. It was a sweltering summer afternoon – and he was unused to such heat. By the time he reached the green, his head had started to spin, and sweat was pasting his shirt to his skin. He felt mildly unwell. A slight indisposition, he thought. Actually that is my word; he would never have said "indisposition", but I have no idea of what word he would have used, even though it is my job to know what words people use. "Indisposition" will do, as long as the boss agrees, and my current one is a right arse – one of those sickly pedantic creatures who make up for knowing nothing by constantly sticking their drippy noses into a dictionary or an encyclopaedia or a thesaurus or a God knows what.

The young man steadied himself against a tree and breathed in hard.

"Can I help you?" I said, munching on a crisp or two. "You're looking a little peaky, if you don't mind me saying."

He was still steadying himself and seemed to be having difficulty in focusing on me. Eventually, by which I mean after a period of at least two minutes, time enough for me to eat two more packets of crisps, he managed to enunciate a few words, "Who the hell are you?"

Now this was not as rude as it might seem, because I do cut a rather strange figure: I am enormous – all these crisps, I suppose – and I never feel the heat. Even on a day like that, I was dressed in a heavy pullover, corduroy trousers and a woolly nightcap with a bobble at the end. I have an obsession with matching clothes, so my red hat has a purple ball of wool at the end, my jumper has a red and purple check, and one trouser leg is red and the other purple.

"Would you stand still for a moment! Would you stop leaping about like a rabbit and talking to yourself in all those different voices!" he commanded in a weak, slightly pleading voice.

Actually this was not as rude as it might seem either, because I do have this habit of leaping around – bit of a tic really; you know, an uncontrollable, spasmodic, muscular convulsion. It's as though I can never stay on the same subject for more than a few seconds. But that's what they tell me to do: don't lecture people, they get bored, and you've got to entertain. You're not doing essays or histories or any of that fancy and well thought-out stuff; you're leaping around and keeping the attention of you-know-who.

"God, my head hurts," he said in a tired voice that suggested real suffering.

I stuffed a few more crisps into my mouth and said, "Would you like a crisp? They're pickled Worcestershire bacon with horseradish sauce – my favourite."

He just looked at me in disbelief, and didn't even thank me. So I started to cartwheel around the green, such is my *joie de vivre*, such my tireless energy. In my line of work, you've seen it all – after a bit, you've seen it all. You get very detached and just enjoy things. What else is there? Of course, I can moralise, if that's what they want of me. I can moralise as well as the next man, but there's no conviction – not in my line of work.

By the time I had cartwheeled my way round the entire green, right back to where I started, he was as white as a sheet. Sweat was pouring off his face, and he looked as though he was past caring. He glanced at me with an expression of complete bafflement; people can do that sometimes, so I don't take a great deal of notice. "Who the hell are you? How does a fat man like you leap so high and then cartwheel the green. It makes no sense... I said, who the hell are you?"

That last bit he said quite loudly, angrily even. So I decided to put him out of his misery: "I am..." I paused to increase the suspense – you learn how to do that in my line of business. "I am..."

"Come on, spit it out," he said grumpily.

"Well for starters, a lot of the academicians, the prescribers of good English don't like you doing that!"

"Doing what?"

"You know: loudly, angrily, grumpily – all those adverbs. They don't like them."

"What are you on about?"

"I'll have you know that I am the Narrative Voice."

"Away you go, you numpty."

I ignored this expression, which was clearly outside the realm of Standard English. An insult, of course. And not one that I was willing to let pass. "That's right. I'm the Narrative Voice and I'm telling a story about you."

"Me?"

"That's right, we live in democratic times – more's the pity – and so I no longer mix exclusively with the gods and godlike heroes. And this time I have got myself one of those writers who write stories with no story."

"Defeats the object."

"You can say that again."

"Plain speech?"

"Not this one. Says he doesn't like mimesis."

"What's that when it's at home?"

"Realism. Copying from life."

"What's wrong with that?"

"Nothing, as far as I'm concerned."

"And no story?"

"That's right. My remit is clearly stated in the contract. I am to describe your journey from the moment you left your home until you get round the corner."

"Round the corner? You're pulling my chain. You mean the corner just after the library?"

"The very same."

"That's not five hundred yards."

"Correct."

"And what happens after that?

"I'm afraid that's not the kind of thing I can divulge."

"Is that right? So you can't tell me what this writer fella has got in store for me? Nice one. I bet you can't tell me, because it's something bad."

"Not at all, but there are regulations that have to be adhered to in all circumstances."

"Really? Well, there's a council regulation about not throwing your empty crisp packets on the green or any-where else."

I chortled politely and then cruelly gave him one of my withering stares to remind him of who was in the stronger position. "By the way, what's your name?"

"Tom… Tom Cunningham. Why do you want to know?"

"I don't, but I need to let the readers know. It'll help them tie things up much later in the book."

"Do I have a good part then?"

"Not really."

"What's the book called?

"*Do the Gods Cry?*"

"Who's the author?"

"You won't have heard of him. He's back at his desk, chewing his pen and fretting like the fool he is. As writers like him are more attached to ideas than genuine emotion, he gives himself great airs and struts around declaiming great chunks of poetry – mostly his own – and claiming that he has no sense of who or what we are and his god has died."

"*His* God no less"

"Indeed, the arrogance of the literary type. *Poseurs!*"

"Posers, you mean?"

"Sorry about that, he – the man chewing his pen and reciting poetry – is having a bad influence on me."

"And who is this god who's died? This god he holds so dear?"

"The god of compassion. That's intellectuals for you. Society moves an inch and they think it has moved a mile. To my mind, there was only ever a trickle of compassion, and if it's changed, it hasn't changed that much. Besides, if God does exist, He exists beyond time and doesn't change with every passing fad."

"A wee bit off his head, is he?"

"No more than any other writer I've worked for. He doesn't know whether gods exist, but he says they are definitely real."

"So he talks in riddles?"

"Well, they like that sort of thing. They like to sound profound. Deep voice, gravitas and long pauses between words, and then they get me to do all the work," I said and then did a few cartwheels to distract him. "Sure you don't want a crisp?" were my first words when I suddenly popped back up in front of him, giving him a little start. "Madras curry with organic coriander. Not at all bad."

He declined with a slight move of his hand, which seemed to tire him.

"Suit yourself," I said with just the right dose of "See-if-I-care" affectation of having taken offence. I drove this point home by consuming five packets of the stuff noisily with a great display of the pleasure it gave me. He stood in silence, almost absent. As he refused to be riled, I returned

15

to our previous subject, "You see, the writer claims that gods keep human beings together. They may be mere constructs of the human brain – who knows? – but they affect people's actions and that is real enough. Warrior tribes have warrior gods, peasants have gods of fertility and good harvests, and these gods tell them how to cooperate. Even the nineteenth-century atheists had a kind of god – an anti-god, if you like – who was a gap on the wall where a picture has been removed or a broken statue. A god whose presence was his absence, but what have we got now?"

"We're to think things out for ourselves, I would say."

"But do you? Do you really?" I took out another packet of crisps and looked as though I cared. "Look around you. Listen to the words we use? Are we really a more thoughtful society than we were before?"

"Who knows? I've never lived in any other. What's this writer fella like anyway?"

"He lives in a shack at the top of a mountain in Sutherland and talks to the birds."

"A recluse."

"That's it. Writers say they need peace to meditate and develop their arguments. Such fragile beings."

"And that's what he came up with after all this peaceful meditation: the gods not crying? I hope he didn't get an Arts Council grant."

"I'm afraid he did."

"I'm not sure I'll read it – his book, I mean."

"Well, as he recently said to his daughter…"

"His daughter? He has children?

"Yes, he lives with his wife and fourteen children in a converted Presbyterian church in Achnabotail and suffers from alcoholism. Writers always have this idea that they have to live life to the full and drink themselves to death. They say it helps their creativity."

"Fourteen children? I thought you said that he lived on his own."

"Did I? Listen, the author is of no importance. Who cares about the author and his biography? There's too much of that crap, these days. Plastered over the back cover as though anybody gives a damn. A writer's biography is always going to disappoint. The only important people are me of course, you the character and the reader, and God knows who she is, poor bastard."

"I'm not a character!"

"Oh yes you are, if I'm putting words into your mouth – I can do that," I drew myself up to my full height.

"God, what am I doing here? I should be off to work. None of this makes any sense."

"Why this hankering? – this crazy hankering for making sense of things. I'm in the business of making people not understand things they thought they understood very well."

"A contrarian?"

"Yes, yes, a contrarian. Well done. That is the right word."

"Well, you can be a contrarian without telling silly stories."

"That's true," I had to admit.

"So, you'll let me get on with my day," he almost sneered, conscious of his little victory.

"Go on then! Who's stopping you? That's how people live now – all TV and Internet. You have a chance to know about not just any book, but a book about you. Even a philistine like yourself should be interested in that."

Predictably he stopped and turned again. "I do read," he said. "I read a lot."

"Yeah? Like what?"

"Everything: fiction, non-fiction, thrillers, detectives, politics, literature. Anything that comes my way. Why else would I be hallucinating about a narrative voice?"

"Hallucinating indeed." I leapt up and down, half in anger this time, and then, calming down I removed my nightcap and studied it. "Listen to the tinkling sound."

He came close and concentrated on listening. "There is no tinkling sound."

"Exactly."

He lost his patience and started to turn away.

"It's the new issue for narrative voices," I said entreatingly. "Just a woolly ball. No cluster of little brass bells. No tinkles," I looked up with a sense of something important to say. "It's all the fault of television. Those voiceovers they have, with their careful, actors' voices that hold your attention, they make readers feel inadequate. Everything is smooth, everything is presentation. What space is there for readers to feel they can invent their own voices in their heads and hear that tinkle?"

"Was there ever a time in which all narrative voices had a tinkle? Many I can think of had a rather moralistic tone and certainly no tinkles."

I felt a little offended; I had opened my heart and given away secrets, something that the authorities would not have approved of. I have been around for a long time; I was invented before feedback and interactive keys and buttons. "Any good narrative voice has to have a little fun: the tinkle might be ever so slight and even be drowned out by weightier matters, but it should always be there. The tinkle, you see, is in the background; often the most important things are. But now they've taken it away. Not a nuanced time we live in."

"You're looking a little sad, as though you've just remembered a beloved grandmother or the taste of apples when you were small. But narrative voices can't have childhoods, and I pity the author who gets stuck with you. They certainly took the tinkle out of your nightcap."

I found myself a bench, sat down heavily and started to weep.

Tom came over and put an arm around me. "I didn't know you were so sensitive. You seemed so full of yourself, so able to see everywhere and form an opinion on everything."

"Do you think this is an easy job: spouting off like a ventriloquist's dummy?"

"I'd no idea."

"All that omniscience and all that cruelty they make us inflict. Think of it." I turned and adopted a confidential manner. "Tom, do you believe in heaven and hell?"

"No."

"Why are you so sure?"

"Well, hell is absurd. What could anyone do to deserve an eternity of Auschwitz? What kind of religion comes up with that?"

"Interesting point. What about paradise?"

"Aren't they a pair? If you believe in one, you have to believe in them both."

I smiled because I knew something that he didn't know and that the reader doesn't know yet. It is such a pleasure for those in the know to smile at those who aren't.

"I've had enough of this. I'm off," he huffed.

I let him go, but followed along behind. Occasionally he staggered and once he turned round to look at me. He seemed upset to see me still there, bouncing along behind him. He tried to quicken his pace for a bit, but he was still poorly. He sunk back into his thoughts. At the corner where the library is, he decided to ignore the traffic lights with their green men and went to the edge of the pavement on the busier road. Someone who is utterly lost in his thoughts has no place in this world. He started to cross the road and ended up in another...

Aras and the Redistribution of Wealth

What a place to be, this Florence in the one-thousand-nine-hundred-and-seventy-third year of Our Lord. I can work for two months in a factory or as a waiter in a tourist restaurant, and earn enough to go without a job for one. Not a bad ratio that. And though the hours are long, you can get work and leave it easily enough. Take the last job I had: throwing the smallest bits of leather into a huge press – quick, damn quick or your fingers will be as thin as a postage stamp. I never quite understood what it did to the leather. Makes it softer and smoother they said, but you didn't have time to make the comparison, you just had to keep throwing them in and then getting them back, and all the time the huge German press just kept going at its own urgent rhythm. And all the time the old man who was working with me – Dario Chiappatopi was his name – was venting his spleen: "Are we so short of workers in Italy that we have to go and get some abroad? Of course not and some of our own boys still can't find exmployment." He was remarkably loquacious for a bigot; what was wrong with "Go home, you foreign scum!" He never worried me. In fact I rather liked him, and thought he might have a point. What am I doing in Florence? Can't be bothered to move on, I suppose. Why should I? It's not exactly cushy and you occasionally have to jump over a meal, as they say in Italy, but the company's good and the times exciting. I'm sure that not every age would have found such a benign Florence: I wouldn't have wanted to live here when those fanatical, finger-wagging, killjoy kids, the *piagnoni*, were running Savonarola's religious revolution during a few years of the last decade of the fifteenth century – a bit like those youthful Red Guards and Mao's Cultural Revolution, whose social hysteria has not entirely passed even now. No, Florence at the moment is not just as good as any other place; it is one of the best. The flood sent the *bien pensants* packing – for the moment at least – and it is a cosmopolitan little village of a city made up of students, foreign drifters, hardworking southerners with odd little businesses and the local lumpenproletariat which thrives on those petty and relatively innocuous crimes that blossom in a tourist town. Can you think of a nicer place to stay? I'm not talking about that moneyed cosmopolitanism that just makes everywhere look the same – InterContinental Hotels, dinner jackets and Anglo-American pop music – I'm talking about that old-fashioned cosmopolitanism that happens by some chaotic accident, and then just fades and fade it should. Nothing good ever lasts.

And what am I talking about? Dario Chiappatopi, of course. The leather factory was so good that I stayed for four months. The money on the factory floor was crap, but the owner would occasionally take me over to his office, and have me do a bit of correspondence in English, or even interpreting with visiting American buyers. Crafty bastard. Language services on the cheap, but he did pay me extra when I was there. So all in all, things were good, but Chiappatopi got it all wrong. Three weeks after leaving, I went back to the factory, drawn by an invisible thread of desire to the girl who works in the department where they glue and sew the various bits of the wallets and purses together. She turned me down. No surprise there. Why would a girl like her with a family, a culture and a network of friends want to hitch up with a ragged foreigner who can barely pay the rent for a shared room where the noise of the bars and the noise of the traffic mingle deliciously? Of course they make their own autonomous din, but together they find synergy: when people leave the bar, they leave slowly and this process usually involves sitting on a motorbike, scooter or moped, turning on the engine and occasionally opening the throttle as punctuation for a half-hour conversation before the eventual departure. There's a verb for it; there would have to be, and it's *sgasare*. The inventiveness of our languages: a word for aimlessly revving up and burdening the clear Mediterranean night with the howl of a mechanical beast.

I want to talk about Chiappatopi and keep getting distracted. But this story is not about Chiappatopi at all; it's actually about Aras and the redistribution of wealth, but I don't want to put you off. You might think that the redistribution of wealth is a not a fit subject. That's for economists and politicians, and has nothing to do with Aras, because Aras doesn't think along ideological lines with long words ending in "i-o-n"; he thinks in terms of right and wrong, which is very quaint, like the Geneva Convention. Anyway I went back to the factory and after getting the kiss-off from the nice girl with the tight faded jeans (and she did do it in the nicest possible way), I bumped into the foreman who greeted me like a long lost brother: "Garry," he said, "promise me this, never stop moving around the world, just keep on drifting, while we just rot in this rotten factory making wallets and purses for the tourists." This, of course, was from a guy who a few weeks earlier would have been complaining not too severely about my output. Now I had been promoted to "free spirit who shows us how to live, if only we had the courage", and of course I felt a fraud, because I have stopped travelling. I hardly ever go beyond the city limits, and when I do it is usually in someone's car on the way to one of those weekend parties in a *casa colonica* in just another pleasant valley surrounded by cypress trees and open fields. And then he told me about Dario Chiappatopi: it seems that the old man got angst-ridden over what he had said to me and thought that he had driven me away. "Not at all," I said. "I never stay long." "I know," replied the foreman respectfully, now I was no longer under his charge, "I know that very well." The old man wanted to contact me, but no one knew where I lived, not even in the office, as I was working without papers and the owner was paying me cash at the end of the week. I don't have a phone. And in the end Chiappatopi could take the guilt no longer and left the factory, even though everyone was calling me a drifter with the hide of a rhinoceros. He'll have come across a lot worse than that on his travels, they said. And they were right. How silly, he left for no reason at all. Besides I hadn't been listening. I had been concentrating on two very important things: keeping my fingers in their present form and marvelling at the beauty of the lady with the tight, faded jeans. I didn't have time for his mutterings.

But you have to admit that this Florence place is not at all bad. Even the xenophobes have half a conscience. That's called landing on your feet.

So maybe Aras is right. He's always singing the praises of this city. "I've lived in Paris and it's shit. Either you live in the ghetto or you have to put up with the racist French all day. Here even the police leave you alone." It does occur to me that it might not always be like this. Here in Florence, most foreigners have fat wallets and are just passing through. Here in Florence, Florentines are too busy feeling uncomfortable about all those other Italians who don't know how to speak Italian, cook a meal or run a country. The Northerners are always putting on airs and the Southerners – well, they're just Southerners. Who cares about the odd guest worker cleaning the windows and waiting in restaurants?

Aras and Krim are both short, wiry men with Mediterranean looks; they could easily be Sicilians, but equally they could come from almost anywhere in Europe. They are in fact Algerians, as is the third member of the group, Tufik, who is a tall handsome man with light brown skin, African features and a smile of friendly insouciance. But he is a Berber, which attracts a degree of ribbing, incredulity and admiration from his fellow countrymen. For me Tufik resembles the stereotyped portrayal of the genie in the lamp: strong, silent, a little inscrutable and glad that someone has finally released him from his millennial prison. For some months we have been sharing a dormitory, shall we call it – a room with nothing but a small wardrobe and four *reti*, as they call the utilitarian metal beds consisting of a metal mesh held in a metal frame with metal arches underneath to lift them slightly off the floor. To wash we have a basin in the same small room as the lavatory. They wash every day and are impeccably turned-out. I find the process of washing one part of the body at a time arduous and time-consuming; I am forever asking people for use of their shower, and when I succeed it is like a liberation.

Our common language is Italian, but they also speak French and Arabic incessantly, switching mid-sentence between one and the other. Tufik, they tell me, also speaks Berber, which seems to Aras and Krim like a defiance of history: "*They* were in Algeria before us." The prize possession in our room is Krim's ghetto-blaster, which only has two tapes to blast – both of them by Fabrizio d'André, who fortunately I like. Aras works in a *tavola calda* in Piazza Santa Maria Novella. It is at the back of an upmarket Sicilian restaurant, and uses its left-over food. When the owner wants to throw people out of his restaurant, he takes them out through the *tavola calda* rather than the main entrance. He does this very politely, using the extremely decorous form of address, *loro*. He moves them forward by agreeing with their angry remonstrations and at the same keeping up the momentum towards the street door. Once they are out, he turns, allows himself a sigh of contempt and then gathers himself together for the rest of the battle fought with solicitousness, measured smiles and the merest suggestion of menace.

That is one world I inhabit. It is spartan, friendly and reliable. It relies on mutual help and an ability to cohabit in a very small space. I am probably the least comfortable in it because I am the double foreigner: not Italian, not Algerian. But at the same time, I like my not belonging – or rather I want to belong to this new place, because what I am supposed to belong to does not attract me.

The other world I inhabit is the world of revolutionary politics, which is actually rather staid and takes itself too seriously. Its activity principally consists of attending demonstrations and the weekly meetings in the *sede*, the headquarters of the Revolutionary Communist Groups, Italian Section of the Fourth International. The headquarters are in fact an abandoned shop complete with shutter but very little else. Inside there is a desk, a dozen chairs (more than sufficient) and the clutter of left-wing politics: old leaflets no one can be bothered to chuck, banners often with wonderful slogans, placards of course, and various oddities which someone sometime thought might come in handy.

Our meetings are always more or less the same. They start with Eugenio, who sits behind the desk. Perhaps that is the purpose of the desk, because I have never seen anyone writing at it. He takes out a Gauloise and licks the length of it on one side. This strange gesture has always intrigued me and I think it's supposed to slow down the burning of the tobacco. He lights up, inhales, then looks at us fiercely and says, "Allora 'ompagni!" That is just, "Well, comrades!" but he aspirates the "c" forcefully in the manner of the Florentine working classes. For thirty years this former member of the Italian Communist Party has been working in one of the large industrial plants on the outskirts but not as a worker; he is in the sales department and travels the world. He has clear intelligent eyes, and can lead you on a wonderful path of logic and analysis towards the same inevitable truth: the imminent collapse of capitalism. His arguments might vary from one week to another, but the end result is unchanged. This speech, often delivered perfectly without notes, is then followed by open debate. I always feel tongue-tied because the excellence of his analysis appears wasted on us six or seven disparate members of his audience, many like me, just foreigners who have drifted in and will eventually drift out.

One is a Belgian woman, whose motives for living in Florence seem as elusive as my own: simply the joy of living in a place that is still itself and unselfconsciously beautiful, but for how long, no one can say. Every year the tourist buses find it more difficult to find a place to park in the cathedral square they clutter. Rents in the city centre are going up, although once a tenant, your rent is frozen. Those who have been renting from just after the war pay tuppence-ha'penny, and even those who have just started can still manage easily on a worker's pay, if they're willing to pile in. Michelle is perhaps just glad to be away from some damp industrial city of Flanders, and she is most earnest in her own tirades, which are as impenetrable as Eugenio's are compellingly lucid. This is not because of her heavy accent, although that does not help. She speaks in jargon and appears to have swallowed Trotsky's Transitional Programme and a do-it-yourself manual one after the other. Not that Michelle isn't attractive in her vehemence, and after Eugenio it is good to have a chance to switch off and enjoy her Gallic stylishness, which could place her in a chic restaurant if weren't for her heavy boots – whose function, I suspect, is to remove all doubts about where her political loyalties lie.

Another is Gaetano, a heavily built young man with a bushy beard whose strands he twists incessantly throughout the meeting as though he intends to plait them. He looks like a pirate and possibly wants to give that impression. His obsession is with partisan warfare as fought in the Second World War, and his contributions to the discussions always contain that evocative phrase, "...

when we go back into the mountains." At that stage I always imagine all six or seven of us clambering up the wooded slopes of the Apennines in military fatigues and carrying rusty machine guns. Michelle will be berating us for not walking fast enough and Gaetano will be telling us how they did it in 1944. I don't find the image very convincing – or attractive. Besides Eugenio would need lots of notice to arrange his holiday dates. Perhaps Gaetano's dreams take him up the mountain every night to fight his brutish father; not to fight him with difference, but to fight fire with fire, machine gun against machine gun and knife against knife. Hatred can do that and in his case, his machismo reflects that of the father he detests. A fascist gang attacked and beat him to a pulp, and he believes that his father sent them, because they ignored the comrade he was with. His father, everyone knows, is a powerful figure in the city and never abjured his fascist credo. Gaetano ended up in hospital for several weeks, and has never been the same since. Of course the rift cannot be healed now, and to us he says, "You are all my family now." Poor Gaetano.

Then there is Patrizia, a handsome, slightly masculine woman with leather jackets and military trousers. She is bright and well read, and her interests go far beyond her political activities. She and Pino are a couple. Pino too is an intellectual, but he has more flair for political discourse, negotiation and conspiracy, not so much against the state as against those who disagree with him within the "party". He has a quick, incisive sense of humour which he uses to good effect, particularly against Eugenio, and he is the only one to challenge the leader, who might never have been elected, because for as long as I have been around Eugenio has been in control and behind that desk. Pino believes that Eugenio is guilty of economic determinism. He might be right, but Eugenio does whatever he does superbly –

from the moment he licks a Gauloise and enunciates, "Allora, 'ompagni!"

Finally I should mention the most enigmatic figure of them all: Giancarlo. He is a tall youth with an already receding hairline, and the hair clearly allocated for early deforestation is of an anodyne brown. He speaks with a slight lisp and pronounces a French "r". He wears a tweed jacket or sometimes even a suit. He never says anything in the meetings, and always remembers what everyone else has said. He treats his comrades with an air of condescension and in some meetings likes to read Goethe in the original German, presumably to fend off the boredom. Goethe doesn't seem to impair his ability to remember our words and cast them up, usually with a sardonic grin. Some comrades, offended by his sarcasm, think he must be some kind of police spy. But what kind of police spy would so signally fail to fit in with the behaviour patterns of revolutionary life?

Today Aras and Krim are particularly excited. They have asked me if I would like to meet some Palestinians. Aras and Krim are not political, but they do follow events in the Holy Land. "You're probably not interested," they say questioningly – expecting me to support the Israelis. I certainly did, but I have become a little agnostic on this issue; there are so many conflicting versions. These are not just any Palestinians; these are young men who travel from city to city to speak to sympathisers, mainly Arabs as Palestine comes a long way behind Vietnam and Chile. Tufik is coming too, mainly for the company. He still wears his smiling features and talks of other matters. Aras and Krim are tense as though attending a presidential visit. They dress smartly and comb their hair, but the venue for this meeting turns out to be the cathedral steps. There are about fifteen people waiting and the two Palestinians arrive on time. They are self-confident young men with stubbly beards, keffiyehs and black leather jackets. Aras introduces me to one of them and we shake hands.

"England?" he says in English.

I nod, having long ago given up the specifics of where I come from.

"Do your parents have a house in England?"

"Yes, they do."

"What would you feel if people came in from another nation, took away your parents' home and just started to treat it as their own?"

I take this to be a metaphor: they have been thrown out of their native land – displaced. "In war people get displaced. They will get compensation."

"Compensation!" The idiocy of it makes him laugh, but good manners stop him short. "No, they don't pay compensation; they just throw you out, and either destroy the house or start to live in it. No compensation."

"I cannot believe that! That's rubbish. Jews would never do that."

"We've nothing against Jews, it's the Israelis," he pronounces the "a" and the "e" in the word Israeli separately, and the guttural tone seems to express all his anger. "We took in the Jews when they were escaping persecution in Europe. We have always respected them. You Europeans were the anti-Semites and you landed us with your problem, your inability to get on. We're paying for your crimes." He didn't flinch when I challenged him, called him a liar in so many words. That means, I think, that he is used to Europeans turning a deaf ear. "You're an intelligent young man," he says on the basis of absolutely no evidence at all, "and I think you'll discover one day that I am telling you the truth." Fortunately Aras and Krim don't understand English. Even if they did, they probably wouldn't hold it against me. They know Europeans. Europeans are stubborn. Peel away one layer of prejudice and you discover another underneath.

Pino comes to my door. I'm lying on my bed in the airless room on my own. I'm reading. Reading Federico Chabod's book on the factory occupations. When I see his face, I slip it under the *rete*. Chabod was a liberal. Eugenio would not approve. Pino probably doesn't care a damn, but you never can tell.

"We're going to meet a comrade from *Potere Operaio Linea Rossa*."

"Who the hell are they?" I raise an eyebrow and feel as though I'm going to be put upon.

"A split from *Potere Operaio*. We look on it as a positive move. A move in our direction. They're still a little spontaneist."

He spoke as though I had joined the Revolutionary Communist Groups after a careful study of all the programmes and dogmas of all the many, many left-wing organisations we have here, while in fact it was all due to a drinking bout at the bar on the corner opposite the Red Garter nightclub where I occasionally worked. That was when I first met Pino and Patrizia. My sympathies were already in that direction. I was ripe and they plucked me from the tree. Now they are telling me what to do.

I went to a disciplined school. I know how to take orders. I get up and am ready to go. Pino starts to brief me but it's not what interests me. Each sentence is unnecessarily oblique and seems to call for that Italian idiom: "We're four cats," meaning "What does all this matter, when we're few in number and barely have the resources to put out a badly typed and rather dogmatic leaflet each month." Still, it's a chance to stretch my legs. We cross Florence with a purposeful step, two revolution-aries pushing hard against the columns on which capitalism rests. We go through the centre of the city, the tourist area, past the *Duomo* which always delights and along the central drag where shoppers struggle with bags worth more than I earn in several weeks – months perhaps.

Just before the station we take a left and come to a very plain, post-war block of flats. Pino presses a bell and after a long wait and extended clatter as a receiver is lifted, we hear an uninviting voice through the intercom, "*Chi è?*" – Who is it?

"Pino."

"Who?"

"Pino Matozzo."

"Never heard of you."

"*Sì*," Pino's humiliation can be clearly heard in that one syllable, "you know – the Revolutionary Communist Groups."

"Of course, come in by all means," the voice does not do cordiality. The lock mechanism clicks and Pino pushes the door open. The dusty stairs made of metal railings and *graniglia*, as they call the heavy slabs of stone and marble chips in cement smoothed to a marble finish, could be found anywhere, but the sense of premature decay is unexpected. When we get to the apartment, the door is open but there is no one at it.

Pino is now rattled. He steps through the door uncertain that he has got the right one. "Anyone in?" he shouts foolishly.

"Sure. I'm in here."

"Here" is a spartan room, even by the standards of the circles I move in. It is large and contains just a wooden box and a dilapidated sofa, whose torn red fabric is covered with dark stains. There's no disorderly pile of left-wing newspapers, no poster of one or other member of the communist pantheon, no books at all, no flyers for radical theatre. From the sound of his aggressive voice, I was expecting a burly youth; what I find is a delicate little man of at least thirty. His ageing white skin contrasts with the dark hair of his wispy beard. He seems to blink at us, but I also feel that this is someone who knows his business, someone who, in spite of appearances, could eat us both for breakfast. Where the hell did Pino find him?

He motions us to sit down on the sofa and with surprising, even disconcerting agility, sweeps the box close to the sofa so that he can sit down and eyeball us from a distance of no more than three feet. I can see his unpleasant pasty skin and am surprised that so much sickliness can harbour so much energy. He is unaware that he is rotting away. His breath is acrid and his teeth blackened with neglect. As he speaks, you sense his intelligence and also that this intelligence has no flexibility, no humour, no other mood beyond his outrage at oppressive regimes. Here is fanaticism that should never be given power, and fortunately for us there is little chance of that happening. In other times, perhaps... I wish that I had stayed with Chabod, who writes a lot of sense, even if I don't agree with every dot and comma. And he knows how to argue against himself.

Pino and the man, who for me still has no name, embark upon a kind of dance in which they methodically expound their various positions on just about everything. Pino is defensive. I want to go. He probably does too, but he is manful in his struggle to hold the pass. Apart from regretting Chabod, I am now thinking about lunch. This is going on a long time, and Pino is much more amusing over a glass of wine and a plate of spaghetti. The last time we went to the absurdly cheap trattoria just round the corner from where he lives, he accused the owner of watering down the wine. She, of course, went into a fury.

"Who do think you are?" she cried...

"Someone who can taste watered-down wine," he replied, while they were both ignored by her other regulars – council workers, mechanics, students and the transvestite prostitute looking very feminine in the men's clothing she wears during the day; at night she looks absurdly masculine as she marches up and down the road outside Pino's flat in a short dress.

That dispute turned out to be easier to resolve than the one that suddenly breaks out between the two comrades. Pino's tact and lack of it are not able to smooth this one over. It starts with Pino – on whose authority I do not know – offering the man and his comrades the chance to become part of the Revolutionary Communist Groups.

"What are talking about? Are you mad?" the man stands up. He is furious and at last some colour has come to his face. "You have to fuse with us."

"But we're an international organisation with thousands of members."

"On the whole, your organisation is run by jerks. Your Florentine branch should combine with us."

"There's been a misunderstanding," Pino remonstrates, also climbing to his feet, which is a relief and I follow suit.

"There sure has. You've been wasting my time," the man says, and I try to think what he might be doing if he weren't here talking to us. But I fail.

Pino has sensibly decided to shift towards the door. He senses that the man is unpredictable and the situation could turn nasty.

It does. The man produces a huge flick-knife which he triggers to produce an equally terrifying blade. He waves it in front of our noses as we slowly back off. "Such a pair of make-pretendy revolutionaries. You people just get in the way. I could slice you up but you'd make a terrible mess, and someone would have to clear it up. Get going!" He makes a final, slightly less aggressive sweep of his knife, which presumably means, "Get out of here before I change my mind."

We run for the door and leap down the stairs with hands on the rail. "The man's crazy!" Pino shouts. State the obvious, I think, but the man's right about one thing: we are a pair of make-pretendy revolutionaries.

I go to the *tavola calda* bearing a *caffè corretto sambuca* for Aras. This is his favourite drink: an espresso coffee with a measure of anise-flavoured spirit. He drinks it in a single gulp and looks busy. I turn to go. "Wait, wait!" he cries.

He takes some money, gives the change and dismisses his customers as if they were disorderly schoolchildren. "I'm joining the army," he says.

"But you're not Italian," I object.

"The Algerian army," he laughs. "I'm joining a volunteer regiment for the next war against Israel. My mind is made up."

"You're leaving?" I was shocked

"I want to give you my job."

Today, I meet the boss who is sitting in the main restaurant. He only needs to check me out briefly. "He's okay," he says to Aras, and Aras takes me into the *tavola calda* to show me what the job entails. All very straight-forward until the end, when I remember that he hasn't given me any prices.

When I ask, Aras looks put out – as though it's an act of insensitivity on my part to bring up such a question. I should be able to work it out, he appears to be implying by his reticence.

"Prices, well you know. How would you do it?"

"Prices. Just give me the prices. It can't be that difficult."

Aras sighs, checks the door and starts to explain, "Listen, this is how I do it. It works and the till is full at the end of the evening. That's what counts and the boss is happy. So, as I say, this is what I do, but you can do what you want. It's quite simple really."

By this time I'm getting a little restless. Why doesn't he come to the point? I'm a Scot, I believe in directness.

"The thing is," he continues, "this *tavola calda* in the middle of the tourist area and the smart shops gets all sorts of customers – particularly tourists in a hurry, so we have to cater for each situation – we have to adjust to ... You get it?"

"No, I don't. What are the prices, Aras? It can't be that difficult."

"Okay, okay, let me explain: if the customer is an American tourist, you make him pay a lot. If he's a European tourist, he pays a little less. If he's Italian middle class, still less. If he's Italian working class, you charge him a pittance. And as for Gypsies, ..."

"Yes, the Gypsies."

"Well, I don't make them pay anything. They're very sensible: there's never more than five of them at a time and they're different people every lunchtime and every evening. They sort it out amongst themselves. As I say, that's how I do it..."

"And that's how I'll do it too," I say suddenly understanding the brilliance of the whole system. "Does the boss know?"

He shrugs, "As long as the cash desk is full, he's happy. So you have to keep the customers happy. At lunchtime, it's mainly tourists and in the evening, it's mainly Italians."

It works like a dream. It took a little getting used to, and I soon learnt just how far you can squeeze an American tourist. Thirty-five thousand lira, that's the sum the boss wants to see in the till when he comes in to check it at the end of the evening. I never quite make it, but I probably don't have Aras's charm and ability to gather in a clientele. The first time the Gypsies came, they looked worried to see my face in place of Aras's. They nearly made straight for the door, but decided to order small dishes and went to the stools to eat their food quietly. When they asked for the bill and I told them it was free, relief spread across their faces. As they left, one of the two women in the group turned to look at me, as though she wanted to memorise my face.

Hers was not an expression of gratitude or, for that matter, of hostility. It was a glance across a void, between two worlds that never meet. It chilled my heart. How can human beings become so divided? It seemed to me then that no amount of human solidarity can bridge the centuries of distrust: however tough my life is – and I have chosen to make it tough – theirs is tougher, much tougher.

The hours are long. Fourteen hours a day. The money is pretty miserable, but not lower than the going rate, perhaps marginally higher. The boss is a reasonable man by the standards of an unreasonable world. And the customers are fun. Most fun of all is the bricklayer Giuseppe; you can hear his voice while he is still walking under the *portici* leading to the other side of the vast square. The sound is muffled by the tunnel-like colonnade and when he turns into the square the volume increases and bizarrely you can hear exactly what he is saying from inside the *tavola calda*. Normally, when someone speaks as loudly as Giuseppe in Scotland, they are up for a fight, but he just wants to talk, argue and occasionally sing; I was once threatened by a Neapolitan and he spoke in a very cool, quiet voice. Truly, all types exist everywhere, but they express their similarities so differently.

Giuseppe, however, does not want to fight. Such a thing would be unimaginable; like a cardinal in full regalia wearing boxing gloves, it would be amusing, surreal. This is in spite of his size and his hammer fists that dance and plead in tune with his stories, his jokes and his lengthy outpourings of ideas, anxieties and slightly simulated outrage at the evils and injustices that surround us.

Usually I make him pay in accordance with the dictates of Aras's social tariff, but sometimes he performs so well that I shrug my shoulders as if to say, "Why the stupid question?" I stare at him and smile, "Tomorrow will do; you can pay tomorrow." Already I am beginning to talk as though I were the owner of this *tavola calda*, and I understand how Aras's system is not only an act of generosity, but also a means to turn oneself from a passive employee into a free agent who judges, decides and implements a personal moral code. It is an act of emancipation. And I wish that I could take the credit for it.

"But I have the money," he usually protests, but his complaint is postiche like many of his mannerisms, or so they appear to a Northern European like myself. He is not a Gypsy who has learnt how to accept humiliation without harm to personal dignity. He has to push away humiliation, albeit very weakly. The right to live without humiliation gives rise to arrogance, something Giuseppe lacks completely. That absolute right is the prerogative of the rich and powerful; all the rest of us have to compromise to some degree. Somewhere out in the city there will be a sunless room with a malfunctioning shower, a *rete* and a stinking mattress. For that discomfort he will pay part of his meagre wages, which probably also subvent relations back in Naples. He is clearly a man alone because, if not, he would hardly work so hard to amuse and ingratiate himself with the shifting, motley population of my *tavola calda*.

"Tomorrow will be fine," I reassure him, and with a smile and perhaps a hearty clap on my back that has all the excessive emphasis of his speech, he is off before I can change my mind. It is that easy to make some people momentarily happy – but then Giuseppe is nearly always above or only just below the happiness level.

Now my hours are so long, the meeting is breaking up when I arrive at the *sede*. No doubt they have covered the usual territory: the imminent collapse of the prevailing economic system, the joys of a partisan's life in the mountains, and the niceties of the transitional programme. My arrival causes Eugenio to call the meeting to order. "'ompagni, I forgot to tell you: we have a particular subject for discussion next week. It has been suggested by comrade Lochrie."

"What is it, Garry?" some of them ask unenthusiastically.

"The redistribution of wealth," I say brightly, but they look like a class that has just been set its homework. And I think to myself, Aras is the one who should introduce this subject; he has done more to redistribute wealth on a tiny scale than this lot will be able to do in their entire lifetimes, but he is on a ship to Algiers because he wants to fight in a distant land he has never seen and probably never will.

I Am Not My Body
(with apologies to William Makepeace
Thackeray and to the readers for retaining
his Pumpernickels and silly surnames)

Maeve King has the sad face of a spaniel, as her slightly swollen jowls sag under a hidden weight. Her body too appears unequal to the struggle against gravity. Her head and slim shoulders are the point of a triangle whose base is her wide hips, standing on the other smaller and inverted triangle of her heavy thighs running down her short legs to her dainty feet. And you, my reader, have already dismissed her – have you not? – in spite of all your "political correctness". You would never call her a "dumpling", "hefty" or, good heavens, a "lump of lard", but with all the delicacy of your class – you are middle class, aren't you? we are all middle class now that the Thatcherites in both parties have declared the working class no longer to exist – you might suggest a better diet and the odd workout at the gym. There is no real excuse for being fat. Obesity is an optional condition, we are told. Surely we can all make the effort? Why were we put into this world, if not to look after our bodies – to ensure their enduring attraction and longevity, no matter how many pots and potions it takes, how many trainers and track suits always shiny new and how many days lost in sweaty activities we detest or in thumbing through glossy mags in search of the latest advice.

You think she looks a fool and cannot keep on top of life. Well then, you've made the same mistake as many others. Take another look. Maeve's piercing eyes express a real intelligence and energy. Those who believe success to be associated with such virtues most likely fail to notice them, because of Maeve's timidity and reticence.

That was Ms King when she started to teach German literature at Southdown University, an oasis of learning, tolerance, good manners and the occasional sit-in, situated in a pleasant, affluent but rather uncultured county. She did not work out, it's true, but she did work (the foolish girl). Her young colleagues in the department were two ambitious men with Scottish names and pronounced English regional accents: Harvey McBride and Cameron Murray. McBride was permanently outraged over many things big and small: from the lack of appreciation afforded some minor women writers of Pumpernickel in the eighteenth century to the lack of appreciation afforded himself after having made his discovery of them. Indeed his outrage in a world of wars and starvation appears to have pivoted around a peculiar mismatch between the objects he most appreciated and those appreciated by almost everybody, who stubbornly persisted in their ignorance after he had produced more than three kilos of learned articles. Nevertheless the head of department was happy enough with the research points.

McBride was also considerably aggrieved that the human generality failed to appreciate his selfless parenting: when the train pulled into the university station one morning and he had to button up the coats on his small herd of toddlers, he lectured the impatient students who wanted to get off and did so by addressing his prodigious progeny in the following terms: "You see these people, they're always in a hurry; no time for anyone but themselves. But we don't have to be rushed. No one can make us rush. No one. You might well ask why they're in such a hurry. Their classes? I don't think so." The guard was now moving down the platform and slamming any unclosed doors as he went. The surprisingly numerous offspring for so young a man stared at their father uncomprehendingly, but the students understood well enough. In part they felt impatient and in part resigned to going on to the next station, where they would have to take a train back in the opposite direction. The departure whistle was surely imminent and the whole scene had something theatrical about it. All things considered, this was more amusing than the average morning journey to their studies. But McBride had not finished: "These lads and lassies are going to be straight off to their various coffee shops to loll around and talk indescribable rubbish to each other." Now he was becoming abusive and his rhetoric was strangely old-mannish for someone who had only just completed his first score and ten. The students were becoming more restless. Some were heading back up the carriage to the other door, some were eyeing the door he was blocking as though they were about to rush it, and some were just enjoying the spectacle.

"You have to do up every last button," grinned one of them. "When it comes to children you can never be too careful. That's a fearful cold wind out there!"

"When I want your advice, I'll ask for it," said McBride rather weakly, but then he stiffened, "and don't think you know how to look after kids; you're no more than a snivelling little kid yourself."

If it was intended to wound, the barb bounced off uselessly. The student, who now appeared more determined to stay on the train than McBride himself, had a taken up a more permanent position leaning against the back of one of the seats with one foot propped up on its toe, like an Edwardian gentleman at his fireplace. "No one understands children, least of all their parents. The child a parent sees is a mere construct in the parent's addled brain, and has nothing to do with the reality of the child. By the time the parent becomes aware of his or her own idiocy, it's too late: the child has grown up and is ready to challenge the parent." At this stage, the student disentangled himself from his Edwardian posture, leant right

41

down until his mouth was close to McBride's ear and hissed, "And then the fun starts!"

"Watch yourself," replied a startled McBride, "watch you behaviour. I'll have your name."

The young man was unmoved and resumed his gentlemanly pose, "Of course, when it comes to understanding children and always admitting that they remain pretty impenetrable for us all, I believe that the closer one is to childhood, the easier it is; having witnessed your performance this morning, I am absolutely convinced that this is the case."

At this stage, McBride had had enough; gathering the living proof of his fertility around him with a protective gesture that suggested the student's words could be construed as offensive to those of tender age, an implication belied by the children's continued expression of complete bafflement over the entire exchange, he opened the door and took them with him. The stationmaster's whistle blew as the students piled out, and he began to wave his arms about in a state of extreme agitation. Health-and-safety was being ignored, and the culprit, wearing a highly fashionable long raincoat of the kind used by American sleuths in the thirties, slipped away with his infantile retinue, like the Pied Piper. You have now been introduced to our heroine's tormentor – not a demonic one, and in the end he turns out to be not all bad. That is the thing about tormentors, they are very rarely all bad, which confuses matters considerably.

But Maeve was not alone. She had a champion and a very remarkable one at that: the tall, dark-haired and attractive Anne Bartlett, a German historian. She immediately understood that Maeve not only had a fine mind but, also and more importantly, a very good heart. They enjoyed each other's company, and what little social life she had revolved around her protector. Anne was one of those people whose intelligence never interferes with their

42

profoundly decent instincts. The white charger was always waiting and, when she mounted it, her own self-interest was entirely disregarded. When it came to Maeve, it was an open and shut case. Here was a woman of undoubted talents whose execrable colleagues were pushing her around and worse: their put-downs were articulated with the slightly weary tone of people who are trying their very best to be kind and to show understanding. Maeve, whose mind ran along strictly rationalist lines, was of course utterly outsmarted and unable to understand exactly where she was being wronged. In heroically holding them at bay, Anne did not use the sword of truth and the trusty shield of fair play so beloved of some right-minded politicians; such weapons would have been far too heavy for her, but she was handy with the rapier of sarcastic comment and a virtuoso with the very down-to-earth broomstick of common sense, which can be used for prodding or simply lateral beating around the head – a very humane instrument of warfare as it causes no lasting damage to the adversary.

Like so many of her kind – her wonderful kind – Anne was less adept at running her own life than at running other people's. She did everything on impulse and believed her own innate decency to be found amongst most people. She was having an asymmetric love affair with a young Czech called Lech, who was intermittently studying for a degree in German literature. He would occasionally come over to England to get drunk, an experience that differed from getting drunk in Prague only in this respect: in England he could complain incessantly about the poor quality of the beer, which undoubtedly added to his pleasure.

Unwittingly Lech was to bring about changes in Maeve's life: such is the fragility of the threads that hold us together. The timing of this momentous event was that season of drunken silliness, that Yuletide whose ebb leaves behind a clutter of empty wineboxes and beer cans. But its place was far more complex, and it requires me to make a little detour.

A few years earlier, the university had decided that it needed to catch up with the more entrepreneurial times. They appointed a go-getting vice-chancellor to further the successes of our illustrious, liberal and, might I say, candid seat of learning with its dreaming towers and cloisters of poured concrete and ceramic pools of shining water, redolent, I think, of some Mediterranean marvel – Venice perhaps. Why not? Well, perhaps because they had to fill in so many of these pools that tended to catch all the falling leaves that autumn brought and then began to turn all shades of brown before blooming in midwinter into a bright algae green.

And this genius of business management they hired was none other than the now infamous Lord Brown of Envelope. He was a Tory in those days when Labour life peers were lagging behind in the corruption stakes, and Lord Envelope was leading the pack: not for him the odd night at the Paris Ritz and a few thousand the tax man knew nothing about. No, he was a man of taste and couldn't possibly restrict his life of luxury to weekends. I will not tire the reader with the details which had three KPMG accountants working full time for two and a half years. For our purposes, I must only mention the wine. The university was the owner not only of large structures in reinforced concrete and endless "villages" of student accommodation, which must have kept the London Brick Company busy for several weeks or possibly months, but also a sixteenth-century hall it rather neglected and had allocated for postgraduate lodgings. No sooner had the building come into Lord Envelope's vision than he started to dream up the most perfect dinner parties in a refurbished version of the hall. And so it was, much to the anger of the post-graduates turfed out of their eccentric accommodation and those pedants at English Heritage who thought his porch with Doric columns not in keeping with the ancient Tudor build. But as Lord Envelope constantly liked to point out to the university authorities, they needed to pay the "going rate for the job", if they wanted a well-run institution with an international reputation. He always drove this important point home by telling them that he had turned down a much more lucrative job in America as the Chief Executive of the Coca-Cola Corporation, and had done so solely out of his great love of learning, instilled in him by his mother, a writer of popular whodunnits who had been unjustly neglected in favour of Agatha Christie. The good men and women of the senate committee were very impressed and indeed cowed by his generous sacrifice and kept opening the university's purse wider and wider.

But I have promised not to burden the reader with all that dismal minutiae of greed, and restrict myself to the one element that was to affect the fate of our plain but unhealthily virtuous heroine, Maeve King – unhealthily for herself, of course, and not for society, which would be much improved if there were more plain Maeves around.

An old Elizabethan hall has, of course, a cellar, and a cellar has to be filled. In the case of Lord Envelope, it had to be filled with the best. In all, the accountants sent in after the vice-chancellor's arrest found 9,738 bottles of the finest claret, mostly Chateau Latour, and the invoice that went with this modest drop of hospitality was considered so scandalous that the senate decided to sell the entire collection of claret (we won't mention the whites and the other reds here) to an enterprising young French historian called Tom Viticult for 25p a bottle (I will leave you to do the sums and choke with envy).

Tom did not have a wine cellar, but his terraced house in Brideton, Southdown's seaside capital, did have an unused coal cellar, which certainly helped out but did not suffice. The surplus was distributed around the house at the bottom of wardrobes, under sinks, in the cupboard under the stairs, beside the cold-water tank in the attic and underneath almost every item of furniture: beds, tables, desks and the TV stand – much to the irritation of his wife, Claire, another scholar of French culture.

Such a quantity of wine could not be drunk by Bacchus in his eternal lifetime – nor by Tom in spite of his comparable thirst for the red liquid full of dizzying dreams, vivacious conversations, happy palates and the odd sore head. There was nothing for it but to organise the mother of all Christmas bashes, and what better place to hold it than in the Elizabethan hall which was having its newly acquired Doric columns removed, a cost the university was defraying by renting it out to the public. The cleverness with which we manage to keep wealth circulating around our advanced western economies is something we never fully understand or appreciate as we should. Thus a small part of the booty was earmarked for immediate consumption, much to Claire's approval as she saw an opportunity for re-deploying part of her invaded wardrobes. By now, the reader must be aware of how fate was manipulating persons and the concomitance of events in order to deprive Maeve of her one support.

So the time was Christmas and the place was the Elizabethan Hall with the partially dismantled Doric columns. Lech was feeling that life was a good adventure. The stifling regime that had run his country since shortly after the war was staggering towards its end. He was abroad again, and visitors like himself were still un-common enough to attract great interest. He had a beautiful girlfriend, although a touch serious for his liking. A childhood full of rank moralising made her stern principles unendearing to him. Good fortune, he thought, is like a woman, and you will do much better if you take her forcefully – none of that namby-pamby sensitivity for her feelings. Sensitivity is something we leave to women; it is not a male virtue. And women, like good fortune, love youth – vigorous youth that doesn't think too much – youth with a good hard body that makes them slightly fearful. Lech had steeled himself with a few foul-tasting English pints before thinking these princely thoughts that can be found in any of the back streets of our towns and cities when the nightclubs empty on a Saturday night, but also in the works of our great European philosophers, lovers of knowledge and civilisation. Lech had the feeling of being elected to great deeds and happiness, which he mistakenly believed to be interconnected.

The entrance to the hall was guarded by the austere head of the Italian Department, Professor Pino Pinguino who must have got up at five in the morning to present the world with such a well-ordered appearance, ranging from polished black shoes to a beautifully coiffured head on which it looked as though each hair had been laboriously placed in position to match a perfect cascade of thatch. There are worse ways to waste one's life, but few that express so compellingly the inanity of our vanity fair. Lech waited for the tall professor to make eye contact with a guest requiring a double dose of sycophantic effusion, and then boldly ducked under his line of vision. Fate must have arranged that too.

As Lech got drunker and discovered the English right-thinking classes to be stuffy, puffed-up and, worst of all, unnaturally incurious about Lech himself, he became increasingly obsessed with the idea of reciting the bawdy poems of the infamous satirical poet from Pumpernickel, Otto Pornovsky, considered a degenerate by the Nazis, not least because of the suspicious ethnicity suggested by his surname and not sufficiently redressed by a Christian name harking back to four Holy Roman Emperors no less,

47

and one of them garnished with a "the Great". What Lech could not possibly have known was that during the eighties feminism had passed from its virtuous radical stage to its tiresome finger-pointing one, in which deviation from the new norm could not be tolerated. Pornovsky is famous for his unremitting depiction of women as mere bodies and objects of male desires, an attitude that was not exclusively Pornovskian and could not be banned by diktat. The cheerless Doctor Joyce Graves, also of the Italian Department, started to bang doors to broadcast that her finest sensitivities had been unpardonably affronted, even though she had been known to eye up the talent amongst the first-year students at the beginning of each year and then report every physical detail to the diaphanous Doctor Cecilia Atrophy from English Literature who looked as though she didn't have the energy to eat her breakfast, let alone make love to one of the sturdy lads depicted by the good doctor of philosophy and defender of our new morality.

As the Czech boyfriend could not be summoned before the school committee, it was Anne Bartlett herself who had to respond for his bad behaviour. Anne, of course, could have made short work of that committee, and many a time she had done just that on behalf of other people, but on this occasion she felt that a grand gesture of solidarity with the part-time student and full-time drinker was in order. It was difficult to reconstruct the exact course of the senate proceedings after the event, as reports were conflicting, but the result was that Anne handed in her notice. Lech repaid her loyalty a few months later by marrying Sophie Witleston who, as far as bodies are concerned, was very well endowed with the upholstery required to set the male hormones racing. The content of her cranium was somewhat limited, unlike her bank account which had been overflowing since her father had sold off his razor-blade company to an American corporation. And all of this, of course, was fine by Lech who knew a good thing when

48

he saw it. Besides the contents of Anne's cranium and bank account had been the other way about, and that can be tedious for a man, particularly one who wants a quiet life and freedom to indulge his pleasures.

But the greatest loser in this tragic end to Anne's academic career was Maeve, who lost her closest friend – and worse, that rare friendship that stimulates and keeps the mind alive.

Anne would marry a doctor – a real one who cures patients – and during her happy years of motherhood, something she had never really hankered after, she started to write a satirical novel about a Northdown University and characters not that dissimilar from the ones we have encountered here. After lying some ten years in a drawer, it has now become a huge success. Anne appears on Newsnight Review, and seated on their low and uncomfortable chairs, she can be heard to reel off inanities in clipped tones to the grinning assent of the presenter whose mind is elsewhere of course – on such matters as who should be the next speaker, who would best enliven her programme, how to make the speakers perform and, dear God, the desperate urgings of her producer channelled directly to her ear. Anne, meanwhile, falls prey to belated ambition and resentment. Her treatment by the university, which she had rarely thought about for more than a decade, has become an obsession, and more inexplicably, she feels that she has wasted her enormous talents on an ungrateful family, which in reality is both grateful and admiring of her success. So it is clear: the vanities of our fairground world can corrupt even the best and brightest of our sons and daughters, so what hope for us lesser mortals?

But what the reader really wants to know is Anne's opinion now of that Lech for whom she sacrificed her career. But don't you know? – We, the vainglorious *homines sapientes*, would lay down our lives for someone whom in all probability we would detest six months later in the happy (or perhaps unhappy) event of our surviving. We are motivated by vanity and impulse, although we dress up our vain and impulsive acts in all sorts of fine clothes. And as for the past, we are forever rewriting it.

So now we come to the really weepy part of our story. Our heroine has been deprived of her *caballera* in shining armour (I'm afraid we have no word for a woman knight in our native tongue, which is no less lacunose than any other language, despite chauvinistic beliefs to the contrary), and is now defenceless against ruthless men who do not want their way with her body but are quite capable of stealing her research results and impugning the integrity of her academic work (in no other field of human endeavour have so many been so dependent on the rumours of so few). I hear you objecting that you hear very little about Maeve; what a predictable lot you are! It is sufficient for a heroine to be virtuous. That is her principal task, but you have to admit that supercilious academics, wayward Czech students and corrupt university vice-chancellors are much more fun to read about.

As the most junior member of faculty in the department, the now unprotected Maeve was summoned to the offices of both Cameron Murray and Harvey MacBride, descendants of a people who could never distinguish between forename and surname or foreboding and surly moaning. Cameron Murray was to see her first and had her sitting around for three-quarters of an hour while he interviewed students. "So sorry to keep you waiting," he would say, with that sly, mock solicitousness he had so expertly mastered. But stop, I'm not a military historian and I'm not an academic. I would never tire you with a battle scene, and describe the clashing steel, the parrying shield or the copious bleeding from fatal wounds, so why would I discuss the even more monotonous cut and thrust of an academic single combat with its purring niceties, wicked jokes, subtle sarcasm and brutal demonstrations of the will to power (and power over what)? We know the outcome: Maeve was put upon. Ah! you say, what a middle-class form of oppression; she was hardly breaking up bricks for aggregate on a Bengali roadside. You're right; but though evils are relative, they are all evils. Leave criticism to the critics and let me introduce you to one last character.

Letizia Rubicondi looked like a beauty in a sixteenth-century Italian painting, and such beauty terrifies most men, except for the occasional oaf who has not the sensitivity to fear it or, at the opposite extreme, refined and self-confident natures such as that of MacBride who made her an offer she could refuse: promotion from *lettrice* to permanent teaching staff in the following academic year in exchange for allowing him to share her bed – his being occupied by the stout, agreeable and extremely loyal lady who was his wife and mother of the well-buttoned offspring. Letizia was a new friend – not a replacement for Anne, as she was not inclined to quixotic demonstrations of solidarity, but she had a fiercely independent character that Maeve admired and learnt from.

One day, Maeve plumped herself down on an armchair in Letizia's study and said, "These shells, our bodies – what an effort it is to lug them around, and they need such pampering even when, like mine, they're overweight and unattractive. Fed, watered, scrubbed, clothed and covered with all sorts of pongs and potions. How many industries flourish, how much commerce feeds the assets of wealthy men, and even how many wars are fought to secure the safety and comfort of these fragile bags of flesh, which must wither in all events?"

"Well, off you go like the anchorites into the desert to eat berries. You'll forgive me if I don't join you," laughed Letizia Rubicondi.

"But it's all right for you," said Maeve indicating, not without a little distaste, Rubicondi's well-styled and wellgarmented form. Why, she thought, are Italian feminists allowed to dress like man-killers in tight shirts and high heels, with perfectly made-up faces and manicured nails? "Look at what I have to drag around. And why do all men, whether ugly or good-looking, think that all of us, unclad and defenceless to their amorous needs, should resemble the latest Hollywood anorexic."

"Defenceless to their amorous needs? Oh dear, you are fucked up," Letizia passed sentence. "Personally I have always thought that they would like to put it anywhere, and find making love to us only marginally more attractive than doing the same thing to a watermelon." Letizia demonstrated once again that, contrary to popular belief, Northern Europeans are more romantic, while if you want truly unromantic and indeed cynical attitudes to sex, you need to go to the south of the continent. "Although it has to be admitted that a watermelon is no good when it comes to decorating a bar stool. That is why I never go out in the evening accompanied by a man: they always want to parade you like a trophy. That's why I keep my sex life and my social life entirely separate."

Maeve, who had been to bed with very few men – all fumbling, awkward encounters – and had never known one who wanted to parade her like a trophy, blushed at her friend's explicitness and self-confidence. It wasn't just about sex, and she decided to take the conversation in a different direction.

"Look, the brain is some kind of computer, but you just switch a computer on and as soon as it gets its electric current, which is instantaneous, it starts to work in an entirely reliable fashion. But the brain is so fussy and so dependent on a healthy body. It gets tired. It doesn't like your drinking habit. It absolutely hates your insomnia, and becomes uncontrollable in the face of over fifty undergraduates."

"Well, for starters," came the smiling reply from Letizia, who always found complex subjects reassuringly simple, as her brain contained one of those old-fashioned filing cabinets, the wooden ones with tiny drawers for holding index cards: everything has a category and everything can be filed away. There is no room for doubt or *crossover*. "Well, for starters, our brain is not a computer [it was filed under 'b' and not under 'c', she presumably meant], and it has intuition, which is simply jumping to a conclusion before you have sufficient evidence. A computer doesn't do that kind of tomfoolery. It applies absolute rigour, while our brains are, at best, dysfunctional computers."

"I don't know about that," said Maeve, uncertain as to where she should start her response. It struck her that Letizia was much more impressive when she was talking about sex. "All that defragging business: isn't that a bit like sleep – and dreaming? After all what is sleep, if not sorting out our brains and getting them ready for the next day, but computers do it so quickly; they defrag in a couple of minutes, whereas we lose a third of our life. It is the terrible inefficiency of it all that irritates me."

"So we're in agreement. The brain is at best a dysfunctional computer," Letizia reasserted.

"Well, not really! The brain, like everything that makes up a human being, is both remarkable and rather clumsily constructed. Yet another demonstration of how we must have been designed by evolution, although designed is not the right word. 'Designed by evolution' is an oxymoron."

"I'll argue against myself here," says Letizia grandly. "Computers, if they were designed from scratch now with the knowledge we have accumulated – with hindsight, as it were – would be designed differently from what they have become. Because they too have evolved step by step, and the design of each generation of computer is constricted by the format of the previous one. That is a bit like evolution, isn't it."

"You're right, Letizia, but I was only using a metaphor when I first said that the brain is a computer. It isn't really a computer, because it contains the ghost of consciousness."

"Now, you're being silly. Next you'll be believing in God and all that tomfoolery," Letizia said, displaying that endearing habit of people speaking a language that is not their own: the over-frequent use of a low-frequency word for no other reason than the speaker's irrational pleasure in articulating the word in question, often because that word would be quite inconceivable in their native tongue.

"Is it silly not to know?" Maeve asked.

Letizia sat on Maeve's chair-rest and put her arm around her. "You are far too serious, my dear," she whispered. "That is why I find you so entertaining. You're coming out with me tonight. I'm going to show you off and give you a good time."

Maeve suddenly felt a little weepy. "You wouldn't find it so entertaining if you knew what I have to put with. If you had colleagues like Harvey MacBride and Cameron Murray..."

Letizia removed her arm and stood up. "Come off it, Maeve! What are you looking for? A knight in shining armour. They don't exist and never did." Maeve's eyes began to burn and she thought to herself that Letizia clearly didn't have an index card for Anne Bartlett. "MacBride's a jerk," Letizia continued, "and so is Murray. So what? They're like the weather: you have to put up with them as part of reality. The storm comes in, and then it blows itself out. And you're still here, working away as you always do. I'd put my money on you, any day. You'll pull through, but stop feeling sorry for yourself. You need *le palle* – balls. What you call *guts* in your language. What a strange lot you are! I tell you what: you're coming out with me tonight and I'm not taking no for an answer." And so a kind of friendship grew stronger. Letizia would continue to push Maeve into having a more relaxed relationship with her own body, and Maeve would continue to resist, because her resistance came from her nature and could not be overcome by intellectual argument.

And we might have been a little too hard on MacBride, as who can blame him for the inconstancy of his values, the hypocritical manner in which he displayed them, his bullying of faculty and students alike, and his ruthless exploitation of Maeve, which I have described, albeit somewhat summarily? We have to admit that his behaviour was perfectly adapted to survival in the delightful and enlightened environment we categorise as academia. In no other sphere of activity is reputation so important and carefully cultivated or projected onto society like a magic lantern. In no other trade are personal politics, committee-controlling, grand gestures and conspiracy so important. What? Even worse than politicians? you ask incredulously. Well indeed, politicians are more dangerous because they have real power; if, however, the world were run by academics, there would very probably be more war and mayhem, not less. So we should be thankful that our ingenious societies have found the means of channelling these people into careers where their cantankerous rivalries can do no real harm or lasting damage to society at large.

And the proof of what I say can be found in the history of Doctor Harvey MacBride himself. His self-help book, *Shit on Everyone Else, or How to be a Great Writer or Artist*, so touched the spirit of our times that it became a "runaway bestseller". In it he explained what had already seemed an established fact: everyone has a novel in them or in the drawer or in their soul or in some other place. Presumably we all also have a marathon, a sculpture and a very successful business enterprise in us, if only we could find the right success manuals and be bothered to follow their advice carefully, thus unleashing on the world huge numbers of frustrated writers, runners, sculptors and businessmen. That's already happened, you say. Quite right, but there is still a market for this stuff. MacBride followed a tried and tested formula: success relies on self-belief and is interfered with only when you start to weaken and take other people's feelings into account. Success is a matter of focus and ruthlessness, and the object is to sell oneself as one would any other "product". This populist treatise was followed by the equally successful *Being a Bastard Gets You to the Top or How to Be a Successful Politician or Captain of Industry* and the slightly more original *Method Acting as a Way of Life*, which explained how the skills of dissembling anger, moral outrage, concern and sincerity can be used to further almost any career. He too was invited onto TV chat shows and was such a success that he became a permanent fixture. Of course, his colleagues no longer took him seriously: how could they? – he had written books that everyone wanted to read. To his great credit, he too started to take himself less seriously. He continued his academic career in a very desultory fashion, dropped off all the committees and didn't finish his monograph on whether Goethe visited Pumpernickel for one afternoon in the autumn of 17**. His bank balance grew and he became very relaxed, but the bank balance was not that important as he showed great generosity and gave half of it to a charity drilling artesian wells in Africa. When Cameron Murray, who shortly afterwards would succumb to an unpleasant accident involving a plate of *strozzapreti*, stopped him in the corridor and provocatively said, "You do realise that those books of yours are crap!" MacBride replied, "You're wrong. They're complete crap," and bounced off laughing at his own feeble joke. In short, a bad book liberated its author and made him a better man.

But you the reader and I the writer of these lines have not led blameless lives, and if fate had landed us in one of those pleasure gardens of learning, might we not have behaved just like him? Surely our professions account for ninety per cent of who we are. Our own contribution is slight, although we do not like to think so. And one final word on this subject: when it comes to writers, translators and all those who push a pen for no other reason than to turn an elegant phrase or shape an original thought (if such things exist), keep a very wide berth but read our books, as we are, on the whole, a penniless lot and our egos are made of material fragile to the touch of reality.

And so in the end Maeve became head of department and, wonderfully, was reunited all day long with the studies she loved. She took joy too in the successes of the staff she recruited, even when they eclipsed her own. And they rewarded her by relaxing into their work and putting aside those university politics of which we spoke. And they loved her dearly and few would countenance the idea of leaving because, although we humans consume our lives in bickering and plotting and spreading false rumour "to better ourselves" and our families, the thing we really desire is to work in harmony and concert with each other. It is circumstance, shall we say, that makes us do what we do aided, no doubt, by that weakness we so often call strength or ambition. But always we want for something better.

And how uplifting are these light satires? I am weeping while I write, as I seldom indulge in happy endings, as you will find out if you persevere with this book. What's this? You're not happy? You say that her emotional life is not complete. I am not writing for Hollywood, and not every happy ending requires a man and a woman to get together (or two men or two women, for that matter). Look, if you want heterosexual heaven along with an estate and an income of three (hundred) thousand a year, forget it or read one of the classics.

For us sweet cynics of our modern age, the emphasis has changed – and for the better I would say: a shred of progress now that progress seems an unlikely claim.

The Difficulty Snails Encounter in Mating

25 September 2004

Dear Gottfried,

Since you have joined International Comestible Commodities, I have been very impressed by your honesty, intelligence and dedication. I feel that you are similar to the young man I was when I joined the firm fifteen years ago, and I will go further: I see in you a worthy successor to my own post. It is only a matter of time before I am promoted to Head of Commodity Movements, as green tea has for many years been outperforming all other commodities in spite of its marginality.

For this reason, I have chosen to give you some advice, so that you can avoid some of the terrible errors I made during the first ten years of my career. I probably appear to you as a person who has always known his business – destined, as it were, to success and position. What I am going to tell you will reveal the weaker side of my character that has now been conclusively overcome. I will reveal my sufferings in the hope that you will avoid similar ones.

In our line of business, we must avoid the distractions of permanent personal relationships, and I have no doubt that my story will convince you of this undeniable truth. We understand it intellectually, but so often we allow our irrational feelings to govern our sound intellects. Remember, the market is the great teacher and there is nothing outside it that is not a distraction, although distractions fall into two categories: those that are pleasant and recreational – to be indulged in to a proper and measured degree – and those that are offensive, nauseating and ultimately dangerous. It doesn't matter, really, what commodity you trade in; it is by trading that we perform an essential function for the betterment of our societies and it is this that justifies our high salaries and the privileges we hold. We owe it to society to keep ourselves focused on the primary task – for us and all those people who rely upon us.

I know that you come from a rural background in Austria, and you must find K***, our beautiful city in the heart of Europe, at times overwhelming and full of allurements and deceitful temptations. I was born in this city and yet I fell into one of its snares. How much more difficult it must be for you, a relatively unsophisticated country boy.

So I write in a spirit of brotherhood and solidarity with a fellow human being setting out on this exhilarating career of hard work, conquest and wealth for the sake of a society that is often envious and dismissive of our achievements. We are a more civilised and evolved version of the medieval knights. Daily we fight to protect the borders of our civilisation which are now virtual rather than geographic, and those who struggle in their mundane lives beneath us can never understand the risks we run and the sacrifices we make.

The first thing you must understand is the importance of a regular and cleanly life. I generally wake early, about three hours before I go to work. The reason for this sacrifice is quite simple: I need to defend my flat against myself and against anyone else who might enter its agreeable, spacious and whitewashed walls. I, Robert Finnick, am required to defend my own home against Robert Finnick for the sake of Robert Finnick. This may seem very strange to those who have not thought about it in any great depth, but my behaviour, far from odd, is based on very sound science. The problems start with the fact that Robert Finnick is in the habit of breathing – that is inhaling healthy air and exhaling an unhealthy version that replaces the oxygen content with carbon dioxide. I am not concerned about my own minuscule contribution to the greenhouse gases that are apparently destroying our world, a question that I leave to the United Nations, G8 and all those politicians who are paid good money by the taxpayer precisely to worry about such matters. What concerns me is that every exhalation contains warm, moist and corrosive air that attacks everything I have paid for with good money. Then there is the question of my footfall across the well-polished floors of my flat. These jolts constantly erode the fabric of the building in which I have invested considerable wealth earned, I might add, at the cost of not inconsiderable effort on my own part. I am, it is true, very careful to tread lightly and wear the appropriate footwear, but the laws of physics deny the possibility of a zero-attrition footstep. I am of course very careful to invite as few people into the flat as possible, which, I think you will agree, is a very sensible precaution for many reasons. My only regret is that my flat contains a few items of undeniable good taste – both twentieth-century art and ancient chinoiserie. I would like to share these objects with similarly appreciative minds, but it is my experience that such sensitivities are hard to find, even in a cultured city like my own. Finally and most treacherous of all, our fingertips exude nasty, acidic oils that cling to every surface we touch. We are a creative species, but are betrayed by our own hands that methodically set about destroying everything we make. Unlike the lucky man whose touch turned everything to gold, our hands can make gold disappear. It could be said that my fingertips are consuming the flat while the rest of me is having to pay not only the huge mortgage but also the bill for the damage they cause.

I have thought about every possible solution to this terrible problem, including the "decapitation" of each fingertip, but this would merely cause new skin to be formed further down the finger with the same disastrous results, while creating the indisputable disadvantage of reducing the efficacy of my hand movements. Wearing rubber gloves is a costly but effective way of dealing with the problem, but I find that my hands sweat more and I have a niggling suspicion that this simply postpones the damage until the moment I remove my gloves and let loose my white, swollen hands on an unprotected environment.

So on rising, I open all or nearly all the windows of my flat, according to the season. I then vacuum the entire flat in the most meticulous manner, by which I mean that every piece of furniture has to be moved. I then dust all surfaces to remove traces of the deposits caused by my innate vices of shedding skin and breathing. Once order has been re-established following the relative anarchy of the night during which I have been obliged to drop my defences against myself or indeed any invited or uninvited intruder, I make myself a well-earned cup of chicory ersatz coffee. A thermometer that always hangs above the cooker is employed to ensure that the milk is heated to exactly the right temperature. I then eat a health-giving plate of cereal with added vitamins. These are not sufficient. I line up an alphabet of vitamins on my side plate: A for my eyesight, B to prevent nervous breakdowns, C to prevent colds and flu, D for healthy teeth and bones, and E for healthy skin. Life is not only about accumulation; it is also about conservation. This means conserving our financial assets through sound business practice, conserving our material assets by careful maintenance thereof, and conserving our bodies, which, in order to achieve maximum longevity, we should treat as though they were eternal. In spite of this devotion to my personal health, I have to admit that at the time of writing this instructive story, I am suffering terribly from the common cold and an unsightly eruption of red pimples decorates my face. The body is the most stubborn and contrary of our assets.

After breakfast, I then walk a mile and cycle two in my custom-made gym. I walk and cycle while staying in exactly the same spot, using exercise to trim my body while avoiding the unpleasantness of travelling through places inhabited largely by walking and breathing people with dangerous fingertips. The only problem is that this traps the sweat and hot breath I produce, within the confines of my own flat. After gym, I go for a shower and the pleasure of well-scrubbed skin, which nevertheless persists in producing the occasional defiant sore.

I leave for the office and all that involves: the company of often foolish and ungrateful people who have no sense of guilt about their walking and breathing. I am however extraordinarily good at what I do, and no one dares annoy me too much, because the directors very much appreciate my profound knowledge of the spot market in green tea. All the great tea houses look to me as a kind of god – the man who has his finger on the pulse of the new markets, the ones driven by our very sensible desire to rid ourselves of free radicals through the massive ingestion of antioxidants. I am the future.

I have my detractors, I do not deny this; indeed some people call me a "cold fish", which reflects the foolishness of those who cannot look below the surface and into the complex mechanisms of the human psyche. And yet, I think I can say without risk of being called arrogant or boastful that I am not only a handsome man but one irresistibly attractive to members of the opposite sex. I have no problem in finding lovers, although I am disciplined enough to keep my encounters with each one to a maximum of five. I strongly believe that we only have freedom for as long as we act as entirely independent individuals economically and socially. I do not wish to restrict my liberty or theirs by forming permanent attachments. And yet on not one but two occasions I allowed myself to be entrapped in that psychotic state of dependency we like to call "love". This all occurred in a period of just over six months, and the intensity of it was such as to impart a harsh lesson that I have never forgotten and think I never will during the rest of my long and successful career.

I met the first of these two sirens while taking a brisk walk in order to digest my food and keep my body trim. Usually my work-out in the gym is more than sufficient, but on that particular day I felt the need, for whatever fatal and fateful reason, to get a little more exercise. There was a group of women tourists outside a shop, and two were staring avidly at a display of leather bags, wallets, purses, key rings and the typically wide choice provided by shops in our advanced civilisation. Another, my lovely Jessica, was standing impatiently a few steps away and staring at one of our ancient churches. "I think," she said in the ringing tones of a powerful American accent, "you'll find the best deals are south of the river. Come on!"

She was a tall, well-built, handsome woman with long, frizzy red hair. She looked intrepid, and her intelligence was obvious. Had she not just expressed an immediate and quite truthful assessment of the tourist market as it operates in our historic city? The best deals definitely are on the south side of the river.

So I did something quite unprecedented, something that is totally alien to my nature: I started to converse with persons entirely unknown to me. This is the first lesson of my story: always suppress any spontaneous impulse; it will only lead you into trouble. "You are quite right, madam," I emphasised my European good manners to create an image of quaintness and solid old-fashioned values. My feeling that the American lady would find this appealing was also a product of rash spontaneity. "The best deals are indeed to be found on the south side of the river."

An enormous, white-toothed smile widened her mouth by a factor of at least 150 per cent, which of itself was a quite extraordinary phenomenon. I felt sure I had made a conquest. "Jessica," she stretched her hand out to shake mine, "what's your name?"

Again my rashness overcame me and I offered to act as their guide and take them to the market area south of the river where they could purchase the desired items at more favourable prices. "We'll pass by the early Gothic cathedral, one of the finest in the country, and then cross Prince Charles bridge. That is a slight detour, but the prolongation of our itinerary will be handsomely repaid by the exquisite architecture we'll encounter."

The other women looked as though they hadn't quite understood what I was saying and appeared to consider me an unwanted intruder. Jessica, on the other hand, seemed smitten, and was staring at me with what is called a "doe-eyed expression". I have this effect on women.

"I love art and architecture," she said. "Did you say early Gothic? That's incredible."

So we set off on our trip and I thought I would make myself useful by pointing out the various buildings of note as we went. I tried to engage with the whole group, but I was coming up against increasing resistance. So after the cathedral, I suggested that we stop at one of our better cafés – a touch on the expensive side, it's true, but the coffee is superlative. This achieved a happy outcome – or perhaps not, depending on how you look at it. The other women decided that they had no time to waste and split into two parties: the first, the more provident one, went off to find the south-side market, while the second, wishing to make a point no doubt, turned back for the shop whose window they had been marvelling at when I interrupted their commerce. Jessica and I found ourselves alone with two excellent cappuccinos with croissants. I decided to give Jessica a lecture on how we make croissants in our city – a very particular process – and on the health benefits of only consuming decaffeinated coffee. She seemed impressed, and I could see that she was a woman of considerable sensitivity.

We found the market and after two and a half hours meandering amongst the stalls, she finally made her choice. Of course I admire the entirely rational thoroughness with which she carried out this transaction, but my feet were protesting. I like to walk, but at a fairly brisk and steady pace. Sauntering and idling are for me something of an ordeal. Still, I have a generous nature and was only too happy to sacrifice my day to this bright but ingenuous foreigner. Besides, the purchase proved to be an outstanding bargain. I removed my pocket calculator and determined the ratio between it and the identical bag in the shop outside which we so fortuitously happened to meet. My timely intervention had saved her no less than 23.86% (not the exact figure, but two decimal points are sufficient here). I told her of this achievement, and once more she seemed impressed, although her smile was somewhat weaker on this occasion.

All in all, we had had a wonderful afternoon, notwithstanding my guilt at having ignored my work for such a prolonged period of time. I invited the young lady to supper in one of our better restaurants, without going over the top. I have achieved wealth precisely because I understand the need to be careful about all outgoings, and I keep meticulous accounts of every transaction I make, however small. She, of course, happily agreed, flashing one of her fullest, full-on smiles. We parted happily and knew where all this was leading.

No sooner was I back at my desk than I started to fret. I would have to ask her back to my flat. I sensed that Jessica would not be amenable to a brief romp in her hotel bedroom. She would want to be courted, and I had already set the tone with all that old-world courtesy stuff. This would mean doubling the breathing, as there would be two human beings instead of one, and sexual intercourse also increases it by an unknown margin. She would of course be wandering around my flat, and although not above eighty kilos in spite of her height and build, her footsteps would have some impact. And being American, she would put her greasy hands over just about everything in my home. Just as a snail leaves its trail of slime wherever it goes, so we human beings leave a more complex and probably even more noxious trace of our existence. How did we live before cleaning fluids?

Fortunately half a bottle of wine each smoothed out the way for the start of our relationship. Otherwise I don't know how I could have endured that invasion of my space by another body. So sexual intercourse took place and it was good. This was confirmed by Jessica in the morning, as she hugged me closely, told me how intelligent I am and flashed her amazing smile. I have to say that I found all that hugging a little unnecessary and was desperate to get back to work. While the day before I had been providing most of the conversation because I wanted Jessica to benefit from my frankly exceptional knowledge of our city's history and culture, she was now dominating the conversation with her inanities. Yes, I know that I am good-looking and intelligent, and I don't need some American mediocrity to come over here to tell me. She seemed to talk as though she had moved in, and my worst fears were confirmed. All the time I couldn't wait for her to get out and get on with being a tourist.

After she finally left, I started to polish the genuine silver photograph frame containing a picture of my ex-wife. I loved her still, I often told myself, although there had been a real compatibility problem she had not been willing to confront. She really did leave a trail of destruction behind her. She had an extravagant mind and it deposited all kinds of detritus around the flat: books, magazines, pens, scissors, lipsticks, used coffee cups, undrunk coffee cups, plates with toast crumbs and plates with pieces of uneaten, cold buttered toast... These objects had no boundaries, no fear of invasiveness. They colonised the flat like a disease. Then she left, after having screamed the most terrible abuse at me. She had said the unkindest things, but she could not have really meant them. She was offloading her own problems onto me. Now she is living with a plumber who plays in the local rugby team. He thinks he's a local hero, but actually he's a bit of a clown. And he leaves behind him an even bigger trail than she did, and most of it consists of empty beer cans. God, she must have regretted leaving her husband, but she couldn't come back because she was obviously too embarrassed by the terrible things she had said. I would have forgiven her, I think, but I was fearful about her breathing, treading and touching, because she always seemed to do a lot more of those things than any other person I have known, and I have lived a full and varied life.

, Are humans really designed to live together? I ask myself in my more reflective moments. And the answer has to be no. The whole history of marriage is a history of misery and regret. Of that I am certain. Even I was unable to make a go of it. It is a nice enough idea, but entirely impractical.

I consider myself to be the ideal modern man. I work hard and consume efficiently and rationally. I keep myself to myself, and live entirely within myself, which takes much more courage than that wife-and-kids stuff and that sharing out. That's for people who can't stand on their own feet. I am uncluttered by children and I look after my health scrupulously, so I demand hardly anything of the state. Why, I ask, should I help out the less fortunate? There is a very good reason why they're less fortunate.

As the day went by and I occasionally thought about Jessica, I started to change my opinion about her. She had a great body. She may not have been very cultured, but I could work on that, and she did appear to have an innate sensitivity. I think that was why she was drawn to me. She clearly wasn't as slobbish as my ex-wife, as I had carefully noted when she was clearing up after breakfast. She adored me, and that was entirely understandable. Surely my expensive flat could cope with an extra human being. Why should I turn her away? Why should I not let her stay for a few months? Do you see how easy it is for a man to be led astray by female wiles?

The first thing I did on getting home in the evening was to remove my ex-wife's photograph and throw it in the bin. The second was to ring Jessica on my mobile and ask her over for a meal at home. And so it was: we lived together quite happily for six months. She proved to be extremely accommodating, submissive even. I found that I could get her to do most of the cleaning chores. There was a good chance that the arrangement was home-friendly – that any damage caused by her presence was undone by the efficacy of her cleaning skills. When she announced that she had cancelled her return ticket and that the immigration people probably wouldn't notice her for a long time, I wasn't at all upset. In fact, I was actually happy about it. Jessica's photograph found its way into my prized silver photograph frame.

Then came the second woman and it was Jessica who invited her into the flat. As I say, about six months had passed – possibly the happiest cohabitation of my life. Do you see the snare? Sometimes you only notice after you've become irreversibly trapped. The woman was an Italian called Elena Fuoristrada, and she literally draped herself across my sofa, while she fingered its borders and put one foot on an armrest. And I didn't mind. In fact I was charmed. She wore no bra, and her breasts hung down lazily, occasionally swinging under her loose cotton dress as she made one of her sudden movements often for reasons of emphasis. Normally I find such things not just unattractive but positively repellent, yet there was something about those free breasts that was unmistakably arousing. This was slightly embarrassing as Jessica was by now examining my every move. I think I know why those breasts were so attractive, and it was nothing to do with themselves or the rest of what was, after all, a youthful and energetic body. It was her, her entire persona and, most of all, her boldness. Everything about her said, "This is who I am. Accept me as such, or take a running jump. I care not for you, and in fact I find you somewhat inferior and servile. There is nothing you can do that will ever please me." How could any red-blooded man fail to fall in love with that?

Jessica took great pleasure in telling me that the woman had said she thought I was a creep and a *fico lesso*, which apparently is the Italian for a "boiled fig". "Meaning?" I asked, entirely unaffected by the whole matter. "Meaning that you are a persnickety little wimp – the kind of person who worries too much about the silly little things."

"I wonder what a fig looks like when it has been boiled," I said, as my passion for Elena only grew, in response to I know not what absurd sexual mechanism. They say that opposites attract, but I cannot say that Elena was showing any signs of being attracted to me. They say a lot of things: most of them untrue or so general as to be worthless. The reality was undeniable: Elena was my new passion. Jessica was my old one and therefore an encumbrance. "I believe that a boiled fig would probably be bloated and bleached."

"Very attractive," said Jessica. "That's you to a tee." I believe that was her first remark that did not express unalloyed devotion. But such is the psychotic state of love that I wasn't even offended. I didn't heed it. What clearer proof do you need? And surely you too have found yourself in this irrational state? One that ignores the clearest signals of trouble ahead. Evidently Jessica had noticed something.

Well, a man in love is capable of anything, and for me the solution was very simple. I waited until Jessica was having a shower and then looked through her address book for Elena's number. I then waited for her to go out and rang Elena, who eventually replied in an insouciant voice that could melt your whole body. I was stuttering like a schoolboy. Would she come to see me alone? Would she come now because Jessica would be out most of the day? After a little thought she said she would.

Five minutes later, Elena was there. Five minutes! Surely she was as desperate as I was, although such a cool character gave nothing away. She threw her collapsible umbrella into the Chinese vase on the hall table and her coat on top of it. She could not have known, of course, that the vase was worth half a million euros and was one of my most prized possessions. She lost no time in draping herself once more on my sofa – and I didn't care. She had slipped off her sandals and her naked toes were digging themselves into the leather upholstery – and still I didn't care. "Very comfortable sofa, this," she said and then her buttocks jumped up and down in the middle to test the springs. "Yes, very comfortable."

"It cost six and half thousand euros," I announced proudly.

"Really?" she jiggled around even more vigorously. "So what can I do for you?"

"Well, nothing really," I answered pathetically.

"Nothing!" she shouted. "Are you some kind of tease? You ring me up in a state of panic, ask me to come round and tell me it's a good moment because Jessica is out. I think we know what we're talking about here."

I blushed and decided to bluff myself out of my confusion. "What are we talking about here? You tell me."

"Okay, I'll tell you! It's blindingly obvious: you want to go to bed with me."

71

Why would this embarrass a sophisticated man of the world like me? Such was the psychosis... "It's true," I said at last. "I do, I do terribly want to go to bed with you. This, I'm afraid, is a minor passion."

"Only a minor one? Well, I don't think you're for me then."

"No, no. What am I saying? A major passion. An all-consuming passion. A passion that has completely taken hold of me and makes me disregard things I hold most dear."

"By 'things you hold most dear', I assume you mean Jessica. Some credit to you for that, but I don't think you should refer to her as 'things', do you?"

I was baffled for a second or two. "No, no, I don't mean Jessica," I smiled, "I mean 'things' – like my Chinese vase and my sofa."

"Oh," said Elena, looking a little baffled herself.

"God, yes! What I feel for you is in a completely different category from what I have ever felt for Jessica. Elena, I really think that you are the love of my life. I know it now."

"But you're still struggling to put me before your 'things', aren't you?"

"Not at all," I cried. "I said that I disregard them. That really is unique, I promise you."

"What can I say? I'm very moved. I'll have to think about it, though."

"You mean you're not rejecting me? It's not out of the question? Thank you, thank you," I enthused.

"If I come, I'll come at two o'clock tomorrow," she dictated, "so make sure Jessica's not going to be around. No nasty surprises, my friend."

"Oh Elena, my sweet."

Did I see Elena's lip curl, as she leapt off the sofa. "I have to be going," she said and very soon she was quickly and carelessly lifting her coat off the vase and fishing around inside it for her umbrella.

"Elena, give me at least the warmth of your embrace."

Again her lip moved. What a strange lady she was! "Let's leave that until tomorrow. I'm in a hurry."

"Yes, yes. Anything you say. Until tomorrow!" I moaned. Do you see the degradations a man can heap upon himself? This is my warning.

I have to confess that I did slightly neglect my work over the ensuing twenty-four hours. We are all made of flesh, and just occasionally I fall below my usual professional standards. In the evening Jessica didn't help matters by acting strangely. She was untypically grumpy and left our plates on the dining-room table. In the end I had to wash them up myself. However, she didn't put up any resistance to my idea that, as part of her ongoing education, she should visit the art gallery in L***, which is an hour's journey from here. Even when I said, "Make a really good day of it!" and gave her four hundred euros, she did not appear to be placated. She didn't even thank me, and this is another lesson you must always hold dear: women are an ungrateful sex, and that is pretty much a universal rule.

I was at home before two, waiting for Elena and making a few last-minute adjustments, including the removal of Jessica's photograph, which I put in a drawer for safe-keeping. She was punctual, which you wouldn't have expected of her. She breezed in carrying several bags, and went straight to the bedroom, where she undressed. This was almost instantaneous, and she just slipped off her dress, kicked off her sandals and was wearing no underwear.

She then produced a nurse's uniform. I have never understood the attraction of these things, but with Elena I was willing to try anything that took her fancy. "Are you going to wear that?" I said.

"No," she replied, "you are."

Yes, yes, I know what you're thinking: how could I humiliate myself still further? There are no depths to which we will not go when we are a prey to this psychosis. That is the most important lesson in this letter. Never form a permanent relationship with a woman; never give your heart as I did to Elena.

But it did not end there. She then pulled out a dog suit. God knows where she got it from. I was entirely covered in this suit, except for my face. She asked me to kiss her feet, her tits and her buttocks, and in each she angled herself in a certain direction, for what reason I could not be sure.

I won't tell you all of the humiliating poses, positions and postures she inflicted on me that afternoon. I eventually tired of her arrogance, and demanded we went to bed. To my surprise, she agreed demurely and jumped under the covers, but even then I sensed her expression of expectation to be more humorous than amorous. The phone rang. I intended to leave it, but she looked at me and said, "It might be important."

I lifted the phone just to get rid of whoever it was.

"Robert, where have you been? I have been looking for you everywhere." It sounded like Pierre from Human Resources. What could he have wanted with me? He had no right to bother someone of my seniority.

"I'm at home. Whatever it is can wait for the morning," I replied testily.

"But this is important. The green tea market is in freefall."

"Which means exactly," my head began to race. If this were at all serious, I would have been facing ruin, not only at work but also personally, because so sure was I of the upward trend in the foreseeable future that I had been betting on this and not covering it in the opposite direction.

"Well, it looks as though the bottom has fallen out of the market. The Chinese have just dumped huge quantities."

"What is it with the Chinese? Always the Chinese. Pierre, I'm coming over to the office straightaway." I dressed and rushed out of the house. Instinctively I did not stop to kiss or say goodbye to Elena who was maintaining her bemused smile.

On arriving at the office, I rushed to see the colleagues on my section, who I expected to find in a crisis meeting. Instead they were chatting and laughing over cups of coffee. I soon realised that the market was, if anything, rather bullish. I went to see Pierre who denied having made the phone call. Threatening to speak to his superiors as soon as I returned, I rushed back home, now fearing the worst and uncertain as to what Elena's game might be.

They had acted with great alacrity. I have to admit that Elena is an operator. By the time I got back they were gone. As was my Chinese vase. My sofa had been ripped with a knife. Apart from that, there was little damage. Perhaps I should say there was little other damage to my house and property – to me the damage was colossal. Everywhere they had strewn photographs of myself and Elena in absurd positions. A letter on my persecuted sofa made the blackmail explicit: "Your silence will earn our silence. Sorry about the sofa and the vase, we know how much you cared for them – more than you did for Jessica."

Further examination of the flat revealed the plot. A hole in the wardrobe must have been used by Jessica for photographing us. Pierre was looking relaxed because he knew that I would never report him. I was obliged to swallow my bile, and look on as they spent their ill-gotten gains.

After selling my vase for over 800,000 euros – a much higher price than the half million I had paid and yet another demonstration of the range of my business acumen – Elena and Jessica bought a large restaurant and adjoining building in a run-down part of the city. They turned it into one of the most chic establishments we have, and converted the rest of the building into a theatre and arts centre. The dregs of society all collect there and criticise wealth-creators like myself. They married and their "gay" wedding was the society event of the year. I rarely see them, but Jessica is a changed woman. I have to admit that she looks even more attractive, although these days she has the same neglected air as her partner. You probably wouldn't want to get too close.

I am very conscious that I have a highly evolved sensitivity and harmonisation to the civilisation in which I live. I realise that there is no woman worthy of sharing my space. I am happy to spend the occasional night with different women. This is part of being a healthy man. Every week I have a game of squash and every week, usually on a Friday, I go out to get myself a woman, which is not difficult. I perhaps owe that higher form of consciousness to my terrible experience with Jessica and Elena. They taught me the utility of the one-night stand. I of course threw Jessica's photo away and put one of myself on graduation day in the genuine silver photograph frame. I was on my way to the top and to immaculate solitude.

Gottfried, I urge you to follow this same route towards the only state of consciousness and knowledge that can make us happy.

Yours fraternally,
Robert Finnick

A Dream of Justice
(or of as much justice as we can ever expect in this world)

"That's right! We Jews were complete bastards," Leon says with weary sarcasm, although no one can be sure that he has thought out his reply; it seems more likely that he has simply responded with an instinctive verbal reaction to a matter he considers both tiresome and unimportant.

"That is not what I'm saying," his father-in-law Mustapha mutters with the irritation of the misunderstood. "But the Israelis were bastards; they really were and they made my childhood a misery. A misery I tell you. If you had told me at the time that my daughter would marry a Jew and that my grandchildren would have some fancy European surname, I would have spat in your face." And then in a lower tone half to himself, "I would have died of shame."

"Shame, father. That is a terrible thing to say," his daughter Fatima says with a complex laugh that expresses embarrassment, impatience but also a tiny part of solidarity and respect for the old man.

He brightens and apologises, "Of course I have no shame now. Leon is Leon. I don't think of him as a Jew."

"But I am."

"Of course you are. But for me you are my son-in-law, the father of my grandchildren, and the husband of my only surviving daughter. I have got used to you and your strange ways. We speak Hebrew in this house. That is how the dice landed. I have no problem with that, but ..."

"... but leave it alone, Old Man," Leon interrupts. "It's history now. No one cares. This is the new Palestine. Arabs and Jews live together – if not in complete harmony – at least without blowing each other up. It's best not to revisit all that stuff. There must have been faults on all sides, but now it's in the past, and we need to forget."

"You need to forget. Of course you do. But I can never forget. I can forgive, but I cannot forget. I cannot forget the people they crushed under their tanks on the most important …"

"Crushed under tanks? Come on, you tottering old fool."

"Leon, show a little respect!" says Fatima.

"Yes, but crushed under tanks? Let's get real."

"I know because I was there, and the tanks that crushed over three hundred non-violent protesters lying on the ground stopped just next to me. If the tanks had moved just six more inches they would have started to crush me."

"He has finally lost his head," Leon guffaws.

"No he hasn't," his wife turns on him angrily. There is suddenly a light in her eyes, and Leon, who is normally happy to dictate to his wife, albeit in a manner he considers loving, sensitive and even solicitous, knows that he can go no further. He senses there is an area that always divides them and which they have very sensibly decided to avoid. "Tell him," she shouts at her father. "You tell him what happened."

The old man adjusts himself and his clothing in his chair, settling in for a long story that needs to be told patiently, because he believes that his listener will be hard of hearing. "It was back in 2012 and there was a Palestinian leader – a Christian who believed in non-violence. His name was Ibrahim Safieh, who you have heard of."

"Of course."

"Well, you know that he was run over by a tank, but you don't know the circumstances. He came out of nowhere and he had a way with words. Now, I think that he was perhaps a fanatic and that many people died for his principles, but then again, he did change things. Or he started the changes. He was a tall man with a long beard, and he always wore robes. At first some people thought he was ridiculous. He was full of his own importance and yet he had a funny voice. It was shrill, and he was always telling us what God had told him to do. But in spite of this, many young Muslims like myself, as well as Christians of course, started to follow him. He seemed to offer an alternative to the endless fighting against an enemy we could not possibly defeat. He held rallies in Ramallah. They grew bigger and bigger. The Israelis did not like him, but following the massacres in the Gaza Strip, they were beginning to be a little more careful about international public opinion. America was broke and less inclined to bankroll the country. They let him speak. It was odd, because he used a lot of references to Judaism, to what Christians call the Old Testament. He said he was the new Moses and that he would take the Palestinian people out of their captivity and lead them back to their own lands. But he was also very vague. I don't think we will ever know what Ibrahim would have done with Palestine if he had ever had the power. In spite of his non-violence, I think there was an edge of intolerance in him – in his manner and his absolute self-belief."

"But he is our national hero?" says Leon.

"And quite rightly. He brought about the Change. I am just trying to tell you what really happened, because I was there."

"Go on, father," come Leon's respectful words.

"Well, one day there was a huge rally – perhaps two or three hundred thousand. This was quite unheard of. People could not easily meet together even in much smaller numbers or move around. In many towns and villages most of the men had been picked off the streets and imprisoned. That was why so many young women were somehow coming in from the surrounding towns and villages. Ramallah was even then a continuously built-up area reaching to East Jerusalem, and where most of the intellectuals lived. Everyone thought that day would be like every other day. Who knows if Ibrahim already had plans or if, as he claimed, he had awaited the word of God? He spoke at length, and once he got going, you no longer heard his squeaky voice. He spoke well, but as I say he was very vague about what he wanted to achieve and how he was going to do it. He used to speak of our sufferings and say that everything was God's will. God would not make his people suffer forever, and we were being tested. If we believed in God and the goodness of his deeds, we would not only survive, we would prosper. But on this occasion and after having spoken at length, he suddenly fell on his knees and screamed that he had had a vision. His face was white, his eyes turned skyward and his lips were trembling. If he was acting, he was a convincing actor. An angel had told him that we should all march northwards to Jenin. This may not seem strange now, but at the time the Israelis had military checkpoints all over the place. A great wall extended far into what were called the Occupied Territories. We would have to pass through highly populated areas and barren desert, through areas reserved for Jewish settlers who wanted to murder us and through these checkpoints which were manned by well-armed soldiers. It was folly. And yet we set off."

"This was the March of the Hundred Thousand."

"That's correct. For a while the Israelis let us pass. They thought we would get hungry and turn back. Perhaps they thought that was the time to punish us – when we fragmented into small, vulnerable groups. Ibrahim's entire plan, in as much as it existed, was based on the assumption that the Israelis could develop a conscience over their treatment of us Palestinians. Nothing had ever happened that could have given us the slightest hope of their even beginning to empathise with us. Leon, I have to say that, with the exception of a few very unusual and courageous individuals, the Israelis were wholly racist in their attitude to us. Their views may have varied: some would have liked to annihilate us, some would have liked to drive us out from what remained of our lands, some would have liked to bludgeon us into submissiveness and

80

that was pretty much what they did, but almost all of them considered us a problem simply because we existed. They could not and would not perceive us as human beings with rights. That was heresy, and the few who tentatively argued our case were treated as pariahs – as 'self-hating Jews'. So when we set off for Jenin, we did so in a state of desperate elation. Elation because Ibrahim's words – his irrational dreams and simplicities – seemed to be our last hope, after everything else had been tried. Life was so miserable, the injustices so enormous and the world's silence so total and unfathomable, that death held few fears, especially for us young people who had all grown up with jangled nerves – witnesses and often victims of Israeli violence."

The old man stops and studies his listeners: one who knows the story by heart and the other who hears it for the first time. She is nervous; he is gloomy. Leon has agreed to suppress his instincts and resents the imposition. Nevertheless he listens attentively. He does not intend to either encourage or discourage the old man's story, and only stares to show a continuing sense of annoyance.

"We walked for twenty miles – a long way in a small country. The Israelis abandoned their checkpoints, but they monitored our movements from the air and their military vehicles were never far away. But we kept going and the people came to give us food, blankets and clothing. We camped and built fires to keep ourselves warm through the early spring night. We sang. We ate a little food. Not much of course. We were many, and even the generosity of the Palestinian people was not enough."

"This is a little one-sided," says Leon. But his wife's eyes silence him again.

"I am not saying that the Palestinians are inherently better than every other people. Nor are they any worse. But suffering does temporarily make a people better and more introspective, just as power makes them smug, uncaring and materialistic. Jews, of all people, should know that, given how they suffered in Europe."

"Okay, okay. So what happened next? How did Ibrahim Safieh get crushed by a tank? Was there violence? A lot of people say Israeli soldiers were killed."

"Not by us. But I will explain it all in good order. You must be patient, Leon."

"So you camped out like a bunch of boy scouts. What next?" Leon isn't used to the old man adopting such a confident and didactic tone. He, Leon, is the educated man. His father was an industrialist, but he is a professor of Russian literature. A wealthy man, he feels that he has done a great deal by taking in the old man after his mother-in-law died, and nobody can deny that Leon is a kind and decent man in all his dealings. He is a man almost without prejudice, but he has his own reasons for not examining the past. His maternal grandfather spent fifteen years in prison because he failed to report to the Truth and Reconciliation Committee that he had taken part in the unprovoked massacre of ten Palestinian farm-workers and a child in a remote part of the West Bank. He liked – indeed loved – the man, who was generous to a fault, but not when Leon married an Arab. For five years the grandfather would not speak to his grandson, and he has never wanted to see his great-grandchildren. Leon's other grandfather had been possibly less racist – or at least less violently racist, but he made himself wealthy from the confiscation of Arab lands. A skilful businessman with good political connections, he has never had to return a single hectare. Leon is a direct beneficiary of stolen wealth. Somewhere in his psyche he is aware of this, but no one – not even the Arabs – want to revive the programme of restoring land to pre-1948 owners. It proved to be as corrupt in the reversal as it had been brutal in the original expropriation. Only the powerful regained land and it was often not their own. False papers were created. Together,

Jewish and Arab lawyers grew rich out of the restoration of Arab lands to the "wrong owners". Powerful Jews and powerful Arabs became even more powerful, but at least the demarcation between the powerful and powerless followed racist distinctions less closely. The powerless were ignored.

"Well," the old man continues, "the next day was very different. We awoke with a sense of victory. It says a lot about those times that a twenty-mile walk late into the night was considered a victory. We were tired but exhilarated. The Israelis had set up a provisional checkpoint during the night and it was flanked by a large troop of soldiers and military equipment. Ibrahim, unusually devout for a Palestinian Christian, said his prayers publicly and was joined by some of our own clerics. He gathered us on the road again and formed us into a column that was fifteen to twenty people wide. He then asked us to march to the checkpoint. When we reached it, an Israeli officer came forward and ordered us to stop, but Ibrahim simply removed the pistol from his hand, emptied the magazine, and threw it away. He then embraced the owner of the weapon and called him his brother, before continuing briskly on his way as though the checkpoint did not exist. The officer grimaced, not knowing how to react. We followed and, copying his gesture, we embraced the other soldiers and disarmed them if they would allow us to do this without force. After passing the checkpoint, we found a second line of soldiers with rifles already pointed.

"A single shot rang out and the man walking next to Ibrahim fell to the ground. When a second shot killed two men, Ibrahim speeded up his already brisk pace, but did not break into a run. He had a tactical instinct which did not however make up for his lack of strategy. Soon it was clear that the Israelis had orders not to shoot Ibrahim, because the riflemen were now cutting down swathes of human beings on both sides of him. This caused some people, particularly those who had always been sceptical of his non-violent methods, to accuse him of conspiring with Israelis, but events were to prove them wrong.

"We were now on top of the soldiers and some broke into a rout. Others kept their positions, but their arms were no longer of any use. This was a crucial moment, and we were still relatively undisciplined. We had suffered and were angry. It would have taken very little for that anger to turn into revenge, and the non-violent movement would have died there and then, as the Israelis no doubt wanted. But Ibrahim wasted no time. Again he hugged a soldier who had fallen into rougher hands. 'Leave him,' he said, 'he was following orders. One day the court will try those who today have broken the law. They will be punished in accordance with the law. We are not the law, and we must act peacefully at all times.' He said these things in Hebrew, so that the soldiers would understand. They were visibly relieved, as they were now all surrounded by a great mass of incensed Palestinians. They did not grimace in disgust, as the first officer had done at the checkpoint, but often returned the embrace enthusiastically. 'These are the orders,' said one of the officers as he held up an envelope. Another officer shouted, 'Traitor.' We began to realise the extent of our victory and how we had disoriented our enemy. The orders confirmed what we already knew – the soldiers had been instructed to open fire and to provoke our violent reaction. In this they had failed.

"We lost sixty-seven dead that day. I can remember many of them. One was a cousin of mine. He wasn't that interested in politics, and I was the one who had persuaded him to come. I no longer felt elated, although Ibrahim and some of his close followers clearly did. They were right, I suppose. We had achieved a lot, and if we had killed even one of those soldiers, we would have lost everything. They were right, but it did not feel like that to me. Whatever way we did this, we were going to pay a high price.

"We met few real obstacles on the rest of the way to Jenin. The Israelis sent negotiators, and the international press were allowed to follow us. The Israelis understood from these negotiations that we would disband on reaching Jenin, and they were now determined to show the world how liberal they were – something that did not come easily to them. They tried to stop the people from supplying us with food, and they forced us into a tortuous and gruelling route, but we still got to Jenin. Ibrahim organised one of his rallies, and it may be that the Israelis were not entirely wrong when they said that he had agreed to disband the march once he got to Jenin. They still thought that this was an interlude, rather than an event that would change our lives and theirs.

"Ibrahim delivered one of his typical speeches. In fact, he was in some ways very predictable. The crowd was massive. At Jenin there was a huge refugee camp. You would have thought that things could not have been worse for Palestinians, but they were in these camps. The only water was rainwater, and the eight o'clock curfew brought terrors every night: light-bombs and soldiers running on the tin roofs above the refugees' heads. They were always dignified people – dignified by terrible suffering. They broke out of the camp to join us; perhaps they sensed that something at last was going to change. Once again, Ibrahim fell on his knees and spoke of a vision. This time we would march on Nablus. The Israelis were furious, and we were a little perplexed. If we marched on Nablus, we would be marching unarmed towards some of the most ruthless and murderous people in a land not known for its restraint. Nablus was a large city with a small but vicious settler community, and nothing achieved there would be lasting. By road we would have to return the way we came and then take one of the roads leading to the east. The alternative was a gruelling overland journey with few supplies and ideal terrain for the Israelis to harass us without restraint; surely the press would not follow us across such open country. Everyone had thought that after Jenin, we would march on Jerusalem, where decisions were made and the Israeli community was more divided. Some of the Jews there were quite happy to close their ears and eyes to things happening in other parts of the country, but if they happened in front of them, they would not approve. Some would object, and as soon as we had a reasonably substantial Jewish constituency on our side, we would be halfway to achieving what we wanted.

"Along the march, some people had been leaving, but others had been joining. After the announcement of the march on Nablus, many people slipped away. I thought about it, but did not know what to do. I think I would have returned home, if my cousin had not been killed. I felt guilty. But also, I think, I wanted to see how it was all going to end. I was no longer confident, and mass hysteria had given way to more rational argument. We were angry with Ibrahim, and perhaps I was even stupid enough to believe some of the rumours about him. It was a long time ago. He was a brave man, no doubt of that. Although I also think he was a deeply damaged person and probably half mad. But it takes a madman to change a mad world.

"We had only walked about ten miles out of Jenin when we came up against a column of Israeli tanks. A pompous Israeli officer came forward and told us to return to Jenin. He hectored us in Hebrew and ungainly Arabic. When Ibrahim tried to disarm him and embrace him, the officer responded by punching him in the stomach and then hitting him over the back of the neck with his pistol. At first, it appeared that Ibrahim was unconscious, but he soon started struggling to his feet and wiped a little blood away with his hand. He announced in perfect Hebrew that the officer was still his brother, although he kept his distance and did not attempt to embrace him another time. Ibrahim had just quarter of an hour of life left: that was the time the officer gave us to clear the area, before he marched back to the tank with a ridiculous swing of one arm, while the other held up the pistol in an equally comic position. On his return to the tanks, the officer started to shout a series of orders, as though he were a skilfully devised automaton. When the engines were started in all the tanks at almost the same time, Ibrahim decided to deploy one of Gandhi's tactics. We were to lie on the ground at right angles to the direction of the rough path we had been walking on.

"Just before I lay down I saw the first tank jump unsteadily forward. Black smoke came from an exhaust somewhere at the back. In part it just seemed like any other motor vehicle setting off on a journey; in part it was a great grey box of evil, as though the Israelis had designed a container for all their hatred and inhumanity. I was unprepared for what was going to happen. Those who were watching from the side described what happened next. The column slowly approached our unprotected prostrate bodies. Ibrahim had said that no one would drive over people lying on the ground, and so when the first tank was close to us, everyone expected it to stop. Perhaps the soldiers would get out and beat the people on the ground. Instead the tank suddenly accelerated as though to do what it wanted to do, it would have to take a run at it. There was screaming and then machine-gun fire and explosions. Suddenly the tank stopped. Why? I had no idea what was happening. Someone pulled me up from the ground, touching me as though desperate to know what a person so close to death might have felt like. I too, I suppose, perceived myself in a new light. That is how I have continued to feel that terrible event – throughout my long life I have always considered myself to be someone living on time that no longer belonged to me. Possibly I have enjoyed life a little more precisely because I no longer expected much from it. I was alive and that was enough. I looked down at the base of the tank and saw the blood leaking through the black grease of the tracks. Human bodies and human machinery. Defencelessness and the metallic technology of death."

"That's enough," Leon says while standing up. "This all happened fifty years ago. Bad stuff was done on both sides, and nothing is to be gained by going over this again and again. We became the Republic of Israel-Palestine and then the Republic of Palestine. We have changed, and frankly you Palestinians have won, so why don't you show a little magnanimity and put the past in the past."

"We haven't won at all," Fatima shouts at her husband. "You Jews still own most of the land you stole, you run most of the industry and are in all the positions of most influence. Don't tell us that we won. We still suffer."

"Are you happy now, old man?" says Leon. "You've caused an argument between husband and wife. We never argued before you came to live with us. This can't work, if all you want to do is talk of the misdeeds of my people – my people who have suffered at least as much as yours."

"I have no wish to cause a rift between man and wife. I am telling the story as it was. Israelis and Palestinians. Both have their good and bad, and it was Israelis who stopped the tanks. This is what I want to tell you and more besides. Because the story is more complex and more interesting than what you find in our school books, which are themselves the result of yet another absurd negotiation. Not that I am against negotiation: if we can only get along through endless negotiation, then so be it. Better that than fighting, far better. But I am telling you, my family, what really happened. Do you want to hear it?"

"Yes," says Fatima, "it's about time Leon heard it too."

"What do you mean the Israelis stopped the tanks? How could it be otherwise? They were driving them."

"Ah, but not the same Israelis. The Israelis who stopped the tanks were not the ones who were driving them."

"Explain."

"A group of Israeli infantrymen jumped on the first tank. The tank crew had left their hatch on their turret open as they did not expect an attack by armed men. The infantrymen opened fire down the hatch and started to climb in. The soldiers in the tank behind had seen what was happening and fired their machine gun at the men still on the tank. Five of them died and fell to the ground. Then more infantrymen attacked the other tanks. This was not just a fight between right and wrong, between racism and integration and between humanity and fanaticism; it was also a fight between two military units – one infantry and one motorised artillery. Grenades were thrown down the hatches and machine-gun fire from other tanks mowed them down. Eventually the infantrymen took control, although I think they sustained more casualties. Forty-six of them died that day. I know that because we buried them. It was more difficult with our dead. We think that there were three hundred and eighty-five, but the bodies were so pulverised that we had to count them by asking people who was missing. As the march was made up of family groups and friends, the dead were often from groups that were entirely destroyed, so we cannot be sure about the exact figure. It was probably more."

"But this is extraordinary," says Leon. "This could be a founding story. How come no one knows about this? This is a story of Israeli soldiers killing each other, while Arabs stand by. Come on, this would be dynamite if it were true."

"It is true. Why does no one talk about it? Well, the answer is simple. Politicians. Politicians wanted to keep their own ethnic constituencies. On that both Israeli and Palestinian politicians were agreed. Perhaps it was the only thing they fully agreed about. They fudged their agreements on unification, a secular state, universal suffrage, equal property rights and an integrated army, but they wanted to keep some of the tensions, because they all represented certain groups. As the Palestinian community grew much larger with the returning refugees, Israelis wanted them divided into Muslims, Christians, Druze, Bedouins and so on. Stories of cross-community solidarity were not what they wanted. They wanted continuous argument, jostling and negotiation, negotiation, negotiation. But then again, I have seen many things I would never have dreamt of, so I don't complain. We have come a long way, but I have always believed that every people is better than its politicians."

"But how do you cover up something like that?"

"It hasn't been totally covered up. You don't know it, because you haven't wanted to know about it. It is not part of the mainstream myth, but it is part of real history, and many Arabs and Jews must know about it. There were many witnesses on both sides, many books have been written and many documentaries have been made, but the majority did not want to hear about it after the establishment of Israel-Palestine. They were difficult years of continuing racism and unfulfilled expectations. Even when history moves quickly, it moves slowly, because people do not really change overnight. They pretend to change, but they have been brought up to see things in a particular way and cannot change in their hearts, even if they would like to. Change is generational, and I am happy with what has happened. Only in the last ten to fifteen years do I feel that we could never go back. That's why I welcomed your marriage. Everyone told me that I, as a veteran of the March of the Hundred Thousand, should have been angry. I should have felt betrayed. But I said, 'Why? They are in love, and that is what they want to do. No one will stop them, and anyway I don't want to, because this is the way forward. If we don't want to be divided forever, we need to intermarry; we need to mix, but we haven't mixed very much. Too little, in fact.'"

"You're right, father. Sorry if I'm a bit prickly. You're a very wise old man. Thank you for telling me your story," Leon says with doubtful sincerity. The experience has been unpleasant and he would have preferred to have avoided it. Having been subjected to it, he now wants to bring it to a swift conclusion.

"But it's not over. It's only just beginning. I haven't even finished telling you about that one incident. You said something about Arabs standing by. That's exactly how it was. We were unarmed, and besides we were sworn to non-violence. We were like spectators, but the most stunning incident was just about to happen. The infantrymen brought the pompous officer to us. He was very arrogant and kept threatening them with all kinds of punishments. Another officer pointed to him and said, 'This is Captain P, who is known to all of us for his brutality. He riddled a wounded girl with bullets, and was even tried by one of our courts.' 'And acquitted?' one of us said. 'Of course,' the officer said, 'but this time there will be no impunity.' Captain P laughed, 'And what court will ever try me?' A young soldier moved forward abruptly and said, 'This is the court that will try you.' He had dark skin, and must have been a child of Arab Jews. He raised his gun and pointed it at Captain P's head, and the captain immediately fell on his knees and tugged at the soldier's trouser legs. 'A Jew should never kill a Jew.' 'It has already started,' and he took out a pistol to dispatch the captain at short range. The captain wept as he understood the inevitability of his death, and we just watched unable or unwilling to intervene. He fired one shot and the captain's kneeling body crumpled the short distance to the ground. Then the soldier lifted the pistol to his own head and shouted in heavily accented English, 'Israel is fucked.' He shot himself and his body collapsed across that of the dead captain. Who was he? Why did he shout in English? I will never know. The only press at that stage was a lone reporter from the *Jerusalem Post*. It could be relied on to distort and massage the truth. As far as I know, no one reported that dramatic incident. You, Leon, are used to Haaretz in three languages: Hebrew, Arabic and English, with 'The Voice of Palestine' under each masthead, but it wasn't always like that. "

"My god. It was a massacre."

"Oh, we were used to massacres. We suffered them all the time. Ibrahim had been right when he said that non-violence would cause the Israelis to fight amongst themselves, because they would no longer be able to believe their myths and would have to confront their own morality. But Ibrahim was dead. Did this mean it was all over? We had no idea of what to do next."

"You marched on Jerusalem after all."

"Of course we did. That is official history, but it was not a simple decision. I was appointed to the ruling Committee of Twenty."

"Come now, old man, you are making fun of us. The tank stopped just before killing you, and then you become one of the leaders of the movement that changed our nation. And which particular cabinet post did you have, father-in-law?"

"The position of the tank was crucial, and it was the reason why I was appointed to the Committee, which consisted of the twenty living people closest to the tank after it came to a halt. Who made that appointment? That is the important thing. Have you ever heard of Yusuf Khalidi?"

"Vaguely. But I can't place the name."

"Of course you can," says Fatima. "He was an important leader at the time of the March of the Hundred Thousand. He was shot by a member of the Kach Party shortly after the establishment of Israel-Palestine."

"He was not just a leader," Mustapha continues, "he was the leader of the whole successful movement. He was the real Father of the Nation. He is the one we should all revere, but he was too clever for the vested interests. It may have been the Kach Party who actually killed him, but many more mainstream politicians would have wanted him out of the way. While Ibrahim was the mad tactician and showman, Yusuf was the strategist and arch-schemer. He understood that Ibrahim had hit on a weakness in the enormous Israeli military machine, but he also had a very clear idea of where he wanted to go and how to achieve it. The Israeli military command must have been shaken by events – by the internecine killing – but they were most certainly relieved that Ibrahim was dead, and they probably gave orders to the tank crews for exactly that reason. They thought the movement was Ibrahim. First they wanted to avoid making him a martyr, but once the movement looked strong and also unpredictable, they wanted him out of the way. They were right in the sense that he had created the movement out of nothing, but I strongly believe that had he lived, it would have floundered. Yusuf spoke to us from a burned-out tank. Our aim, he said, was not a tiny Palestinian state but a united country covering all the territory of the old mandate, in which both Jew and Palestinian would live together in complete equality. It would be a secular state, and Arabic and Hebrew would be the official languages. It was he who ordered the burial of all the martyrs, both Jewish and Arab. Ibrahim and his fellow martyrs were originally buried amongst the infantrymen, but the Israeli army later removed their own dead to another cemetery. Now, of course there is the Ibrahim Mausoleum, but then it was a more modest affair. Still Yusuf had it done in style while he quietly worked to have discipline reimposed along with a sense of purpose.

"His idea of making a committee of twenty random leaders was also a clever move. He had ideas and we had none. Most of us were young, and we soon adored his clever mind and generosity. It was said, and it could well be true, that he had never previously supported non-violent action. It was even claimed that he had been an official of some importance in Hamas. This too is quite believable, because he had the kind of organisational abilities that are rarely innate and are more often the product of training. I also believe that he had never been particularly religious, but he was wise enough to know that the movement had been born of religious passions, and he would have to maintain the illusion of religious orthodoxy. He was therefore punctilious in his prayers and as strict in following the outward dictates of Islam as Ibrahim had been in following those of Christianity. Above all, he understood the importance of not threatening Jews. He had learned from Ibrahim that they had to be won over – or rather enough of them had to be won over to make a difference.

"He immediately told us that we would be marching on Jerusalem and not Nablus. 'That was madness,' he said to us. That was the only criticism I heard him make of Ibrahim, but I think he had been exasperated by the man's reliance on the word of God rather than the rational considerations of a human brain. He invited the Israeli soldiers to join us and throw away their weapons. This too caused many different reactions. A few did just that. Others said they were returning to their units and would accept whatever punishment was inflicted on them. Others still were very conscious that they were now effectively outlaws, but quixotically wanted to protect us. They marched along with us but at a distance. They carried their arms and kept a great deal of military supplies in trucks they had commandeered. Their presence made Yusuf very nervous, but he stopped short of giving them a direct order to leave. 'A group of highly trained military men without a ions in Israeli society, and our guardian angels inued to defend us. They too lost some of their men, others joined them. Yusuf let them fight. He just ted the Knesset. We marched in. That is, five hundred s entered and Yusuf told the others to stay outside. He ounced that the parliament was dissolved and then e was bedlam. The Knesset members ranted and raved, he immediately began to concede. Half of them had to e said, and an equal number of our people would take place. The new Knesset would be a constituent mbly for a new country called Israel-Palestine. The lis were happy at least that their name came first; they colluding in the demolition of all they held dear, and elt they were gaining concessions. Yusuf's master-e was that he did not have himself nominated."

o were you, as a member of the Committee of Twenty, mber of this constituent assembly?"

was."

atima draws in her breath, "But father, you never told at."

t was not a big deal. I followed Yusuf's instructions t was all over very quickly. He said that new elections the most important thing. They had to be held before stablishment got over its shock and woke up to the hat it had released the reins of power when there was no need. Those elections were held three hectic s later, and I was not re-elected. My party, the Islamic list Party, got very few votes and my political career ver before it even started."

he Islamic Socialist Party?"

es, that was a mistake. Don't mix religion and s, you're quite right. But after a political earthquake, arties coalesce in a very erratic manner. I did not e that party; it chose me. Anyway my heart was not I am quite political, but I am not a politician. That ot my world and I was glad to leave it. The party split

clear purpose is always a risk, and our plans rely entirely on the avoidance of violence. The Israelis will eventually come up with methods to defeat us, that is why we must strike at their heart immediately.' The Israelis must have thought they had destroyed our movement by destroying Ibrahim. They probably thought that having him out of the way was worth the upset his death caused amongst increasingly hostile 'international opinion'. But actually they had given us a superb leader. That was luck and that was the randomness of history.

"On the road to Jerusalem, the Israeli government continuously sent negotiators just as it had done on the road to Jenin, but this time they were very senior. Ministers appeared and left exasperated. They were beginning to realise that Yusuf was dangerous. He was always polite, and liked to joke with them. They forced themselves to laugh, but were at a loss. Should they kill him too? Wouldn't that just produce another even more formidable leader? I don't think it would have. We Arabs were lucky to have had Ibrahim, and now we were even luckier to have found Yusuf. I doubt that our luck would have lasted, but the Israeli leaders were not clever men. For sixty-four years they had relied on military superiority, and that superiority had grown to a level so absurdly colossal that they no longer had to think. Suddenly the situation appeared to them much more complex than it really was, and Yusuf was an expert at knowing when to show his hand and when to keep it hidden. These negotiators rushed off not because Yusuf had not offered them something, but because they were quite incapable of making a decision. They also believed that he would be stopped by the wall, but when we approached it was suddenly demolished by explosive, just like God divided the Red Sea for the people of Israel. Yusuf once appeared to suggest that it was the work of our infantrymen who hovered around like our guardian angels, and in any event

Yusuf did not leave things to divine intervention. He just quietly said in his elliptic manner, 'I was right not to offend them, and they have proved their worth.' This showed how close he had come to getting them to leave. It must have been a difficult decision for him, but in the end he got it right. We members of the ruling committee just rubber-stamped his decisions, but he talked us through his reasoning and always treated us with the utmost respect, as indeed he did almost everyone he met.

"We read in the papers that the Israeli army had shot the infantrymen who returned to their barracks. This was not only a terrible act; it was also stupid of them. The army was made up of ordinary people, and ordinary people were now beginning to shift in their opinions. You might not know about these events, Leon, but at the time there was not a person in Israel or the Occupied Territories who did not. The executions merely alienated the army, confirmed the resolve of the deserters who protected us and increased the disorientation on which Yusuf was relying. He knew it could not last, and that he had to bring about an immediate change or everything would be lost.

"At last we approached the city, and I shall never forget that moment. It was one of fear – not for oneself but for our momentous movement whose aims now looked achievable – and one of incredulity, as after all, there were only a few weeks dividing us from the rally we had attended in Ramallah and a time when there was not even hope of one day being able to hope. I thought then that if I survived I would speak of little else for the rest of my life, but instead the rest of my life has been about survival – not the survival I thought of then, which was no more than prolonging one's physical existence, but the survival we all struggle with even in affluent countries that are not riven by conflicts. It has not been a bad life, because, as I said, I have not expected very much. Many of my fellow marchers have felt cheated and constantly tell me so, but then they

did not feel that tank get so close. They [...] many friends and relations. They did not wi[...] closely as I did, and therefore they do not k[...] run it was.

"The army never stood against us again[...] was a decision from above or simply a lac[...] amongst the ranks is something I can[...] probably the soldiers did not know that th[...] the end of their racist state, and if they h[...] their privileges would at least be weake[...] might have acted differently. Maybe that is [...] part. I think that they were like Ibrahim; th[...] where their actions were taking them, and [...] were no match for Yusuf. It is firm lead[...] cruelty and military might, that overcomes [...]

"Sounds like an argument for a stron[...] says Leon. "I think your Yusuf might ha[...] you, if he had lived."

"You might be right, but I think not."

"You clearly loved him. What did you f[...] assassinated?"

"Devastated. I was devastated," some[...] bitterness reawakes with his words. "I we[...] would have taken revenge. That's how in[...] Nearly four hundred men and women[...] beneath tanks, and I had no desire for [...] death of one man almost destroyed m[...] violence."

"But it didn't?"

"No. Because you just get back to life.[...] the difficulties of life. A man's life is always[...] from contemporary history, even the life [...] who for a brief period was at the centre of [...]

"So you didn't encounter any more resi[...]

"Not from the army, but organised gr[...] with weapons and many people died. Th[...]

shortly afterwards, and I think the two factions continued to quarrel for some decades – but without me."

"I have never denied that terrible things were done," says Leon, "but that was fifty years ago. You people fail to move on, and that is what is holding Palestine back at the moment. We simply have to forget the past, however terrible."

Leon feels that the argument is overwhelmingly convincing. It should be the end of the conversation. They should understand. But they don't.

"You think that the Arabs are the ones who can't forget – the only ones who can't forget," says Fatima, "but what about your grandfather? He won't even come to see his grandchildren, your children, but still you're happy that he has decided to speak to you. You chat on the phone to a man who despises your children."

"A man can do wrong without being wholly bad. You have to understand his upbringing."

"I don't have to understand anything of the sort," snaps Fatima, visibly angry, and Leon takes the warning. He has seen her like that on very few occasions, enough to know that the cost can be high if he doesn't read the signal. He met Fatima when she was a personal assistant to one of the directors in the family firm where he worked part-time during his studies. He was attracted of course by her dark hair, intelligent eyes, curved Mediterranean nose and warm smile, but he was doubly attracted by her refusal to ever offer him one of those smiles. She told him later by way of explanation that she considered him "just another arrogant young Jewish boy". He set about courting her with unfailing perseverance, and so she always retains an element of the upper hand she originally held, even after surrendering some of her power to adapt to her wifely role as she sees it. "I want you to go and see that grandfather of yours," she says, but he knows it is an order.

"And you want me to take his grandchildren. Is that it?" he guesses.

"No, I want you to take my father."

"Your father? Why should I take your father?"

"Because he was a witness to the birth of this unhappy country, and so was your grandfather. The only way you're ever going to understand what happened is if you go through with this. There are books on those events in any bookshop, but you will never read them. You prefer to hide behind the 'official version'; you prefer the comfort of ignorance. Our children have many, many relations who died because of those events. How can they ever understand if their father can't? And if they do and you don't, there will always be a rift between you and them."

Leon presses the button on the intercom at the gate to his grandfather's home and vast garden. It has been a long time since he was last there, but the long drive, once a symbol of certain welcome, looks threatening, especially when, in place of his grandfather and now-departed grandmother, he sees two large black dogs barking fiercely and running fast down the gravel. The gate has clicked open but he waits until his grandfather comes into view, walking vigorously in spite of his stick which he doesn't use gingerly to take his weight, but as a prop to tap the ground in front of him – more an affectation of old age. Leon and his grandfather, David Rubinstein, greet each other without their once customary embraces and then the old men shake hands, each with an excess of courtesy. Rubinstein shouts at his dogs to calm them down and gestures that they should all go to his house, a sturdy villa in Californian style. In the meantime, an old woman has also come out not so much to greet them as to announce her presence. She shakes the visitors' hands limply and stares at them with evident disapproval. It turns out that this is grandfather's new partner – a lover for his old age. They process up the drive in awkward silence.

Once inside the home, the guests are seated in comfort and coffees produced.

"To what do I owe this honour?" asks Rubinstein with muted sarcasm. "In the company of your father-in-law too." Leon feels that he is actually rather pleased by this change to his routine.

"I would have thought that your grandfather had made his feelings quite clear," says the old lady.

"Be quiet," he says, "I don't want to upset our guests. I am very happy to see you both. But I am curious about the reason for the visit."

"Fatima – my wife Fatima – has suggested that you only started talking to me again because you refuse to speak to your other grandson, who must now be what? – twenty?"

"Twenty-one," he replies, his face darkening and whatever good will he had fading quickly. "Your wife clearly makes it her business to be remarkably well informed. Does she know the reason why I won't speak to him?"

"Very possibly, but she asked me to ask you."

Rubinstein does not like the way this unknown woman appears to be manipulating their conversation from a distance, but he allows the conversation to take its course. "The reason is quite simple: he refuses to speak to me."

"He's become a radical," says the old lady grimly. "He wants us Jews to pay for what he calls 'war crimes'. He's holed up in a squat in East Jerusalem with some other down-and-outs, and you can't get a word of sense out of him."

Rubinstein looks shattered. "It's not something I want to talk about. If you're interested, go and see him. He might speak to you, if you take your father-in-law."

"Oh yes, the father-in-law will go down very well," says the old lady, whose sarcasm is unashamed. "They'll probably make you an honorary member of their revolutionary group."

"Revolutionary group?"

"Yes," says Rubinstein in a tired voice, "it seems that he is mixed up with the people who last year kidnapped Michael Adler, the chairman of the Confederation of Palestinian Industries."

"Christ, he could be in prison."

"He could ..."

"... and they should throw away the keys," the old lady interrupts.

Rubinstein ignores her, "He could be and they only leave him out because he's an Ibrahim and not a Yusuf. He's got a big mouth and has no idea what he's about. He's more useful to them out of prison. With the noise he makes, they'll never have any trouble finding him."

"My father-in-law knew them both," says Leon.

"Who? Your cousin and who else?"

"No, Ibrahim and Yusuf. He was on the March of the Ten Thousand."

The old man brightens and turns to Mustapha; history has that power to ennoble even in the face of the most entrenched prejudices. "What did you say your name was?" he asks, but gets no reply other than a fixed stare.

"Mustapha was on the Committee of Twenty," Leon continues.

"Was he now?" Rubinstein is genuinely respectful, as though in the company of, yes, an enemy, but also an enemy of high standing. Generals have something in common, even when on opposing sides.

"I can take no credit for it," Mustapha speaks at last. "It was purely a matter of chance."

"It is always a matter of chance," Rubinstein smiles.

"Mustapha says that Israeli soldiers crushed hundreds of peaceful protesters with their tanks," Leon continues to push the point.

"Of course they did," the old man doesn't hesitate. "Of course, everyone knew that at the time. We were led by idiots. They should never have killed Ibrahim, and they should have killed Yusuf immediately. Instead our highest politicians paid him court and ran after him like children. If only we had had a Yusuf! Every step he took was quickly calculated and carefully executed. Even his own death was engineered, I think. He knew that his death would seal the new status quo, and that his job was done. The Kach Party may have killed him, but he placed himself in their sights. There's no doubt of that. At the right moment for him, he made it easy for them and they obliged. They were as stupid as the rest of us. We were thoroughly outsmarted."

"We were too damn nice," the old lady is red with fury. "We killed Ibrahim, and we should have killed Yusuf, and we should have kept killing until they all went quiet. We had an army and they didn't. Why did we lose our nerve?"

"We are all Palestinians now, my love," Rubinstein smiles at her calmly; the bitterness and cynical humour are there, but almost concealed, and their nuanced presence is carefully calculated. She looks pleased and hurt: hurt because those words – her being a Palestinian, even in some ironic sense – stir up and tighten her intestines; pleased because those other words – "my love" officially announce her position to one of the old man's relations, even if it is the one who went and married an Arab.

"I remember you," Leon suddenly cries, shifting in his chair and horror passing across his face. "You're Eva Argaman, the woman who hit the Palestinian shopper." Everyone knows the details: she was the daughter of a wealthy family, not one of those funding the most extremist settlers but people with moderate views who supported the Peace Now movement. She became notorious for a single event that even now seemed to straighten her back against the pressures of age. A photo of her was discovered and published in the newspapers, and in it she is seen slapping an elderly Palestinian woman in the face. The woman is overweight and overburdened with plastic bags of what appear to be foodstuffs. On the back of the picture which she sent to a female colleague in the army, she wrote, "Teaching respect – the glory days!" A trophy picture, like so many, but unfortunately for her a decade later, her army friend was no longer her friend, and to repay some real or imagined slight she sent the picture to the papers.

"You want to know how I could have possibly done such a thing? Am I right?" there is the slightest trace of defensiveness in her tone, something entirely missing up to this moment. "People don't understand the times. Yes, I enjoyed my time in the army – I particularly enjoyed the friendship, the camaraderie. Young people can't know what they're missing: we were fighting against a common enemy and we were fighting hard. That brings you close together, very close."

"And at no cost, given that the *common enemy* had no weapons – no army, no navy, no air force," Leon is now getting angry too. "A war in which you mete it out, and receive nothing back but the occasional homemade rocket exploding in the desert."

"We had casualties too, and civilian ones. What about the suicide bombers?"

"You mean starting with Baruch Goldstein?" says Leon immediately.

"He wasn't a bomber!" she stops and realises she has said something stupid. More plaintively she says, "It was war. There were casualties on both sides. War is never fair. You cannot pull your punches."

He looks at her quizzically and holds her own self-confident gaze. She breaks first, exploding in a fit of anger, "You young people understand nothing. They gave our land away to the Arab. We could still be here and not in this hideous multicultural mishmash, if we had had more balls

– we lost the one place where we could at last be Jewish without fear. We lost our dream."

"My wife was right to send me here. It has been painful, but I now know she was right. She wanted to teach me something and you two have certainly obliged – beyond all her hopes. I call my father-in-law father, and rightly so: he has wisdom." This time Leon means it.

They stand up to go and Rubinstein stays seated. He waves his hand as though shooing animals. "Go, go and don't come back, Leon. I don't want to see you or hear from you again. Go, go, get out of here. Go and see your cousin if you want. He lives at number thirty-five, Gamal Nasser Street, Jerusalem, an appropriate address for a renegade."

As they crunch their way back down the gravel drive, Leon and Mustapha are formulating different reactions to their encounter, principally because they belong to different generations.

"How could he live with a woman like that," Leon feels ashamed of this family connection.

"How could she end up with a man like that," Mustapha retorts. "Hundreds, thousands, even ten of thousands of Israelis did such things. That was a time when they were shooting children, like your grandfather did. Of course, she shouldn't have slapped that woman. If she hadn't kept the photograph and been so stupid as to send it to someone else, she would probably be pontificating about the horrors of those times, keeping a photo of Ibrahim on her wall and celebrating Unification Day with the rest of us. We are so plagued by photographs, because photographs enlarge not just an image but a moment. I prefer her to hypocrites and racists like your grandfather. The photograph only means that in a given moment she was driven by the prevailing conformism to think that slapping an elderly woman was admissible. Things changed but the photograph trapped her in time and forced her to defend what she knows is indefensible. She is in part a victim of those times."

"Victim? Her?" Leon shakes his head in disbelief. "Let's go home. We've done what Fatima wanted. And she got her result."

"I thought we were going to Jerusalem to see your cousin," Mustapha objects.

"You're joking. Why would we want to do that?"

It's doubtful that the famous Egyptian leader would have been very happy to give his name to such an unassuming lane in the centre of the old town. Leon's cousin, Baruch, is a gaunt youth with wavy hair and intense blue eyes. He acknowledges unenthusiastically the presence of Leon and his father-in-law. He saunters over to a corner of the room and signals to them to sit down on a sofa. "Nice of you to come, but a little rash. They're probably opening a file on you this very minute."

"Who's they?"

"The secret services."

"Well, it'll make dull reading."

"Why have you come?"

"Just curious. Our grandfather believes that you're implicated in Michael Adler's kidnap."

"Well, he's wrong, but I don't have any problem with the people who really did do it. This country needs to wake up to the past. It needs to acknowledge the crimes committed in the Occupied Territories before 2012."

"You're crazy," says Leon.

"Then fuck off out of here."

"Young man," Mustapha enters the conversation, "I don't think you're crazy. Not at all. It's good that you want to make people aware of the past, but you can't do it by kidnapping people. It doesn't help. I admire your concern, but reject your methods."

Baruch looks troubled. He signals to a young woman who runs over. This one looks almost sick with intensity. Baruch introduces her as Eleanor and places a proprietorial arm on her shoulder.

"This man is against our methods," he points to Leon's father-in-law with a gesture that lacks his earlier aggression.

She however seems less accepting. "What's your angle? What are you doing here?" Mustapha recognises that arrogance; she seems exactly like those young Israelis who in his youth demanded his papers as soon as he stuck his head out of the door – only now she is asking different questions and defending something else: the sanctity of his own people's victimhood. He knew that it was going to be strange; that is why he insisted on coming. Curiosity, more than anything else, has driven him towards this meeting, but he didn't think it would be this hard.

"My son-in-law is Baruch's cousin. This is a family encounter, but I am also interested in what he's saying. You see, I was on the Committee of Twenty and I knew Ibrahim Safieh and Yusuf Khalidi."

"Well," she sneers, "now I understand it all. Two men who betrayed their people. And you were one of their followers."

"Betrayed? But that is ridiculous."

"They left crimes unpunished and the criminals in possession of their booty. They were merely extensions of Western imperialism."

Baruch, who has now detached his arm from the girl's shoulder, mutters, "Eleanor, that's ridiculous." He has appeared unimpressed by Mustapha's historical connections, but he is nervous about the way she is grilling the old man, who is however capable of defending himself.

"What did you gain?" she asks in a slightly less strident tone.

"Almost everything. Compared with before. I agree that injustices remain, but nothing compared with what our lives had been like. And Israelis too were saved from themselves. Who knows what follies they could have committed? Where it could all have ended up? The Kach Party wanted some kind of final solution – a tragedy that would not only have heaped one terminal, delirious misery on the Palestinians, but endless, indelible, smaller ones on the Israelis themselves. This would have been the ultimate and inevitable lunacy of 'ethnic' nationalism... If you don't get on with your neighbour, you don't move home and you don't burn his one down. You have to work it out, because at the end of the day you're just reflections of each other. Our solution, like the South African one, means exactly that: we have to work it out. Together."

"So the Israelis should get away with their crimes?" asked Baruch.

"I never thought I would hear those words from a Jew," Mustapha laughed, "that is progress indeed."

"You think that I can't transcend my people," Baruch almost implored.

"Why should you have to?" Mustapha retorted. "No one is their people, and any people is made up of all sorts. There are times in history when a people – perhaps a people like any other – can be caught up in some mad ideology that drives quite large percentages to behave badly – brutally – shamelessly, use what word you like, but I now can see that this never goes on forever. Humanity always raises its head, weakly perhaps but unfailingly. Don't take too much on yourselves. Just hearing you admitting to this past is for me a liberation. I don't want you to go much further. Kidnapping, no. And don't have anything to do with those who do! You seem like nice young people." Mustapha knows that this last piece of unintended condescension has been a mistake as soon as he says it.

Eleanor looks furious and shifts on her skinny legs. She looks more like a frightened deer sniffing the air for danger than a revolutionary seeking to overthrow what she considers still to be a racist state. "Don't you believe in progress, and that some people need to risk their lives to achieve it?"

"Haven't we already made some progress?" says Mustapha. "Peace, open borders? At least now you can drive from Tel Aviv for an evening in Beirut. No war, not even a customs post, just one straight road. A motorway. Surely that is progress?"

"Is that your idea of progress – access to a good restaurant? What about justice?" says Baruch, joining the conversation on what he feels is safer ground.

"Justice is fine," says Mustapha, "but its rigid application can lead to more injustice. We should leave absolute justice to God, who is in the business of absolutes. We human beings have to be more pragmatic. I once thought that we had to get all our land and houses back, just as Jews got back all the property confiscated by the Nazis. But then I realised that they didn't: that is, the rich got it back when they could, but all the poorer Jews, workers and peasants with small plots of land and the odd house, they never got compensation of any kind. We're like them: we, on the whole, were poor people and our assets were few: an olive grove, a house, a pasture, pieces of rudimentary agricultural equipment. We're not going to be compensated either. I don't say that it's right, but that's the way of the world. Money goes to money; always has and probably always will. I can live with injustice, just as many Jews, Gypsies and others lived with injustice in Europe. The important thing is peace. You don't understand that, because you're young and want to put the world to rights before you're forty. It can't be done. I admire your stand. I hope you get somewhere, only I repeat: don't bring violence back. The rich never pay for that – Arab or Jew – the rich never pay. The poor always pay for violence, even when it's done in their name; it leads to a crazy tit-for-tat over differences that don't count. There is no difference between human beings that justifies violence."

"Not even the difference between rich and poor?"

"Not even that."

"This is insane. You an Arab saying these things," Baruch looks upset. "This society has got to wake up to the past. And we are the people to make it happen."

Leon, who has been listening with detachment and an increasing admiration for his father-in-law, suddenly looks alarmed: "Baruch, why are you saying these things? Is it because of our grandfather and what he did?"

"Oh, everyone's angry with my grandfather now. Yes, what he did was wrong. Very wrong. He killed an eight-year-old boy, probably to remove a witness. I am not defending him; he is scum, but who amongst the Israelis cared at the time? No one. Now they go on as though he was a monster, a child-killer, but who cared at the time? No one. They were all complicit."

"You're right. I don't doubt it, but ..." said Leon.

"No one cared a damn. They were all complicit," Baruch repeated obsessively.

"Well, not all. There were some – very few, I agree – people who were brave enough to ..."

"Bullshit! They were all complicit. From top to bottom," Baruch's eyes blaze with irrational anger – irrational that is, if you haven't lived his life. "The whole fucking lot of that rotten society from the army judges and lawyers to the whistle-blowing soldiers who could have brought the boy's killer to book, but fell at the last hurdle – at the closed session when they retracted everything."

"What are you saying? That our grandfather should have gone to prison at the time of the event?"

"Of course he should! What are *you* saying, you idiot? He killed a little boy and had a hand in killing entirely harmless labourers. If you're not sent to prison for that, then you might as well close all the damn prisons. There's nothing worse."

"But he's our grandfather, and as you say ..."

"If they'd sent him to prison, as they should have, I wouldn't exist and, what's more, my mother would not have lived, would not have suffered and would not have died the way she did – victim of the belated self-righteousness of the Israeli people. I wouldn't have been brought up by my racist grandfather. Don't give me that stuff about things being more complicated... We were all tainted and still are. Three or four generations, remember. I won't have any kids; they would be child-killers' kids."

"Why so angry, young man?" Mustapha said. "It was all over long ago. Even then it made no sense to be this angry. Anger and hatred never solved anything."

"Don't give me that facile crap!" Baruch sneered, bereft of words to express the magnitude of a thought constructed not from experience but from unremembered fragments of anger – the shards of a world that shattered long before he was born.

"What can be more facile than your Palestinians-good-and-Israelis-bad approach?" Mustapha asked. "We had our collaborators, our traitors and even our hotheads who made things worse by believing too much, by hating like you do. But I repeat: it's all over. The battle has been. We have a secular, multicultural state in which all citizens have equal rights."

Baruch laughed an uncomfortable, bitter laughter, "You're a bit of a collaborator yourself."

Mustapha flinched but said nothing.

"Look around you," Baruch continued. "Do you really think that justice has been done? Who lives in the smart west Jerusalem suburbs? Jews, that's who. Okay, there's the odd token Arab lawyer who made money from turning a blind eye to stolen property – the stolen land that should have been given back. And who do you find in the slums of east Jerusalem where those housing estates – some unfinished at the time of the Change – are overcrowded with those who returned from equally squalid refugee camps? Arabs. All Arabs. That's not justice. Not when the criminal still enjoys the fruits of his crimes."

"Young man, I don't disagree with you. That is an injustice, but there has always been injustice. It is part ..."

"I don't want to hear it. I don't want your homilies on how the world works. I will never learn to live with injustice. I don't want to be just another Palestinian Jew who maybe even wears a keffiyeh during his university years and hangs out in the bars of the bidonvilles, but knows that Daddy's got him a nice position ready in the family firm or an internship at the Knesset. I want Justice. I want to shake this country up and make it look at its past, which it has forgotten now it's so busy making money. They dropped the macho military thing and then became even more powerful through their control of the economy."

"You don't want justice; you want to be justice!"

On their way home, Leon and Mustapha sit for a long time in silence. "Today, I have learnt how little I knew," Leon eventually says.

"And you'll have to go back and see your young cousin. Stop him from getting into trouble."

"He is already, I think. And I don't really blame him."

"My daughter has got her way, but I'm not sure she'll like the new, more politicised you."

"I think you're right, and when we act in the present, we never think about the past we are bequeathing to our children and grandchildren. Each generation is a different country, and when we dream, we should dream sensibly."

Outlook

Day One

I meet here with my thoughts. An appointment with introspection and the populations of my brain. When I sit down I can still hear the wind that rushes up the valley and shakes the wooden building that is my home and hermitage, and I can still smell the dampness of the books whose many words are slowly rotting on their arching planks. All is mine as far as the eye can see, for even the ramblers avoid this lonely and unexceptional place.

In this mineness, I sink into a snowstorm of words that come from afar, living words that come from the dead, meaningful words deprived of their creator's meaning. A dialogue with experiences not experienced. Such is the soul of the writer.

I am not an original mind. By which I mean that I can never start from nothing. In the rush of empty activities that filled my youth, I often didn't think for weeks on end. But give me a sentence and I will produce a thousand. Words spring from words like one-celled creatures relentlessly reproducing under a microscope.

I am not a discerning mind. By which I mean that I can never really decide what I choose, I can never grasp the criteria that really matter, least of all at the time when they have some relevance. I generally decide in a completely arbitrary manner. I choose because a choice must be made, but having chosen, I can be forthright in the opinions which that choice produces.

I can remember what I thought but not why I thought it. That was an emotion that has been lost in the meanders that my mind has covered since.

I cannot remember how I happened to find myself here. This is not the place I dreamt of, this is not the destination that I charted, when disdainfully I shut the door of childhood behind me and set off, as though in search of adventure.

Today I was reminded and disturbed by the past. My ex-wife rang me. I was disturbed for many reasons. Not only had I forgotten about the existence of a wife, I had forgotten the existence of the phone, hidden by the waste-paper basket and covered with old newspapers.

"It's your ex-wife," she announced in a proprietorial manner. She had something of mine that she could never wholly relinquish – my past.

"I was sure you were dead," I returned with the frankness of a child. "Cold and dead."

"Exactly what we thought of you. What have you done with yourself, you anti-social old fool. It's time you started thinking about the practicalities of old age, it's time you came down from your mountain, from your ivory tower, and faced the reality of survival."

"Up here, survival is easy."

"For the moment, perhaps."

Usually I read, scribble and muse. Usually I leave alone time, youth and old age, and gather around the voices of my doubts. Here was a specific woman with a specific voice reminding me of my specific nature, telling me of its ageing, its impending death. One day I would no longer be able to look out of this mind, just as I would no longer be able to look out of the window and down to the stony slope of the valley. I rarely do either, but I am always comforted by the fact that I could if I wanted to.

Have I wasted my life? I cannot remember what I was supposed to do with it. At school, headmasters, teachers, priests and other figures of authority often explained the purpose of life, the duties to be carried out, the rewards, and the dignity to be derived, but I can't remember the things themselves, only that they were and we believed them.

"I am ringing you for your own good, but if you're going to be stubborn, be it on your own head," said my ex-wife who was now adopting a threatening tone.

Was I responsible for my presence here? For my existence on the margin of everything? Or did they send me here? I believe, or should I say that I believed, that we are each responsible for ourselves, that we create our own nature, our own purposes, our own rules. How did I arrive at that certainty? If I followed logical steps, does it matter that I no longer remember them? Everything always slips away, our grip is extremely weak. Did I make a moral decision? Did I decide what people should be like and infer from that some kind of code? Why did I think such a thing could be important? Because society needs such individuals or because of the aesthetics of self-reliance, the image of the hero, the superman who is his own demiurge?

I transferred some of my question marks to my ex-wife: "Am I up here because I rejected society or because society rejected me? Did I perhaps reject it because I was aware that it was rejecting me? Did I drop out or was I thrown out? I hope that I just drifted out unseen."

"Oh, all of those things, I suppose," replied my ex-wife from her own doubts, "but it's all forgotten now. The important thing is that you will soon need looking after."

How threatening is society's amnesia. What is it that has to be forgotten by a society that is only interested in me for my oncoming death, because it abhors the idea that someone could die alone, but is unconcerned if they live alone. The reality of my ex-wife's voice which had travelled from God knows where as an electrically encoded signal, was harder than the stones outside that waited to be dislodged by the winter rains.

"Leave me in peace! The flood of time will wash us all into oblivion, but I stand on the ebb and do not feel its passing."

"You haven't changed. You answer in riddles, affect the intellectual to cover up for your ineptitude. Small wonder the director arranged for your dismissal while appearing to hold you in esteem and the manager spoke openly of your bizarre nature. 'He might be good at his work, but he doesn't care about the company.' That's what he used to say about you. He said you didn't care about anything."

This really reminded me of something. They accused me of affecting the intellectual and not caring. These were possibly the same thing, but seen from different view-points. I, too, accused myself of not caring. I didn't care about things that others cared about and needed to care about. On the other hand, I had never understood the other accusation, as what I really wanted to affect was not an intellectual, but someone just like them. I wanted to affect their normality. I was extrovert in my attempted normality. I would do normal things very purposefully, as though to say: "Look at me, I'm normal too!" But they would only look at me with shock and accuse me of playing the part of the eccentric. In short, I could never perceive things in the same proportions as other people.

"If you don't come down, we will have to come and get you," threatened my ex-wife. Now I remember her. She was always threatening me with some punishment. She would say things like: "If you don't go to see the director about your promotion, I'll have to speak to him myself", "If I can't buy that dress, I won't be able to come to the office party" and "If you don't pull yourself together, I'll divorce you". Yes, I remember her; she had artful expression, and smoked continuously. She smelt of stale tobacco and had the strength of an ox. If she said she would come, she would quite definitely come.

"How long will you give me?"

"A week."

"Is that all?"

"How long do you need?"

"Long enough to forget this phone call."

"You were always such a sweet man. Forever rejecting those who try to help you. Unfortunately somebody has to be responsible. Get your things ready, we will be there in a week."

So I have a week in which to recover my amnesia, to shrink the universe to my circle of stones.

Day Two

I am free to work, to plough the fields of my imagination, to sow the seeds of future thoughts. I remember, too, how the academics enclosed my mind, took the common land for private use, and said: 'You cannot go there! Think this way and survive, or go and beg in the restricted corners of your restricted time.' The literary landlords were so leisurely in their reply to the queries of this depleted earth, while I laboured in a factory of words produced in standard sizes, and only the friendship of fellow toilers filled the day with a sense of living.

But now the day is free, and frightens with the quickening pace of time. I realise my emptiness and the empty circle of my dreams. They will come for the skeleton of my soul, and the empty land will lose even my loneliness.

Good is a laborious task, a stone tower against the chaos of our warring wants. Or is that the state? – that holds the whole machine together and bids me leave the fertile field where my youth dreamed equality. And I do still, but alone in this stony place.

Evil has a more stable base, lurks in the scattered stones of history, and scattered hopes. They always win, the men who act the powerful parts with conviction of their own true worth. Or is it only winning that makes them so? I cannot recall the cause of my disquiet.

I end the day of my first furrow, a solitary groove that scars the landscape of a meagre thought.

Day Three

Even here, much of my time goes on the little things of life that make life bearable. I make my coffee while the stove struggles with the morning chill. All I do is immediately undone. I restrict any cleaning and washing to the bare minimum required for personal comfort. But the unravelling goes on.

My wife with the wily face (was she the only one?) would make me feel an unraveller. Some people are subversive just by being – "I am here" I cried by standing in my narrow space of time. I and others. Other odd-shaped men and women whose ancestral lands were fenced in by the machinery of state, and all required the little things of life that largely drain into the swelling coffers of well-stuffed men.

The stuff of life is this, I fear. They were right, my colleagues and my wife – their simple rule has worked, and turned them into comfortable things that grow in the sheltered pasture of the hemmed-in land. Not even the lily-of-the-field has raiment so designered as they. Nor does the scythe cut deep in those parts.

Day Four

Again it rang. It rang the presence of a past that now returns.

"Who is it?" I cried.

"It's me, Dad. My brother and I are worried about you, Dad." She insisted on the "Dad", claiming ties of kin like a God-given right. "We have forgiven for the past!"

I had a daughter and a son! What had I done that demanded to be forgiven, and was now recalled by that demand? I had given them the finitude of life, and left them in the well-protected pen – the well-machined and metal pen where our children are reared.

Forgive. Forgive the intensity of thought, and the carelessness with which I cast it aside. Forgive for not improving while denouncing all. Forgive the petty banter that blurs the hard reality of things that die. Forgive my sagging muscles that no longer hew.

Forgive me for not having the solidity of well-stuffed men to bear you up on the tide of life.

"What was there to forgive?" I asked.

"The desertion of our normality," I think she said, or did she say:

"Come on Dad! What do you think? Piking off like that to your mountain without a thought for others. You didn't come to my graduation. You didn't come to my wedding. You're a grandfather now, you know! But what do you care! You've always been so wrapped up in yourself! It's really sick. We should just leave you to die up there. You're a stubborn old man who never did anything for anyone, least of all for your own family!"

Close relations are always the most incomprehensible because of the simplicity of their demands – and their pervasiveness. I cannot remember why I would have ever wanted children, but certainly it was not for this. Was it the arrogance of continuing my genes? – mixed with those of the wily woman, so that with wily smiles they haunt my dreams? Was it to love and nurture them, to give a meaning to the expanse of life? Could I not love? Was that why they closed me out, and set those stakes into the ground? For what original sin did wire enclose the Eden of my early dreams, those banal ambitions of family and career?

Tiredness has pulled me early to my bed. I fell with such a force that dust has filled the room like fog. My smarting eyes can no longer focus on the cracks that randomly run patterns on the wall.

Day Five

I cannot move. A fragile stillness like settled dust settles in my soul. The light cuts the air and falls in hard-edged shadows. Outside the bright day is heralded by an activity of birds framed by the stillness of the stones, which now I can only imagine. The fiefdom of my solitude is taken from me by the paralysis of sagging sinews – and the hierarchy of the past stands outside my room and makes way for death.

All that was either forgotten or remembered will shrivel, and the desert of my life will be submerged beneath the waters of oblivion, and become a more fertile land for future growth and more rooted existences.

I cannot move, I cannot eat. All things I cared for have no hold and lose their shape, like the pages of a book exposed to sun and rain.

Day Six

The phone rings persistent and full of things to say, but I cannot reach it. Controlled from beyond the walls and confining forms, an extension of the cultivated world, it calls on my imagination and what might be said.

"Who are you?"

"I am God, the creator of all the universe, in whom you have seldom believed."

"It was not from want of trying."

"You tried all – and believed nothing."

"I had my creed."

"We organise things quite strictly here, and can make no exceptions. We have drawn a line, divided off, and sent our charges to their appointed place."

"Then I was right not to believe in your nightmare reflection of this loveless world. But I would believe in your utopia where the excluded enter in..."

"Prepare..."

"And who are you?"

"Your father, upon whose grave you could not weep. Your father who raised you with loving care, and lacking nothing sent you forth into the wooded world – to adventure, vigour and a strong hold on the future. Instead you wimpishly let me down – and cried on the shoulder of fate. You joined the weak – and then deserted all for this deserted place."

"I remember the hardness of your caring hand that pushed me forward to the empty plain."

"You remember nothing, not even how to die."

"And who are you?"

"Your fatherland, the most betrayed of all your relations, and the one that gave you most. I gave you your language, the landscape of your thoughts; I gave you the smells and colours of your youth – and in return you have ridiculed my heroic and masterly past, the design of my machine and the hardness of my walls. Your feminine sensitivity for those beyond the firm boundaries of our brotherhood has sapped the virile juices for generations to come."

Day Seven

God made the world in seven days, say the clerics, and others, more precise, produce a figure of prosaic enormity that belittles our short scratching on this earth. But we have ordered almost every inch, and set it around with markers of propriety – the narrow etiquette of ownership. This little world of discarded thoughts and deserted memories had seven days to die, and still insists on gasping at the dusty air, wanting to live but wanting to die before the past with satanic ritual erupts into this sacred privacy.

There is no beauty in an old man's death; it hangs in the air, uncertain about the certainty. There is no sorrow in an old man's death, and little tragic in the misuse of such a wealth of years.

I hear the engine, the hard metallic rhythm draws the demonic weight of materialist matters closer to my closing breath. I would die within the circle of my now empty soul, and never face the devil who with weasel leer will cast me into the fire of feelinglessness.

No Such Thing as a Free Lunch

The unsettled elation triggered by a sudden break in the hopeless two-and-a-half-hour wait for a lift carried the hitch-hikers manically forward to where the Mercedes-Benz had come to a halt some twenty yards down the road.

"Ya beauty," Tom cried.

"About time," said Ian as they ran.

On arriving at the car they found a middle-aged man at the wheel who was staring fixedly at the line of traffic that climbed a gentle hill, apparently unaware of their presence.

"He's yanking our chain."

"The bastard."

They bobbed their heads about as though they wanted to look inside, but the real intention was to get noticed. The electric window started its descent and released an odour of sweat and cigarettes, but the man continued to stare in front. He was as still as an oppressively windless day, and it was impossible to sense whether his stillness was relaxed or alert. He said nothing, but waited.

"Are ye gi'ing us a lift or what?"

"Ja!"

"Where are you going?"

"Where are *you* going?"

Tom was now irritated and uncertain. "Where are you gauin', man? If you're no gauin' oor way, what's the point?"

"I am going your way. I am out for a drive, and I wish to go a far distance. Just tell me where you are going." The man spoke in clipped English and still refused to move his head.

"Freaky," Tom whispered to Ian, almost as a question. "What do we do?"

"Calais," said Ian.

"You are Scottish, right?"

"Yeah. What of it?" Tom grumped.

"Well, maybe you are Scottish and living in Calais, but I think you are going to Calais to get the ferry, and very probably you are then going to Scotland. Am I right?"

The tetchiness born of standing for hours in the sun endlessly raising an upright thumb to signal to passing cars, followed by this rambling conversation, now struggled against a tickling sense of the ridiculous that rose like a weak but unrelenting vibration and broke out in strangled laughter. "Is this a joke or somethin'?" Tom said in a voice that mingled anger and gaiety.

"This is no joke," the German said with pedantic forcefulness, still looking up the hill as though expecting someone or something to appear over its brow. "I want to drive somewhere and you want to go somewhere. This is ecological, no? I am not wasting my petrol and polluting the planet for no reason, yes?" he laughed very slightly – the first real movement, but without taking his eyes off the low and distant summit.

"He's a complete clown," Tom said turning away, but Ian preferred the company of a clown to another couple of hours waving his thumb at fast-moving traffic.

"That is very kind of you. And yes, we are going to Scotland. To Glasgow actually."

"Well, please get in. I will take you all the way."

"Come on. He's aff his heid. You're no getting in the car wi' him. He's no right – he'll cut up our body parts and put them in the freezer. And then he'll have us for supper with sauerkraut and *Liebfraumilch* for the next few months. I'd rather travel with a load of rotten fish. No way!"

"You'll excuse my friend," said Ian while kicking Tom in the shins.

The man continued to stare at the road for several seconds before saying, "I will take you as far as you wish to go. Please get in and just tell me where to go."

Ian jumped in and Tom reluctantly followed.

They travelled in silence. Tom and Ian were awed by the bulk of the man. In his big car, his considerable mass had not been immediately apparent. Fat, yes, but also strong and menacing. The car moved at speed – and smoothly like the expensive car it was. Even the smoothness could not be trusted; it felt impossibly, illusorily and profoundly unsettling and unnatural. Strangely it was Ian who felt most disturbed and keenest to break the spell. "You're what we might call a free spirit. A man who takes to the road just to see what happens," he said.

The big man sat solidly in his seat and took no notice. Ian felt that his words hung in the air like a vaguely unpleasant smell that could not fade in the closed environment of the speeding car. He waited and thought of other things to say, but rejected them all. Then when he had given up hope of a response, the man said, "I am not a free spirit, as you call it. I have always been a man with a purpose. If I do something, I do it for a reason. I do not like spontaneity. Spontaneity, I think, is a very modern thing. It is for the young, like you."

There was nothing reassuring about that statement.

On the ferry, the German paid for lunch and then went for a snooze. He seemed perfectly relaxed and confident that they would rejoin him for the rest of the journey north. Ian was not so sure. "You were right, Tom, there's something creepy about the guy," he said as they leant against the railing on deck and looked down on a grey and foamy wake. "I don't think we should go any further with him. We should wait and then hitch again."

"But he paid to take his car across."

"He's minted. That's clear enough."

"At the speed he goes, we'll be home tonight or to-morrow morning. No chance of that, if we go back to hitching."

Tom, short, stocky and strong, and the more quick-witted of the two, was now completely seduced by the idea of a speedy and physically comfortable ride home. Pity about the company and who could credit the man, but for the moment he had given up trying to fathom the German's motives. Ian, a pale and sensitive youth, was now certain that this trip was a mistake, but he had never been able to assert himself over Tom, except on that one fateful occasion – his determination to accept the silent man's lift.

After London, the German pulled into a service station and got out of the car without saying anything. The friends followed him sheepishly, hardly looking at each other. The man locked the car remotely without turning round and strode towards the cafeteria. He moved at speed but appeared nonchalant at the same time. He looked and felt like a man always in control – of himself and everything besides. His expression was almost blank or rather would have been blank if it weren't for a veiled but nevertheless distinct aura of harsh determination.

The man insisted on paying for the rolls and the coffees. The youths did not protest too much, but their consternation never abated. The ham rolls tasted even more plasticky than usual. The coffee made them feel slightly nauseous. Then the man asked Tom if he had a mobile phone; Tom lied that he didn't. The same question was put to Ian, who stammered for a couple of seconds before realising that it was too late to lie. The man then started to say how he liked to help people out: he saw two nice young men and he wanted to help them. He too had been young once, and used to hitch-hike around the country. Surely he could be of help. He could take them home, and that was what he was doing. Now he remembered that he had to ring some lawyers in Rome about a loan he had taken out. His English might seem

125

good, but he wasn't fluent like a native speaker, and the Italian lawyer wasn't that good either. They might misunderstand each other. He felt sure that Ian wouldn't mind helping him out.

"A mobile to Italy," said Tom, "that'll cost a fortune! Why don't you use your own, even if he is acting as your interpreter?"

The man acknowledged the argument by extracting a wad of notes from his pocket and counting out two hundred pounds in ten-pound notes. He then pushed the money across the surface of the table towards Ian. "That should cover it," he said without a trace of resentment.

Ian rang the number asked of him and once he got through to the lawyer he found that his English was in fact very poor. "I am ringing on behalf of ..." he looked up at the man, realising that he didn't even know his name.

"Tell him that it concerns the Libkin case," the man said as though this should have been clear.

"I am ringing about the Libkin case," Ian blushed with confusion.

"Ah! Is too long you are not talking. You people very naughty. Mr. Lo Monaco is not 'appy. Not 'appy at all. You understand."

Ian understood nothing but said yes, and looked at the man.

"Tell him that the funds are now available. We can transfer them," the man said, still absolutely cool.

"The funds are available. We can transfer them." Why did Ian say "we"? He was identifying with one side of a transaction he knew nothing about.

"Good! Is good! But late, too late. Mr. Lo Monaco not 'appy. I will ring you this evening on this phone and tell you where to transfer the funds. You understand?"

"Yes!"

"Good," and the Italian lawyer hung up.

"Well?" said the man.

"He hung up."

"And?"

"And he'll ring with the bank details this evening."

The German cracked a smile. It was not an expansive one, but on that expressionless face it was like a ray of sunlight. It was the first touch of reality. And human reality, we know, is often insincere. "Well, that's that then. Let's return to our journey. Let's get you boys home. Back to your mothers and fathers."

The German had no intention of driving through the night. They stopped in the early evening at a service station motel. He booked them a twin room and insisted that he would sleep in the chair. The only luggage he took from the car was a spongebag and a darts board with three darts skewered into it.

The two youths sat on the side of their beds, incapable of any action. The man found an appropriate hook for his darts board, extracted the darts and threw them. He then returned to the board and removed them. It was unclear if he kept any score or registered his performance. His nature was sealed up hermetically in an envelope of immobility – except where some activity required a minimum of movement, as in driving or walking or chucking darts. He strode back to his starting position. That lethargic stride again. The pace of a big man. One, two, three, the darts thudded into the board. And off he went again. And again. And again. His behaviour was obsessive and possibly designed to unnerve them further. Or possibly it was just to pass the time of day. Tom now knew that they had to get out. He also knew that it would not be easy.

"Why does he do that?" asked Tom. "Is he nervous or is he bored?"

"Neither," replied Ian, "he doesn't have feelings."

"Of course he does. Everyone does. Even a zombie like that. If we knew, it could help us."

Ian's response was a blank stare. He always disliked the way Tom wanted to complicate everything. For him, the man was an inexplicable phenomenon. Any attempt to decipher his behaviour was pointless, nonsensical, even perverse.

They sat for over an hour without saying a word, and all the time the man went back and forth, throwing the darts and retrieving them. Tom wanted to scream at him – or do worse – but he was conscious of his mass and his unchallengeable self-control.

Then Ian's phone rang. It was the lawyer. "You 'ave a pen?" and Ian scribbled down the bank details. "You make bank transfer tomorrow morning. You understand?"

After that the hitch-hikers went to bed, but they couldn't sleep. The man, however, soon nodded off in the armchair, leaving the standard lamp next to him switched on. He snored, but when Tom made a move to get up, one of the man's eyes opened and stared with the empty intelligence of an animal. Tom went back to bed and his worries.

In the morning, the man was slightly more communicative. He smiled again and offered breakfast. Ian found it hard to chew on his muesli. He had little appetite, and Tom was having only a little more success with his bacon and eggs. He knew that he had to be ready to get himself and Ian out of the way as soon as he could.

The man drove them sedately to the nearest town. It was a dull place like many others; a medieval church looked out of place amongst twentieth-century buildings all very similar to each other along a standard high street. The shops all belonged to chains and the people who rushed along the pavements looked as unconvincing as those little plastic people they use on architectural models. They seemed to decorate this newly made toy-town, and yet they were the ones who belonged to normality. They had places to go and things to do; Ian and Tom felt as though they had been kidnapped, but perhaps they had just found a kindly if rather inarticulate man – a foreigner with few words. Why not? There are eccentrics, aren't there, although perhaps not too many in that suburban village.

The man parked and went into the bank.

"This is where we get off," said Tom. He opened the back-seat door slightly. "No point in hanging around."

Ian looked half dead. He hadn't the strength for more hitch-hiking. "Why not finish the ride?"

"Because the man's a nutter, aff his heid, I tell ya. This time we've got to go."

"No way, this is a comfy ride. I'm not standing out there on some lay-by or slip road, waving my thumb at smelly lorries and decrepit vans," said Ian, so tired that his usual anxieties were entirely abated.

Tom could have gone – should have gone. The door was open, and he now understood that something was very wrong. He could not abandon Ian though. Ian was his friend. Friends stick together – look after each other. When he closed the door and remained in the car, he did so principally out of solidarity with his friend – but also, somewhere hidden in the recesses of his mind or, more specifically, his imagination, another motivation was grinding away quietly and unfailingly: his curiosity to know what all this was about: who was this man? why had he given them a lift? It wasn't generosity, but no other explanation made any sense. It's not reason that tells us there's a pattern to this journey; it's our imagination, which loves the coherence of a story.

They sat for some time in silence, and when the man reappeared, he seemed surprised to see them. "Good boys," he said as he got into the car. "You waited for me. I am sorry that I am so long in bank."

Again the silence and the smooth speed of the car. Again the man staring fixedly at the road ahead. However, the man's surprise on his return to the car had confirmed in Tom's mind the foolishness of waiting for him. The danger now felt so inescapable that there was little point in worrying about it.

"Where are you from?" Tom asked as they drove through the Southern Uplands.

"I live in Frankfurt."

"But where were you born?"

Surprisingly the man seemed to open up – relatively speaking. "I grew up in Dresden."

"That was in the GDR."

"Of course."

"Did you work for the Stasi?" Tom joked.

"Yes I did, since you ask," the man answered bluntly. "I was a young and ambitious officer. My career was very good. Very good indeed. I was married. I had good flat."

"Did you torture people?" Tom was aware of the naivety of his questions, but they were producing results.

"No. Other people did that. If it was necessary. I hunted people. But a policeman doesn't hunt people like a tiger; he hunts them like a spider. He leaves a web, a trap which the criminal cannot avoid. The criminal is caught because of his own foolishness."

"But didn't the Stasi go after people just because of their beliefs?"

"Of course. Beliefs are very important to a state. No state likes people to have ideas too different from the ones it upholds in any given moment. It is no good believing what the state used to think ten or twenty years ago, or even what the state might think in ten or twenty years' time – that is even more dangerous."

"So you believe in communism then?"

"I used to. In a way. But I don't any more."

There were a couple of minutes silence while Tom thought this over. Ian was asleep. "Why did you change your mind about communism?"

"Simple. Communism lost, and communism lost because it didn't understand human nature. Capitalism understands human nature much better. What is it your philosopher says? 'There is no such thing as a free lunch.' That is very much right," the man laughed, "so obvious, so simple."

"Reassuringly simple," Tom agreed. "I suppose you're right. There is no such thing as a free lunch. Everybody is out to get something, however small."

"Come off it, Tom," Ian has just woken up. "We got a free lunch three days ago. Remember? That teacher who gave us a lift near the Swiss border. In the hills around Belleguarde. We stopped at this restaurant with a beautiful view. We had as much paté as you could want, followed by steak and chips. It was great. He gave us a lift *and* paid for our lunch. And now you're saying that no such thing exists."

"That's right!" said Tom, reassured that the reassuringly simple had turned out to be wrong.

"Ah, but there must have been a motive," said the German.

"What possible motive could there be?" said Ian.

"Well," said Tom, "he did keep saying that his son was at university in England, and that he was just paying us back for the hospitality given his son, who also likes to hitch-hike."

"You see," said the former Stasi officer, "I am right. There is an exchange of interests here."

"No there isn't," said Ian becoming animated. "He didn't know we were English, British or whatever when he picked us up and, more importantly, he didn't have to buy *us* a meal. We never gave his son any hospitality. This is nonsense."

"You're friend is a romantic," said the German.

"Hardly," said Ian, but he would have been willing to admit that he was less adept at understanding and manipulating this world than the other two in the car. But romantic he was not. Impractical. Cynical perhaps. He simply had the common sense to recognise where a partial truth can be turned into an absurdity by its isolation from all other factors. He looked out of the car and watched the gentle, pleasant and unremarkable countryside fly by. All he wanted now was to be home. He wanted to be reacquainted with the familiar.

"So who do you work for now? The West German intelligence?" Tom continued his interrogation.

"There is no West Germany now. And I wouldn't tell you if I were. They would not employ me anyway. They say that they are different. They say that they have higher standards. But there is plenty of work for people like me."

"Like what?"

"Work for corporations, of course. Corporations are like states, like small, very powerful republics, and there is no democracy to get in the way. People make decisions in private, and their decisions are final. I can work for such people."

Tom and Ian looked at each other, and there was nothing reassuring about that statement.

When they got to the outskirts of Glasgow, Ian announced to the driver that his address was in Bearsden. Home was minutes away. But the German was unimpressed. "I will drop you in the centre of the city, okay? You ring your mummy from there."

Ian worried about the delay in getting to a hot bath, and Tom worried about the German and his intentions. More time in the car was more time to find a solution, but the only way out of the car was to wait for the German to allow them to leave. In the city centre the man circled around close to the motorway exits but was never happy with any of them. He shifted out of the centre, found a slip road, circled a couple of times and then suddenly drew up beside the pavement and shouted, "Out of here, hurry!" The young men obliged and the Mercedes shot away and immediately disappeared down a side road, shortly followed by another car. They turned to each other, and Tom beamed. He was relieved, but his friend was peeved that he still wasn't home. "After all that, he could have taken us to the door. What was all that going round in circles about, anyway?"

"Let's get out of here," Tom said. Some of his anxiety was returning.

On Tom's advice, they moved to a back lane while they tried to orient themselves in a part of the city they didn't know. It was one of those places that ooze dampness even on a dry day. Bins were overflowing. Cardboard boxes had been thrown away randomly. Soapy water dribbled out of a blocked drain. It is easier to miss an important detail in such an environment than in a crowded street. The two friends walked briskly with the intention of getting out into another street of shops at the end of the lane, but halfway along, Ian's phone rang. He took it out and did not recognise the number. He answered, but the line almost immediately went dead. He shrugged and started to move. "That was me, pal," came a voice. A short man in a smart blue overcoat, with a barely visible white collar and tie underneath, stepped into the light and waved his own mobile phone. "I was just giving you a call. Wondered how you were. Was thinking about your health. Besides, I think we should have a wee chat, boys." He waved his hand, but Tom was already hurtling down the lane, his feet and his thumping heart almost in unison, terror coursing through his veins. Two men appeared and effortlessly stopped the projectile of quivering human flesh. One of the men punched Tom in the stomach, and when the poor boy bent double the other one kicked him in the teeth. The sequence was so perfectly timed, it had the appearance of a choreographed system for immobilising a running man. It perhaps belonged to a handbook somewhere. The store of human knowledge is now in a state of exponential growth; it is an expanding universe that is also becoming colder.

Ian looked the other way, and saw another two large men. He was struggling to understand what was going on, and why. Tiredness, loneliness and, yes, still only a mild sensation of fear not equal to the nastiness of their predicament. Ian's world was one in which decency and good manners prevailed; he had no understanding of how things were going to go until he saw Tom's face. They had brought him back and the first thing he noted was that Tom had lost several teeth. But worse than that was his friend's expression of absolute terror.

There followed another car journey – a short one to the other side of the city. The smartly dressed man continued his absurd pretence of chumminess and concern. The reality of the criminal profession is unique for its slavishness to fiction: the four goons possibly recognised the cinematic references in the smart man's speech. Perhaps their minds scanned their own extensive DVD collections in search of the most likely sources. "We had a phone call just an hour ago from a man – I've forgotten his name – 'These boys har very naughty. Mr. Lo Monaco not 'appy. Not 'appy at all. You understand.' Now Mr. Lo Monaco is not a man you want to upset, boys." He laughed, and so did his companions in succession. Their laughter was slightly forced. They didn't seem to extract the same degree of pleasure from their work as the smart man did. "Now, why did you go and do that, boys? Never mind, we get to do him a favour. He'll owe us one, after you guys dish the dirt on Herr Schmidt. Not his real name, I suppose. The lawyer doesn't think so."

Another dirty lane and another back entrance. The seven men climbed the stairs to a sparsely furnished office. Tom and Ian were stood against the wall. "How long have you been working for this Schmidt character? Why was he travelling to Glasgow?" Before the two could answer or even think of answering these bewildering questions, the smart man's phone rang. He took it out and started an animated conversation during which he lost his jocular tone. "You lost him? ... How did you do that? ... For Christ's sake the fucker could be anywhere. ... So you're telling me that all I've got for Lo Monaco is these two dumb-asses. I'll tell you one thing: this Schmidt fella might be sharp but he needs to change his recruiting agency. These guys are shite."

"Right boys," he turned to his victims, "I think you got the gist of that: your boss has shaken us off, and that, my friends, makes things worse for you. So let's go back to my question: How long have you been working for Schmidt and why was he travelling to Glasgow?"

"He was giving us a lift home," said Ian through a dry mouth.

"And we don't know him. We were hitch-hiking," said Tom.

Both got punched in the stomach and gasped for breath.

"So we've got a couple of jokers. You want to do this the hard way. And why the loyalty to Schmidt? He can't be paying you enough."

The smart man could never understand why the two never gave a thing away. So he never did that favour for Lo Monaco. In fact, Lo Monaco was unimpressed with his contacts in Glasgow. Three days later, the badly beaten bodies of two young men were found floating in the Clyde. The police opened a murder case. The guilty parties were never apprehended. Business was not interrupted.

Paradise, Hotel Accommodation, the Kitchen Staff and Sundry Other Things Most Elevated and Sublime

... and ended up in another world. I had been hit by a car. I knew that much, but I wasn't in pain. A middle-aged woman jumped out from the driver's side and a lanky guy from the passenger's.

"I think you've killed him, Mum," said the man rather too nonchalantly. "You hit him smack on!" And he emphasised this concept by smashing his right fist into his left palm.

"Oh my God, what have I done?" the mother wailed.

The son came over with scientific zeal. He was clearly interested in knowing the actual effects of a metal box with a mass of approximately half a ton travelling at a velocity of approximately thirty-eight miles per hour colliding with a stationary object consisting almost entirely of soft organic tissue. The product of this clash between two opposing and asymmetric forces was, it appeared from his expression, rather disappointing.

The mother began to cry. "He just walked out in front of me."

"Don't worry, Mum. He was probably some kind of psycho – wanted to top himself. So you did him a favour."

Then she started to scream, "Is he dead? Please tell me he isn't dead! Call an ambulance." People came over to comfort her, and she was right: I did just walk out in front of her. What was I thinking? I was spooked by that weird guy – the one in the coloured clothing – said he was a narrative voice. I must have been dreaming.

The son crooked his head and studied me with what appeared to be his habitual detachment. "This is not a computer game, you know," I said crossly, "I have been injured and I do need an ambulance. Don't worry, I'm not going to sue your mother. Nothing like that, but could you stop staring at me?"

He didn't seem to understand or even hear a word I said. "Nope," he enunciated very clearly in his best mid-Atlantic, "the dude's not breathing. I'm sure of it."

So, according to the nerdy type, I was dead. And I had to die before encountering the mildly irritating experience of being called a "dude".

A suited young man with spiky gelled hair and an officious expression came up: "I saw the whole thing very clearly from the other side of the road. You," he pointed belligerently at the woman, "were driving far too fast."

Thankfully the son then left me to go and argue with the spiky hair. That became the area of significant activity and I could enjoy a few moments on my own to reflect on my predicament – or what appeared to be my premature departure from the vale of tears. I would miss the evening shift on the garden sheds, I would miss grey days at home with my parents indulging in their harangues, I would miss the joys of love and parenthood, and I would miss the weight of years turning me into my father. I would miss out on life. Still, it appeared that death wasn't the end at all, although no one could hear me and it seemed I was unable to move.

"Perhaps I *was* going too fast," the driver was saying weepily.

"No, you weren't, Mum. The idiot just stepped off the pavement. Come on. There was nothing you could do."

"Listen, you were going fast enough to kill him, and this is a thirty-mile-an-hour zone. I saw it. I'm a witness."

While I was thinking that there was as little peace in this other world as in the one I had just left, a sober man dressed in black leaned over me. He could have been an undertaker. In fact, that was my first thought, but then I noticed two unusual things about him. His dress wasn't really modern; he was perhaps a seventeenth-century puritan. And he looked like a slimmed-down and more empathetic version of the man who called himself the Narrative Voice.

"Tom? Tom Cunningham?" he asked.

"That's me," I answered with an inexplicable sense of relief.

"Good. Come with me then." His answer showed that he could hear me. He put out his hand and bid me take hold of it, "We'd better be on our way."

I took his hand and, to my surprise, I was able to move and stand up. He smiled slightly and said, "I'm going to be your guide. We have a long but not particularly onerous journey ahead." And so off we went.

We wandered down the nondescript, the plain linearity of Paisley Road West, and he instructed me upon my fate, my journey and my immortal soul. No one saw us as we passed or heard the earnest, sweetly ornate but slightly dull discourse that issued forth from prudent lips – of the companion of my initial passage into the afterlife. I wasn't a good student and was more curious about my altered state, my invisibility to a busy and noisy world populated by those whose shades were still suspended in their corporeal domiciles, like the battered one I left on the road beside the two modern men who disputed the velocity of the wheeled projectile that had struck me dead.

"What is your name?" I asked.

"What's it to you?" the wise man said, "what does it matter who accompanies you and puts you right on all the niceties of the other side of death and glosses all the little signs we find along the way?"

"It doesn't matter much to me, but the bizarre fellow who accosted me before my death and perhaps led me to it would think it useful to release such information at this stage."

"Very well, I am John Milton," the man said with his widest smile yet and not without a certain pride, "the great English poet. We're the sort of people who take on this job."

I had vaguely heard of this man. "Are you going to show me around hell?"

"Hell no, there's no hell in the world after death."

"No hell? Didn't the narrative voice mention that?" I thought aloud.

"Hell is what you've left behind: diseases and accidents that can whisk away your friends and lovers, your parents and your children; pain and torture inflicted by circumstance or intention; cyclones, tsunamis, mud flows, fires and armed men wandering with a lust for cruelty; ghastly dictatorships that are overthrown by frivolous and unprincipled democracies so that oppression is followed by anarchy, the one thing that is worse; minds that wish to construct atom bombs so that the apocalypse, which once seemed the ravings of mad monks and insane prophets, can and probably will become a reality. But that is not all; the unequal world you have left behind has many wealthy people who manage to be as unhappy as or unhappier than those who have every right to be so. Sir So-and-so quarrels over the handsome pension his now defunct bank should pay – how many German motor cars can a man buy in a year? That's just the big stuff, and then there are the lies, the false gossip, the rivalries and jealousies, the ambitions, the arrogance, the self-delusion, the affronts and rebuffs inflicted by high and low office, the scrabbling around for crumbs from the table and the conspicuous waste of those who let the crumbs fall while also leaving a great wealth of food to rot in their larders. What hell could possibly follow that? We only have a heaven and that is where we're going."

"So why the long journey? Why don't we fly there on wings with a harp in our hands?"

"This world has its rules and its own scientific logic. You have to learn to accept them just as you did those of the world you have just left behind."

I imagined the heaven that lay ahead of me: high walls like a medieval city, but white and glowing with the goodness of its ethereal power; an adamantine gate shut fast and guarded by angels in Swiss uniforms; and inside pleasure gardens with bountiful orchards and graceful people, all young, glowing with fine thoughts and kindness, promenading by the fountains and through the apple groves, deep in discussion and politely allowing each other to formulate their words, for they have no need to hurry, eternity awaits. Eventually I would be taken to the princely hall whose high vaults depict the histories of all peoples and the glories of holy men and women. Sweet smells of cinnamon and frankincense would lighten my head, already spinning at the divine grandeur of the holy place. At the end of a seemingly endless red carpet, there would be fifty-three steps and above them a throne, and on that throne would sit a vigorous and wise old man – known to us as God. I was filled with joyous energy and ready for my trek. How lucky I was that the poor lady had run me over and released me from the idiocy and banality of earthly existence. I was off on my quest for full knowledge of how the heavens have been built.

"I am ready," I said a little unwisely, and suddenly Paisley Road West faded and we found ourselves struggling across a desert. My feet sank deep into the sand, and the going was tough. Nothing could be seen for miles. We trudged in silence now that there was no one around not to hear us. "How do you know which way to go?" I asked at length, because we appeared to be going round in circles.

"I don't," he replied.

My religious fervour flagged. The afterlife was beginning to look very arduous. "Have you no idea?"

"You are still obsessed with time, which has no worth in the afterlife, but you will only really understand this once you have passed through the sandglass into eternal time. That's what I am looking for now. If we keep going round in circles here, we will eventually come across it."

Suddenly he started to sink deeper into the sand: "This is it," he cried, "follow after me by standing on this very spot."

Shaken and fearful I stepped on what I thought was the exact place where he had disappeared from view. Vicious currents of sand gripped my legs as if they were tentacles of an unknown and unlikely cephalopod and drew my body down. After the initial shock, the feeling was not unpleasant and was perhaps even the exhilarating sensation a child feels in a swimming-pool chute. I was whisked further and further down into the depths of the boundless sands. I laughed. And laughed again when I bounced off a round, balloon-like object in the shape of a black-suited man in a top hat and a moment later off a similar object in the shape of a woman in evening dress, barely visible in the sandy vortex.

Just as I was learning to enjoy the experience for what it was and to be almost unmindful of Milton's explanation and my eventual passing into a different dimension of time, I bumped against a glass surface and started to slide down along with the rush of sand. Of course, it drew me close to a narrow passage or entrance through which I passed, hitting the hardness as I went and feeling not pain but the discomfort of being jarred. Being thin, I passed through without difficulty, and I think that even a fat man would have managed it, but not a large animal similar in size, say, to a camel. After that I floated down in a rain of sand and landed just next to my guide. Strangely there was no sand on the grassy lawn around me, nor above me could I see any sign of the sandglass, only a beautiful clear sky of aquamarine blue. The countryside in which we found ourselves was of an equally rich green such as painters use to suggest the freedom and luxuriance of the primeval woodland not entirely lacking in menace and hidden spirits.

My master leapt to his feet. "The way is not long." At times, this prolix man could be laconic. At times, this slow and professorial guide could be energetic and zestful. He started to walk at a military pace, and when I complained, he pointed to the summit of the hill. Finally he waved his hand once more and said, "It's there. It's the other side of that hill." My imaginings were revived. All I had to do was climb to the top of the fertile mound before me, which was covered with vines, olive groves and those dark, abundant woods from whose interiors you could hear the gurgling of plentiful streams, the myriad songs of myriad songbirds and the plaintive pipes of melancholic goatmen.

We climbed and climbed. And as we climbed, my impatience to see the happy place where we all spend eternity grew to such an intensity, I thought that my immortal soul would surely suffocate in a haze of blissful expectation. When at last we arrived at the summit, I couldn't see anything that looked like heaven – only an enormous hotel in the modern style. The enormity was indeed ineffable, but everything else was banal. It was impossible to see where the hotel ended in either direction of the valley. Every mile or so there was a huge neon light on the hotel roof, forming the words "Paradise Hotel". There were many entrances that could be seen and presumably there were many more that could not. At each entrance there was an endless queue of new arrivals. Suddenly the afterlife no longer felt like a personal encounter with truth and beauty, but more like Butlins on a public holiday multiplied by some absurd celestial factor.

Milton perceived my disappointment. "It wasn't always like this. But what could they do? Populations just kept increasing. In the end, they had to pull the old one down and build another. They used Sir Basil Fence, the architect who designed Southdown University. He came highly recommended when he came up here in the mid seventies. Everything is done by committee in paradise too."

"I thought it would be by divine edict."

"Oh no, we move with the times up here. We don't allow human mortals to get ahead of us. Well, we do actually, because we are a reflection of how mortals perceive things. So we move with the times, but slightly lagging behind. It wasn't always like this."

"But will I get to see God?" I asked, as this, at the time, seemed the most important thing.

"Oh no, no one has seen him in a long time."

"But he does exist?"

"Well, on the whole, I think so. During my mortal life on earth, I was a very conformist non-conformist, but now I am less certain. Of the seven days God marked out as the measure of our time, three find me thinking like a deist, three like a theist and one like an atheist."

"There must surely be more certainty in the afterlife?"

"Not at all," he said dismissively.

"But we know it doesn't end."

"Who knows? As far as you're concerned, I and all that we have done together might just be a vision in the final nanoseconds before you die. In any case, God reveals nothing of himself in this life either. Perhaps down there amongst those busy mortals, a bizarrely clever man will one day discover the scientific explanation for all this – for the strangeness of existence in any world. They seem to have discovered an awful lot of things since I expired in blindness. We keep abreast of modern cognisance, you know. It's really very exciting. Darwin, what a clever man! And who would have thought it? But it's still a conundrum."

It seemed that the distance between the real and the ideal is even greater in heaven than it is on earth. "I'm so disappointed."

"Why? Knowledge is good, but curiosity about the unknown is better. And you'll have a long time to think about these things," Milton said.

"But didn't you write about Satan, hell and the fall of man?"

"I did."

"So you got it all wrong."

"It depends how you look at it," he smiled, "my Satan represents very well the psychology of power amongst humans. His ruthlessness, his arrogance and his courage are well portrayed, I think."

"Never read it myself."

"Few people do these days."

"Does that sadden you?"

"Of course, literary vanity does not diminish once you're dead."

"At least there's no punishment up here, even if paradise does have its disappointments."

"We haven't got there yet," he said, although by then we were getting close, and I could perceive the extraordinary height of the building from below and the stone carvings on the outer wall depicting all kinds of pleasures, although rather consumerist ones: beaches, palm trees, people running, an enormous sun, smiling children and old people, hard-working adults building a utopian city full of cinemas, bowling alleys, restaurants, malls, cafés, ice rinks, tennis courts and the like. "You may get used to it," he said doubtfully.

"I'm not convinced, but at least there's no punishment," I insisted on this one saving grace.

"Well that not strictly true. Someone's resisting the trend, because in spite of all the changes, there are still two punishments."

"What are they?" I said with interest. Even though I had just asserted my intellectual approval of no punishments, part of me – the less rational part of me – was curious to know and slightly reassured.

"Well you know those balloon-like creatures in the top half of the sandglass?"

"Yes…"

"Well they're the souls of very rich people held in a kind of limbo for eternity and buffeted by currents of sands. If you never experience a touch of the hell down on earth, then you never really experience that mortal life at all, so you are then condemned to spend eternity in limbo, deprived of all stimuli other than the gritty blast of shifting sands."

"And the other punishment?"

"Yes, you will find out in Paradise Hotel. They run a self-service restaurant. Well, what can they do with current population figures? And the kitchens are entirely staffed by twentieth and twenty-first-century dictators, potentates, war criminals and other purveyors of human misery."

"I like that idea better. But it seems to me that they get off lightly, while the rich people are dealt with too harshly."

"You're right. But this immortal world is not run on entirely rational lines either. The law is blind, and a rich potentate or war criminal is punished as a potentate or war criminal and not as a rich man, perhaps because someone on the committee who decides this kind of thing thinks that a punishment with an element of humiliation is worse than a punishment that involves the deprivation of sensory experience. But I'm not so sure."

We came to the building, or rather, to a long jostling queue. Everyone was excited and talking about the amazing facilities inside. There was a shiny, slightly kitsch sign with the wording, "Heaven – Eternity is a Wonderful Experience and we guarantee Happiness (conditions apply)." Who could not be excited by such a promise? This hotel seemed to reflect too closely the world I had just left, and I began to wish that I had entered one of those dark woods where the goatmen live and play their pipes. Nymphs and deer, and gods hunting both, no doubt. Fear and surprises. Cruelty and purpose. Generosity and recklessness. Pride and arrogance. So much more real than this exercise in celestial mass tourism.

Milton appeared to read my thoughts, "Pleasure, pleasure every day – for eternity. I warn you that this can become very dull."

Eventually we got inside, where I registered and was allocated a room with an absurdly high number. Milton accompanied me there, and never stopped explaining and elucidating – in modern English but with a slightly pedantic tone.

"Not everyone has a guide," I noted.

"No, there are not many guides. If you are that way inclined, you can go back to the mortal world and pick up souls from dead bodies and guide them back. I like it as an occupation; it gets me out of this – this hotel. Each soul I accompany is different, and I learn from them, just as I instruct. I can make the journey more pleasing. Many souls are terrified when they fall into the sandglass, so I am helping the dead in the moment they feel most lost. Anyone here can do this, but not many do – mainly writers who wrote about these things."

"Then I am indebted to you. How did you find me?"

"By chance. Now let's get something to eat."

"Why do we need to eat in the immortal world?"

"We don't, but here we are reflections of the mortal world and we retain its appetites."

We got our wooden trays and stood in the queue at the self-service, still chatting about the construction of the mortal and immortal universe. "Move along, move along," shouted a man in a striped chef's uniform, "we don't have all day; fish and chips, steak pie or cauliflower cheese? What's it to be?"

"How's your appeal going?" asked Milton affably of the man in stripes.

"Well, I think," he replied, "but it will take time. This bureaucratic mix-up has deprived me of my rightful enjoyment, but what are a few years in comparison to eternity. I bear my trials as a Christian should. With fortitude. It is the foul slur upon my name that concerns me most. It is a cosmic injustice I suffer in silence."

My mentor turned to me and politely explained, "This gentleman – Mr. Blair he's called – has been condemned to these kitchens for warmongering. You might remember the case ..."

"Of course, I thought I recognised you. Yes, I was thirteen when you invaded Iraq. Of course, I remember ... Weapons of mass destruction... Bad luck about the skiing accident."

"Everything I did I did in good faith," the man adopted an expression of suppressed anguish – he played the part of the misunderstood.

Coming from another age, Milton seemed to feel sorry for him. "At least you have a chance to speak with our Lord Protector back there in the steamiest part of the kitchens where they scrub and wash. Something I would dearly love to do." The ex-prime minister seemed perplexed by this suggestion.

Just then a little man with a simian face broke in: "Yeah, you get them kick his ass over there amongst them dishwashers. I'm heartily sick of his pissing and moaning. Of course, he ain't got no chance. I reckon them reds and pinkos got their hands on this place."

Milton might have been moving with the times, but not enough to understand the American gentleman who resembled an American president well known for his accomplished missions.

When we sat down to our meal, I started to reflect on how religions had got it so wrong. No hell. Eternity in the kitchens didn't seem so bad compared with the vicious talionic penance of the Middle Ages. I shared my perplexities with my master.

"Maybe," he said, "there was a hell up here when people on earth could believe in it. Maybe the gods and the heavens are just a reflection of all those minds down below aching to know and to understand at last – and then, most foolish of all, believing with absolute certainty."

"You mean that this paradise we live in is something new – so where were its oldest inmates when there was a hell? Were the occupants of hell trans-shipped to here when it was closed down?"

"Maybe. But I think the past is changed retrospectively to adapt to the new reality. When you're down in your earthly existence, you think – well, if there really is a life after death, we'll eventually find out how it all works, but in fact it all appears even more indecipherable up here than it did down there. Human life after death continues to enjoy an epistemological void – a place for the imagination."

Such were our conversations. Very interesting they were too, although inconclusive for the most part. We walked the corridors and avoided as much as we could the shabbiness of the entertainments provided in Paradise Hotel. We talked and talked, and became close in a way. One day as we sauntered along the dusty carpet and breathed the stale air, we saw an extraordinary man coming towards us with his large retinue. He was tall and had a long, long grey beard, flowing robes of red and gold, and what can only be called a businesslike manner. Just behind two men were pushing a trolley on which lay an enormous parchment covered with numbers. When he was close, Milton bowed very low and said, "Sire, you do me honour." The man beckoned to him to stand and then came close, so close his mouth was next to Milton's ear:

"We have got to number 2,678,432,765,321, all en-suite it appears. I think that we can crack this in another two and a half thousand years. And then what will I do?" He started to move off. "By the way, Milton, start to move with the times – no one says 'sire' these days. Not even 'sir'."

Milton, still in awe, just muttered, "Of course, sir. Of course, you're right. You're always right."

"Who was that?"

"Aristotle. He's counting the number of rooms in Paradise Hotel."

"Why?"

"Because it matters to him. When he takes it into his head to find something out, he is utterly dedicated to his task. Knowledge is everything for him."

"Sounds very dull. How long has it taken him?"

"Well, he's been at it since he died."

"I thought you said that hell might have existed in the Middle Ages."

"Yes, indeed. Although I cannot be sure. Because our memories are also adjusted. Everything is labile here. If there had been hell at that time or even when I died, he would have been stuck in limbo discussing philosophy with all the other Greek ..."

"...windbags," I interrupted.

Milton looked at me sternly as one would at a congenial but slightly unruly pupil. "Remember that the world of immortals is probably just a shadow of the one inhabited by mortals, and when the latter changes, then the former changes not only in the present but also in the past. Time here is of a different dimension; that is why we had to go through the sandglass. When mortals project their imaginations on the past, the future or the timeless, they always do it through the prism of the present."

Just then another bearded man in flowing robes appeared. He was short and fat, and was muttering to himself: "Socrates said... Alcibiades asserted... Timaeus negated... Gorgias insisted..." And in front of him strode a cockerel.

"Mister Plato, good day," said Milton in a familiar tone.

"Ah, Milton. Poets like you should be kept away from any virtuous republic, particularly a celestial one. What are you plotting now? What vain imaginings are you coming up with to distract the tender and malleable minds of the rabble? This place is quite uncontrolled. And the last thing they need is poets wandering around and reciting nonsense."

"Quite right," said Milton, "and that's why I do my best to stay away. I'm back and forth, you know. I'm hardly ever here."

"Glad to hear it. What are you doing with this young man?"

"Showing him around ... and subverting him."

"Thought as much."

"Are we allowed to keep pets in heaven?" I joined the conversation shyly.

Plato looked at me as though I were an idiot.

"The cockerel," I said and pointed to it.

He looked away from me and towards Milton, "Try to teach the boy something."

"The cockerel," Milton explained, "is none other than the famous mathematician Pythagoras in his most evolved incarnation."

"Correct," said Plato, "and we have work to do."

"The reader has just come by – a couple of minutes before you appeared."

"Oh really, the 'counter' we should call him now. How's he getting on with counting all the rooms in the building?"

"Halfway there, he thinks."

"Well, as I say, we have work to do. Sensible work. Good day, sir." And off he went, muttering and perhaps consulting with the cockerel.

"Plato may be a grump, a reactionary you would call him now, but he is the more genial of the two," Milton smiled warmly, like someone touched by the banality of greatness.

"And the one I can read," I said.

"You modern people have very delicate palates. Have you ever looked at the servile prefaces we had to digest in my times? If someone isn't enticing you people with what might come next, you can't read a word. But you're right: the curmudgeon is a good read – a better read than the reader."

"What did you mean by saying that you're subverting me?"

"I am, really. This is what I do. I go back to the solid earth to find souls on the point of leaving their mortal coils and then I guide them back. I like to show them the silliness of heaven with its amusement arcades where people spend eternity trying to make money they can't spend..."

"That is a relative eternity. Who knows what'll happen, when things change down below."

"Quite," he said, always irritated at my habit of interrupting him, "and also observing those large screens they have, the ones that show humans beings in their homes – reality TV, they call it. They look at the real tragedies of randomly chosen individuals and laugh. Their eyes are desperate for entertainment. Always entertainment. There's nothing else. No seriousness. No feeling. No compassion."

"There was little of those things down on earth, too."

"Reality TV, and then of course the group therapy sessions. In which people endlessly rake over their lives on earth. Then, yes, they find the strength to weep. But always about themselves. What their mummies and daddies didn't do. The brutes they met in life. The cheats and scoundrels. All the horrors of earthly existence that made them come off worse. That isn't an existence, and certainly not one you'd want for eternity."

"So what do you want me to do?" I asked.

"Leave the Hotel with me and I shall take you to one of the dark woods and lead you into its deep interior. I will abandon you there, and in time you will become feral. You too will metamorphose into a goatman and play the pipes and wander singing your weird songs of infinite melancholy. I shall not hide from you that there are dangers there. Fierce, mythological beasts conjured up by man's greatest fears stalk the woods in search of prey. If you stay away long enough, you will be freed from the vicissitudes of heaven and its changing natures in accordance with the whims of mortals, but – and this is an enormous 'but' – you will lose some of your immortality, which mathematically means that you will not see out the whole of eternity. The thrill of danger has its price. But you will live. You who lived so little in the world of mortals will live the charmed life of a wild spirit in the dark imagined woods."

And so it was. I followed him dutifully and he abandoned me to go in search of his own prey. Like so many writers, he incites others to folly from the safety of his studied thoughts. But folly is good. Folly brought me here, and my goat legs carry me through the limitless forest, whose distant calls excite my heart. I, who once used a staple gun to join together frail garden sheds, now whittle my pan pipes and scratch on timbers the words of my bitter-sweet songs. I dance in the clearing and laugh in the hollows. I sleep on the boughs and feast on the berries. I drink from the stream and swim in the pools. The green is undying and the woods eternal. I wander the paths of man's measureless imagination. I live.

Or I dream.

This

To *this* and all the sadness of this world I write these words of happy oblivion desired and almost gained! I felt and feared that at some future date I would feel no more. No more hear the cries of pain that sear the night and invade my dreams. But then I felt and always feared that I would never cease to feel those pointless wounds that never brought a balm to those who scream and doubtless suffer out of sight.

This is a struggle to retain – to re-evoke those moments of the past that could slip away like leaves scattered by a gust or simply rotting where they lie, losing all the colours they displayed on the branch or brightened and nuanced during the early stages of their desiccation. Memories take on those bright golds, yellows and reddish browns burnished by their retelling. And then they too rot or let themselves be carried off on the rush of time so they can come flying back into our brains heavy with new meanings. These joys and bitter blows lift or shatter hopes and tell us truths of what *this* is – this crazy thing that we all know too well and yet cannot define.

I try to recall what I witnessed standing safely at a hotel window, while the smallest cogs of history turned and ground another people's hopes to dust, as they always must. I saw that great crowd of sans-culottes, then full of faces but faceless now the image fades – a crowd of Bengalis in their lungis and singlets marching by the million to the racetrack hemmed in on every side by soldiers wielding batons lethargically, beating without passion, without zest, because they had to. And those same soldiers, Bengalis too, would, some months from then, fight and die for a nation they would never see, forgotten in the unforgiving flood of history.

The image fades but not what I have learnt: there are few wholly good or evil men, only individuals swept along and now and then resisting vainly all the vicious power of that amorphous flood.

This is to feel with all our senses sharpened by the will to be – to be in the moment and forget for once the weight of years to come or drawn behind, that drag us down or will. This moment sweet – to lie within another's arms and feel the smoothness of her skin, the involucre of her warm and naked soul. This moment when the wind comes in and bites the cheeks with unrelenting force – the force of nature that cohabits still this manufactured land. This lunch when food plays long and vibrant on our budding nerves and slips forgotten into the abyss of our unending needs. And how we shout and turn upon each other with our cares, our thoughts, our strong beliefs of all the things we cannot know with any certitude. We fret and manipulate our words, wanting to win – but what? And will they understand those words in a century, in a decade's time or even in ten days from now? Who cares? We have the now. We stand in it and declare our truths.

And now those vinous moments of the now are in the past and mainly inhabit my memory of Italy, a land where they know how to talk or did. The flasks of wine, the grated cheese that smelt, the oil so new it stings upon the tongue, and all those heady, heady words that melt within the brain and touch those nerves that for far too long have not had anything to feel or grasp.

This hell, this hole: how many times do we return to the darkness of the past? This earthly hell can surely not be followed by an unearthly one. This feeling trapped within a self, a bag of nerves that jangle not just with our own pain, but also with our compassion for that of others. At least our own pain, if it does not break us, makes us strong and therefore serves a purpose. If ever you foolishly dwell on your pains of the past, then take a look at that pompous prick who pampered all his life now smugly observes from his position of great or petty power his secure kingdom of unappreciated delights and honours granted for his acceptance of all the hierarchical chain into which he so snugly fits. Such people at the slightest slight react with anger or self-pity. They do not know that success merely locks the door to the cell in which the self is caught; it makes a prison of a tight abode.

A trip up who knows what secluded tributary of the Niger, a small ship that carried me and my white-uniformed father, and a baggage of lies so serpentine I could not name them here, is my small taste of hell – a smaller portion than most must swallow in their early years. He did not want me on the trip and he knew why. The boat was working hard, laying buoys and lifting them, running lines of soundings, sextants and numbers called, and inking-in the maps – that evening craft surveyors combine with draughts of whisky well-diluted in that sticky, sweaty clime. And I under orders to keep away, out of sight, he said, what are you doing here? The silent scream, that's the clever trick you learn – to stand aside, keep dumb and smile upon a jaundiced world. The engineer took pity on a little lad who dumbly wandered on the decks and read. I passed the weeks in the engine room on a second chair he put out especially for me. An Irishman, he knew how to talk and listen too. He knew how to laugh and watch the dials all the same. The mindless engines toiled away and shuddered as they did. Perhaps this was the most important place, and not the bridge from which I was banned. Eventually we got back to the same deserted Lagos quay, but not my mother's car. When all had left, my father and I stood on the deck. Powerless, he sweated under the vertical rays of the sun; perhaps he stood aside, kept dumb and smiled upon a jaundiced world. He wore his white uniform shorts and white shirt with epaulettes, contrasting with his dark and hirsute skin. He threw aside his peaked Ports Authority hat, the symbol of his rank, and bared his balding head to the cruel sun. He did not care. The lucky state in which we care no more. He knew. I did not know, but he knew his wife had been lying with another man. Trapped in his solitude, he directed what anger he had at me, who insisted on disturbing the completeness of his isolation. Did he not know the human condition? Did he not understand his adult world? Who knows, for he had learnt well how to stand aside, keep dumb and smile weakly on a jaundiced world. After many hours, a car appeared, an orange Beetle which disgorged a young man running with a letter to consign. My father waylaid him with a smile and lots of chat, and of course a plea for a lift home. I never spoke to the man nor he to me, but I remember him clearly: a redhead with a drawn and freckled face, glasses, bad teeth and an energetic smile. My mother screamed, "I'll not see the boy." Knowing so much and not understanding, I was an embarrassment now. So I waited in the hall. I stood aside, kept dumb and smiled upon a jaundiced world. The servants had fled but slowly returned – Adolphus too. He used to bring discovered treasures from the marketplace when I was very small: drums and strange hats, and painted knick-knacks made at home, nicely carved in soft, light woods. He was sacked on a technicality, because he knew too much. He cycled away without a possession in this world and was framed in the oval rear window of our car, to where I cannot say. What did he do when he got there? Did he scream and shout, denounce the perfidious foreigner and beat his fist on the table? Most probably he stood aside, kept dumb and smiled warmly on a jaundiced world.

This is also made of raptures, those moments of escape when the mind concentrates on one thing and distils its pleasure from some problematic of a kind our passions can delight in. A sport, a broke-down car, a mountain face, a place unknown, a book, a canvas stabbed with paint, these all suppress the self, throw wide the cell door and reveal a limitless plain of infinitudes, of ways and ways of doing, seeing, moving, searching, calling, expressing to others and oneself the wondrous permutations of how we can consume *this*, this elusive thing we never notice until it is at risk.

The artist measured up his work with steady eyes and critically calculated all those marks of paint: the colours, contrast, composition, brushwork, pose, poise, expression of the hurt, pathos of the suffering saint – a noose loosely fitted round his scraggy neck. Then he leapt, large brush in hand heavy with black paint. And how he laboured with that destructive arm, which spread a night across the surface of his work. No dawn would resurrect the fearsome portrayal of a martyred end. But still he paints a lonely figure whose afflicted corpse-to-be stands free of ground, of time, of pain perhaps, levitated by the energy of sacrifice. The hooded hangman's gone; so has the crowd that gleeful jostled and stretched forward to enjoy the show; the light of heavens triumphant has been dulled, so loneliness remains.

This contains those civic moments by which we measure out the passing years: birth, pair-bonding of a kind, birth of children, the repeating cycle of their *this*, and then death. *This*, rather grandly, also posits such events within the timeline history dictates: "two years before the war", "just after the recession", "when they landed on the moon". This is how the micro- and the macrocosm should relate; their unequal trajectories are not mechanic things – the individual can rebel and should. *This* belongs beyond oneself and beyond the triteness of one's age and its conformist certitudes.

Allan Cameron

What is this *this*?

It is *this* little thing that seems so big, *this* life we share, *this* tangle of shattered nerves, *this* string of thoughts that lonely twist and turn, fly up into the airless light where ideas are born and the gods sing, or sink into the deep, depressing water that presses on our lungs and cruel clears away all hope, where drags us down the leaden weight of that elusive thing we call reality. Like all small things, *this* life is capable of endless variegations, and the stack of stuff of which it's made can be shuffled in so many ways; in one small yard behind a block of flats, a history of lives can be played out, and more happens in one small child's brain than in several light-years of space. *This* is a divine gift we have to please ourselves, to please others and to waste… and, of course, regret.

And when you get to the end, it is a book already published – no chance to correct or rewrite, and the pages are already turning yellow. It is a story randomly told, and what it lacks in coherence it makes up for in its tragicomic commerce of traducements and prodigal human passions.

Escaping the Self

Bill Havelock and his buddy were sauntering along a lane lost in a flat featureless landscape. Without any purpose. In the distance they could see a country church with a round, flintstone tower, and a huddle of medieval and modern buildings. There was a railway that divided the land and the immense fields whose different shades of green and yellow declared what kind of monoculture they had been subjected to and what stage they had arrived at in the cycle of growth and harvest. Where the railway went in either direction was not known, and Bill Havelock and his buddy did not pose the question. Theirs was an aimless walk, a chance to chatter and laugh. Mainly they discussed their shared fixation: body-building. This meant how to improve their performance, how well they were doing and some gossip about other members of the body-building community. They looked like brothers, even identical twins. Knots of muscles filled their jackets and rounded their shoulders. Their angular faces looked as though they had been made in a mould. They were, of course, completely unrelated, but if you put together endless hours of workouts with regular injections of testosterone supplement then you get a very similar, plasticky product.

They moved effortlessly, aware of their own power and enjoying it. The only problem with their beautifully sculpted bodies was that they had no idea of what to do with them. And then they found a use or rather it was provided as if by divine intervention, because they hadn't previously noticed the old man bent double and shuffling along with his stick. They laughed, and wondered what game they could play. Not having a great store of imagination, they grinned at each other and decided to do the only thing that seemed plausible in the circumstances. They quickly caught up with the old man, Bill grabbed him by the shoulder and his buddy punched the curved and fragile figure in the stomach. Bill kicked him as he fell to the ground and then the two heaved the now crippled old man into the drainage ditch that ran alongside the lane. They laughed and rubbed their hands together.

Their laughter died in their taurine necks as they watched the old man metamorphose into a creature a lot like them. He stood up and his torn shirt revealed rippling stomach muscles beautifully tanned and glistening in the summer sun that pummelled the tidy monotony of that almost empty land. With a single bound, he leapt on them and banged their heads together as a fierce mother might treat her children. He then hurled them one after the other into the same ditch from which he had just emerged.

The two men were mildly concussed and now shared a terrible secret: they had been drubbed by an old man. A few months later at the gym, they saw the same old man shuffling along with his stick towards the gentlemen's lavatories. Slow to learn but quick to feel revenge's goad, they rushed towards him, just as he struggled through the lavatory door. He was a lamb or perhaps a broken-backed goat to the slaughter. Merriment tingled in their blood and their blood coursed in their vigorous, cholesterol-free veins. Life has its moments, and they felt like greyhounds after the hare – creatures with a smooth and healthy pelt that pounded towards their weakling prey. They bounced into the men's loos panting with desire, only to find a man a lot like them. Bill's buddy was now armed with a flick-knife which he produced with a single movement of his arm and hand. The snap of the opening mechanism underscored the silence of that room. He bravely flung himself at the adversary, who with another single movement grabbed the buddy's wrist, twisted him around, removed the weapon and threw its owner headfirst against the mirror above the basins. Now Bill attacked, and again was turned around. Next he felt the knife's blade sinking into his lower back. He fell to the ground.

The two wounded men were rushed to hospital and the police always remained convinced that they had fought each other. They both received six-month prison sentences and never saw each other again. Whatever may be said about our prison system which locks up the mentally ill for venial crimes and has them rot in an environment more corrupting than rehabilitating, Bill left prison a reformed man. He ceased to spend his life in the pursuit of a beautiful muscly body, always supposing that a muscly body is beautiful. He turned instead to helping others and paying back his debt to society. He could be seen wheeling old ladies in wheelchairs, loading containers with charitable gifts for Moldavia and taking part in sponsored runs. He married, had children and looked after his mother. He worked in a bank and was a model employee. Promotion followed promotion, and everyone said that Bill was an upstanding citizen. And the years went by.

Fifteen years went by and there was a knock at his office door. He was leaning back in his comfortable chair and reflecting on his great success. The ex-offender was now a gloriously prosperous and well-liked member of the community. So good to be alive, he thought smugly to himself. His secretary announced that a Mr. Kronovich wished to see him and claimed to know him. Bill could not remember anyone with that strange foreign name, but he told her to show him in. An old man with a stick shuffled in, and Bill immediately recognised him as the old man who had harmed him twice. But Bill, as I have said, was now a reformed character and he stood up to greet the visitor with his usual urbane kindness. The old man returned his cordial reception with a gentle smile and seemed to grow younger and suaver before his eyes. "I am glad to see you prospering so well since we last met," the not so old man said, "and I feel the time has come for a little chat. In fact, I don't remember ever exchanging words with you; you never gave me a chance."

"So right," Bill enthused, "you're so right. I can only apologise for my unforgivable behaviour and should also thank you for all this," he meaningfully swept his arm to indicate his office, his family, his life and perhaps his happiness; "if it hadn't been for you, I might never have abandoned the worthless existence of my youth."

"Not at all," replied the smiling man. "I'm sure you would have discovered the error of your ways, even without my intervention."

"Can you give me any news of my buddy?" Bill asked.

"I'm afraid not. I seem to have lost all contact with him," the now seated man beamed with mannerly tact.

"Come on," objected Bill, "I cannot believe that you can track me down and not him. That would make no sense."

"Well," the man wriggled slightly in his chair, "shall we say that I have to respect professional confidences?"

"Professional confidences?" Bill raised his voice. "But who are you? And how did you do those things?"

"Sometimes it is best not to know everything. Knowledge can be a burden, you know. It can also be a disappointment. The unknown is exciting precisely because it is unknown. Listen, for instance, to a singing voice and enjoy those shivers it sends through your body. Now they want to isolate the tone and count up the hertz of the voice frequency so that they can then synthesise it for every singer. This simply deskills us and introduces us to the banality of the universe. Wasn't it all so much more wonderful when we didn't know?" He crossed his legs elegantly, stretched himself and smiled a smile that exactly reflected and inverted Bill's own charming smile.

"Who are you then? Are you God? Are you an angel? Or a devil? How can you change form? How can you appear and disappear at will?" Bill began to plead. "Please tell me or I shall never be at peace again."

"Ah, my dear fellow," the man said, "please do not agitate yourself. A moment ago, you would have been happy with some news of your buddy, but now you want to know who I am, and that is not something I could possibly divulge."

"Dear Mr. Kronovich," Bill started to sweat, "you have come here uninvited and, although I don't deny the debt I owe you, I object to the manner in which you have unsettled my life. A life, I might say, that I had to construct anew on my release from prison. In fact, I would say that I am now a completely different man, and while I might apologise for my former self, I need to protect my new self from any danger."

"My dear Bill Havelock," the man smirked more darkly, "am I a threat to you? Of course not. I am your friend and benefactor, as you yourself have admitted. The only danger to you is this terrible desire to have an explanation. This is the affliction of the modern age. Why be so restless? You now have everything, just as you were musing to yourself a moment ago."

"Good God," cried Bill, "you even know my thoughts. How dare you! I demand an explanation. I have a right. My privacy has been violated. We all have a right to the privacy of our own thoughts – to privacy more generally. It is the foundation on which our civilisation has been built."

"If I were one of those beings you have taken me for, then you would be the one without a right to make demands, but I am not," the man clarified with an elegant gesture of his hand. "So what I will do is this: if you can be bothered to climb the highest mountain in Wales, you will find a stone and under that stone there'll be a piece of paper which shall declare exactly who I am. I strongly advise you against undertaking this quest, but I see that you are quite determined. There is little I can do to stop you, though it pains me greatly. Top of the highest mountain in Wales, remember."

The man stood up and politely took his leave. He was of slight build, very much like Bill now that Bill had given up his fixation with body-building. The man's departure left Bill in a state of agitation. He had to know, but how long would it take him to climb Snowdon? Not long, and then he would surely know the key to the universe. A few days and he would know the identity of that magical man – in his opinion, most probably some messenger from God. At the end of their conversation, the man's smile had become slightly demonic however; or was that just his imagination? In these matters it is impossible to say.

Bill set off on his quest to discover the identity of the strange man who had so influenced his life – who uninvited had caused tumult once more in his mind. Those who set off in search of fundamental truths no longer travel on steeds or wander the byways on foot; they take the motorway and Bill took it in his BMW saloon. The car purred all the way, and it seemed a pity that the road did not run over the top of the mountain. He was met by a slight drizzle, but he was well kitted out with all the required outdoor gear. Of course, he was no longer as fit as he had been in his youth, but he managed to reach the summit without collapsing from exhaustion. There he found a large stone, which, once lifted, revealed a piece of paper, barely damp from the rain. Its contents came as a disappointment:

My dear Bill,

On reflection, I think it would be better for you if I placed a few more obstacles between you and the information you seek. You will have to climb three more peaks. Go to the highest mountain in Scotland and there you will find another note.

Believe me, our fates are inextricably linked and I would never do anything to harm you. I strongly advise you to desist from your pursuance of knowledge that can do you no good. By the way, the view from Ben Nevis over Loch Linnhe is quite stunning.

Yours forever.

Bill took the news badly. He had a busy life and now he was being asked to put it on hold to seek out information which, if not a key to the universe, was at the very least a key to understanding his own existence. It was an un-happy man who drove home along the M4, and that mood wasn't brightened by the fact that his reliable BMW broke down and he had to be towed to the nearest garage. On arriving home, he argued with his wife. She didn't have the right coffee for breakfast the next day, and when he finally calmed down and got round to drinking the inferior brand, the liquid spilt down his best suit. The children had broken one of the panes on his greenhouse, and having to listen to the eldest's favourite band suddenly became an unbearable imposition. While he prepared for his trip to Scotland, he started to study the paranormal. Great piles of books were ordered on line, and he passed hours in his office poring over them – without obtaining any illuminations. His experience appeared unique and his life some kind of aberration. Why had it been inflicted on him? Was it a curse or an election? The more obsessed he became about the identity of the old man and his various manifestations, the more he obsessed about himself and his place in the world. He was special, and his family could not appreciate his uniqueness.

Eventually he set off on the next stage of his quest. The BMW purred again and the omens seemed good, but when he approached Fort William the weather changed, and wind and rain reduced the visibility. Muffled up in the best of modern climbing clothes, he set off for the summit once more. The journey was long and wild. Modern climbing clothes are good but little match for the worst of Scottish weather on the hills. Trickles of damp found their way down the back of his neck and the cold started to enter his bones. Halfway up his strength abandoned him and he sought shelter by some rocks. While he huddled up to them in his misery, he heard a cough and turned. It was, he thought, the man whose identity he was seeking out, but this time he looked haggard: no longer his urbane self but rather a middle-aged man worn out by his travails.

"Is it really worth all this pain?" the man asked.

"It's you."

"I feel for your suffering, and have come once more to persuade to desist from this madness. What can you possibly want to gain?"

"Now I know you really are some demonic spirit. I'm sure of it."

"Then desist! If you're so certain of who I am," he urged grimly.

"Perhaps you're right," Bill agreed.

"On the other hand, you are already halfway up – perhaps two-thirds," the man smiled wanly.

"No, I think you're right. I should have followed your advice from the beginning. It was given in a spirit of generosity, and I have been arrogantly ignoring it."

"True, but I have been an important influence in your life, and you shouldn't turn your back on this quest without thinking it through very carefully. Curiosity is the trait that distinguishes humanity from dumb animals, but it always comes with a price – only the pusillanimous ignore its siren call. Life is about discovery, and better the discomfort of knowledge than the vegetal comfort of ignorance. Live, whatever the cost. You have come this far," he argued in a smooth and persuasive voice.

"You're right," said Bill, and he started off into the rain and wind with the determination of a polar explorer. The truth must be uncovered whatever the cost. The truth he eventually uncovered was this disappointing letter:

Dear Mr. Havelock,

You are a man of great fortitude, but I doubt you have the fortitude to undertake the next test: I ask you to go to the summit of the highest mountain in France and find the note I leave you there. Your frustrated friend.

During his drive home, Bill fell asleep and crashed his BMW into a roadside barrier. The car was a write-off. He continued his journey by train. In a miserable mood he staggered home. His wife was distraught to hear of the car. His eldest had dyed his hair pink, which provoked a paroxysm of rage in Bill, but his wife defended the child. Boys do these things now, she cried, and he felt the family were closing off to him. Good riddance. Hadn't he provided them with everything they had? Well, not quite. His wife had a good job too. He sulked in his study and read his books on the paranormal. They still made no sense. Only cranks write such things.

He returned to the gym. This time the aim was not to look like an oversized plastic toy from the eighties, but to train for endurance. He walked for miles and learnt to climb. He started to look at himself in the mirror again, but now his narcissism was not aimless. He knew that his life was a finite thing, and he could make it significant by discovering the identity of that chameleon spirit who haunted his existence. Was this all a punishment for a single act of wanton cruelty? Perhaps, but he could turn his suffering to his advantage. No one could now hold him back from the achievement that would forever be associated with his life. He would be remembered for having revealed the malign spirits that populate our dreams and their physical manifestations. He would be famous and respected, not simply rich and comfortable. The spirit had been right: no courageous soul could fail to be driven by its innate curiosity. This is what it means to be human.

The next expedition took two years to prepare. He planned it very carefully, so that no accident would prevent him from achieving his fated purpose. For most of the climb, the going was very easy, but two hundred yards from the peak a sudden squall of snow obscured all vision and he struggled up the final stretch on his hands and knees. On reaching what he thought to be the summit, he could not find any written message. He crawled around in circles for about half an hour and then he saw a seated figure in front of him. "Where's the bloody note?" he shouted.

The grey silhouette against a white background of swirling snow replied in a deep and terrifying voice, "Why are you crawling on the ground, Bill Havelock? Are you overwhelmed by the elements? If you are, then you should not be here. Those who seek the truth should not be fearful; they should be immune to all feelings and all sensations."

Bill stared at his persecutor: "I am looking for your note."

"There is no note this time. *I* will give you your next task," said the seated figure, whose eyes suddenly flashed red light that pierced the grey.

"Now I know you are a demonic force," Bill uttered in a broken voice. "Why do you torment me?"

"You torment yourself with your quests and ambitions, and then you blame me. Return to your family and forget me."

"I can't. You know that, spirit; that is why you urge me to do what I cannot do?" Bill shouted against the wind. "The devil you are, and who knows where you'll take me? But I no longer care."

"I am no devil," the spirit replied. "I am the one who makes people obsess with themselves and their existences. I am the one that so convinces them of their own importance that they live out their existences in terror – never able to accept their lives as a leaf allows itself to be blown in the wind. Climb to the top of the highest mountain in the world and I promise to reveal myself to you."

"Spirit, why do you torture me? Reveal your secret now. I can climb no more mountains, and the cold has entered my soul. I now believe in nothing except death, and would embrace it happily."

"Come then," said the spirit, "and drink some of my brandy. It will warm you and give you courage."

Bill approached the grey figure, and as he did so the shape took on a clearer form. He could now make out the face and it frightened him. It was skeletal – barely covered with the thinnest possible layer of flesh and skin. What teeth there were, were black and pointed – worn by an enormity of years. The old man – the ancient man – cackled and grinned as he poured brandy into a brandy balloon with a slightly tremulous hand. "Drink it all up, my friend. This will open the way to greater understanding and the solace you crave. Life is not bad, if you know how to live it, and you don't."

Such promises from such a man or spirit should not be relied upon. As Bill drank the liquid his head started to spin and the ancient man took off in a vortex complete with the throne on which he sat. As he went, he laughed loudly and roared, "Beware, Bill Havelock, beware of all you have: your ambitions, your thirst for knowledge – such a fragile thing – and all your property. I can have it off you at any time, and all those things will drag you down to hell – to hell on this earth, so you will beg for death as you did just now."

A helicopter took Bill's body off the mountain, and the doctors were convinced he could not live. But he did, though something died. It was a maddened stare that glinted from whatever consciousness survived in Bill's head. It could hold a stranger and chill a friend's blood. Within six months of his return, his wife and children fled, and he would never see them again. Who knows if this saddened him or even registered in his febrile brain? He set about organising the fourth and final climb towards the skies. This one would be expensive and much had to be done. He worked late into the night on the project and studied the religions and philosophies of the world in the hope of understanding all the calamitous events of his life, but nothing brought easement to his soul.

At the bank he was feared and detested, but his brilliance was undiminished. He had no joy in what he did, as though his nerves had been severed. He saw the world but it did not affect him.

Ten years passed and he aged. His was now a dry and brittle athleticism, but he did not for a moment give up his intentions. The day arrived and he was at base camp with a crowd of hired Sherpas – sulky and badly paid, but too fearful of the man with the maddened stare to rebel. He barked his orders, but it was not anger but a lack of all feeling that drove him on.

They started off and as they went, the Sherpas fell away, in part as had been planned and in part because they sensed that his soul had been sold to the devil who could drag them down even as they climbed. Bill quickened his pace as his goal came ever closer and spoke less and less. Finally, there were just three of them: the madman and his two remaining Sherpa servants. The sun was shining on the peak, and Bill knew that this was where he would finally come to know the truth. Then, as they struggled up the last stretch with their oxygen masks, a tendon snapped in his right ankle. Immune to pain, he wriggled on the ground. "Carry me up," he screamed.

"It is too far," they replied.

"Too far. Nowhere is too far. I would go to hell and back. Lift me up and carry me."

"No sahib, it is too far. We cannot help," they persisted.

"This will strengthen your will," he took out an enormous wad of five-hundred euro notes. Their eyes brightened with desire as they reckoned up the houses that could be built and the cars that could be bought.

Greed sinewed their resolve, although they never thought to steal the cash; he held them with that maddened eye. They lifted him up and hope of wealth lightened their load. They struggled up and never spoke. Life can produce brief moments that silence even the most garrulous tongues. At times they had to slide him up the icy slope like some piece of baggage, but he never complained. The Sherpas worked tirelessly and some small part of their brains was counting joyfully the wad of euros ready to be spent. At last they got there and there it was. A round stone was resting on a single sheet of paper, white and flapping in the gentle breeze.

Bill crawled towards it, grabbed it and then pulled himself upright against a rock. After so much effort, he intended to read it with the dignity of a man who is not crawling on the ground. He looked at it and then started to laugh. After all that, he thought. Each of his eyes produced a tear, and they ran in unison down his pitted face.

"I told you so," a voice declared. "I told you that the truth disappoints while seeking the truth can stimulate. I told you to let go and live, but you would not listen."

"Listen..." he replied and laughed an aimless laugh.

The Sherpas rummaged in his jacket, took the wad he'd promised them and fled, leaving him to commune with the empty air. The man who had been distracted by wanting to be the strongest, the best and finally the most knowledgeable man, now knew that he had simply needed to be a man and care for other men and women.

"Show yourself, you spirit of hell," he cried.

"Hell is in your head," the spirit appeared before him in the guise of the man who had once sat in his office. "Read out those words you have come so far to read. Hear their hollowness and weep some more."

Bill twisted his face in anguish and read, "I AM YOUR SELF, YOUR TYRANNICAL SELF!"

And then, as though he'd recited some magic spell, a crowd of all his past selves appeared: his various childhood selves, his body-building self, his prisoner self, his selves as he evolved through his banking career, his self returned from Mont Blanc, his more recent wizened selves. The crowd of clones began to sing "Sympathy for the Devil", first with the normal manner of "rhythm-and-blues" and then increasingly in an unintelligible wail as they started to spin around the anguished soul. Suddenly they stopped and, in the same instant, disappeared. Bill's lifeless body fell to the frozen ground.

The Essayist

I met murder on the way –
He had a mask like Castlereagh –
Very smooth he looked, yet grim;
Seven blood-hounds followed him:

"The Mask of Anarchy" by Percy Bysshe Shelley
who was "dimwitted" enough to be outraged on
hearing of the Peterloo Massacre, and then
started to bite the hand that fed him.

Let me take time out from these short stories to speak as
the author in an imagined dialogue with Wolfe Henry, a
critic, essayist, television personality, celebrity intellectual
and autobiographer extraordinaire. As I live on a remote
island where conversation is hard to come by, because
there are too few people and too many televisions, I am
known to engage in the odd imagined dialogue. Often my
interlocutor is one of the weekend newspapers; I raise my
voice and they end up hiding somewhere on the floor,
where sometimes they sulk for weeks.

One Saturday, I read a long review of Wolfe Henry's
latest collection of essays, *The Revolting Cubiculum*. Life is
tedious, the reviewer said, and every week great mounds of
dross no one should have even thought of publishing are
heaped onto his desk, but just occasionally a little gem will
slip out of a jiffy bag – and that gem is a work by Wolfe
Henry. The encomium was fulsome and concerned both
the man and his work, but although long, it was so busy
doing what encomia do that it said very little about either
except that they are superlative. In fact the article said only
two things of substance: that Henry likes provoking the
Left, and that Henry hates to come across a hanging
participle, a grammatical error that the reviewer does not
understand but still finds fascinating. In truth, Henry is a
much more amusing and genial Henry Higgins than the
original.

Perhaps I would have let the whole matter rest, had the *Observer* not brought out the following day the crassest possible provocation of the Left that could be imagined. Too strong a statement, you say. Of course, there will be provocations more violent, more dishonest and more illogical, but as crass as this? I doubt it. The reviewer (whose name we need not mention) was examining Noam Chomsky's *Hopes and Prospects*, and the accusatory title screams, "That's typical Chomsky – still happy to bite the hand that feeds him." No one wants to join the ranks of nostalgic old writers – or at least do this too publicly – but such an argument would never have been used thirty years ago or possibly just fifteen. We'll leave aside the crassness of the reviewer's argument that even the bad policies US and Western governments implement are done by people who genuinely believe them noble things to do. Surely anyone with a modicum of experience of the world must know that people even guiltier than Bush and Blair always believe that they are motivated by noble sentiments. Evil is not the product of demonic thought but of banal self-interest, self-belief and self-deception. We'll leave aside the crassness of the journalist's claim that Chomsky "dismisses vast tracts of history in a few splenetic paragraphs, as if no alternative interpretation is worth considering," when actually he appears to be doing just that in relation to Chomsky's book. But we cannot overlook the crassness of the idea that an author should write about his own society as though that society were a medieval patron who has to be flattered and grovelled to, because society pays the bill – whatever that means. And the reason why that title would not have been used thirty years ago was that, at the time, the West was rightly (but also hypocritically, as time has now shown) criticising the Soviet Union for adopting just such arguments. In those days, the West made every effort to display a convincing image of high moral standards, and demanded the application in the

174

Soviet bloc of the very laws we now play fast and loose with in the name of the "War against Terrorism" or whatever the current term is.

It is true that here indigenous dissenters are not imprisoned or tortured. Whatever slights are inflicted are entirely bearable, but that does not mean that we are obliged to provide "some occasional flicker of admiration for the achievements of western civilisation", as the *Observer* reviewer demands of Chomsky. That is not our job. I might very well admire the achievements of the Enlightenment (particularly the early English one) – in fact I do – but I am not in the habit of shouting about it or considering it an entirely unique moment in history. Moreover, I am slightly unsettled by all this shouting about the Enlightenment by people who are bent on bringing it to an end. The Enlightenment is being waved around as the flag of our supposed superiority, but if it has any worth then it is universalist. Voltaire, perhaps the first truly European writer, was unstinting in his satire of every European society, even the English one he so often admired, but Candide can only find bucolic peace in Turkey. I'm sure Voltaire had no illusions about the Ottoman Empire, but he fought his battles at home. Nobody thinks him less French or European because of that; in fact, we are very glad to have him, given our fair share of monsters produced over the intervening period.

Wolfe Henry and the *Observer* reviewer are typical of the modern intellectual. Well, we all want to earn a crust and enjoy a little bit of comfort, but surely in Henry's case, there is no more need to butter up the establishment. Success should bring freedom, even in these conformist times. In any event, I am determined to have a chat with one of these two enlightened gentlemen, and it seems sensible to try it out with the more subtle of the two. It is, of course, a fearful task and Henry's wit is as quick as mine is dull. I ask the reader to hold my hand, which she is quite capable of doing as it will only be a fictional conversation. A real one would be terrifying and Henry might take me for a political stalker and splatter my brains over the interior decoration of a Burger King, as he dreams in *The Revolting Cubiculum* of doing to stalkers more generally. I have read the book of course, and am going in well prepared. Let's see where it takes us.

§   §   §

We arrive at the house one bright summer morning, and I knock at the door. A dainty Filipino maid appears, or is it a young man working on a Ph.D. and acting as the great man's secretary in his spare time. My eyesight is deteriorating fast. I declare my presumptuous intention, give the person my card and introduce the reader, "This lady has kindly agreed to take notes of the conversation." Here I offend the forty-five per cent of my symbolic reader who find the term "lady" condescending and the thirty per cent who are men and dislike being excluded even from such a minor thing. Then Wolfe Henry appears. He has a round, masculine head with fierce little eyes that contrast with his well-rehearsed sardonic grin. Actually I am probably just remembering him from his television days. From the back cover, he looks trim and thoughtful. Now I've put on my bifocals, he does look trim and thoughtful. Like all celebrities, he looks after himself. He has perhaps a private gym, and watches his calorie intake, but nevertheless keeps a good cellar. A question of balance. You wouldn't want to argue with such a substantial fellow as that. He looks so much more in the world than anyone else. In fact he gives the sly impression that he had a hand in designing it. It all makes so much sense to him.

He is actually very amiable. He smiles. "I'm probably going to regret this," he says, "but come in. Why not? Who are you anyway? ... Very sorry, never heard of you. But I am so ignorant about many things. It's hard to keep up."

He is American and retains very little of his American accent, but just enough to give a pleasant timbre to his sonorous voice. Americans come over to Europe either to escape the idiocy of American political discourse or to search for and identify with some old-world snobbery. In other words, we get the best and the worst. I was never quite sure which category he belongs to. American manners are good, exquisitely good, but is that because that most parochial melting pot tries too hard to make a nation of its diversity – rather than enjoy the fact that it contains the rest of the world within itself? Everyone is on their best behaviour because they don't want to be misunderstood. There are simple good manners and complex good manners; the Americans engage in the first and the Indians in the second (beware of an Indian who pays you an excessive compliment, and remember to keep rejecting those offers of a third helping of Chicken Biryani: you're not meant to say yes). It's the difference between syrup and an impenetrable spice. Maybe Henry came over here to get away from all that syrupy niceness; he looks like a man who could publicly insult you so understatedly that you don't realise it until two weeks later. I am now thinking it would have been much better to interview the critic from the *Observer*.

"Fire away," he says or orders, after we have slightly stiffly found our respective seats in his tidy and beautifully arranged study (it must have been a Filipino maid I saw).

"Well, it seems to me that you are very concerned about how posterity will judge your *opus*." Why have I said *opus*? I never say *opus*. Shouldn't I have said *opera*? That's silly. Perhaps I should have said *opera omnia*? Of course not, I'm looking at the wrong language; I should have said *oeuvre*. He likes the odd Latinism though. No, I should have just said "your work". I must have lost my knack for this conversation business. It's so difficult: you can't cross out

177

and start again. "Would you like to enlarge on that?" I end my question weakly. I don't sound like myself at all.

Henry smiles thinly and slyly. I think he has secretly taken offence. "Of course it concerns me. It concerns all writers. You write, I think you said," he adds to emphasise the dubiety that surrounds this circumstance. "I expect it concerns you too." He's right that we all want it to some degree, but I have to be realistic. Mostly I am concerned with finishing the work and paying the bills. I would prefer to ask other questions: will there be books? Will there be readers? Will there be anyone who knows what a hanging participle is?

I move on, "Mr. Henry, you suggest in your book that people find it easier to empathise with others, if they live in a democracy. Could you explain why this is the case? I would have thought that in repressive situations, people can often empathise much better. They are less self-obsessed and more reliant on mutual assistance. We all know what a competitive lot poets are, and this is confirmed by some of your comments. If you read the poems by Russian poets on other Russian poets in *The Page and the Fire*, selected and beautifully translated by Peter Oram, you discover how close they were. Surely if that was true of poets, then it must be even truer of other professions and circles in the Soviet Union."

"In a democracy, I thought it would be clear, people have to negotiate everything. Civil society engages individuals from all walks of life and they need to understand and mediate other people's needs," he looks at me sternly.

"Isn't that a common sense argument that ignores observation of real behaviour? Can you really put your hand on your heart and say that people empathise more with each other than they did thirty or fifty years ago?"

"We were a democracy then too," he smiles condescendingly.

"You're right. But I have lived under a dictatorship and I never noticed any sudden dearth of empathy."

"Your argument is a little unscientific and anecdotal, don't you think?"

What do I know of his brilliance? What right have I to pronounce on the wonders of his brain? I might ask, in my silly way, how much his fame was based on his ability to humiliate those he interviewed – often people whose first language was not English and whose understanding of his overblown and ironic flattery could never match that of his viewers, who were entertained, thank God. That is the most important thing – a good belly laugh in a good belly.

It is generally agreed that the idiot's lantern, as the television business likes to call the box in the corner that keeps it in business, can turn idiots into geniuses, but on occasions it can turn geniuses into idiots. Or perhaps it just makes everyone brilliantly and reliably mediocre. Its Midas touch is quite indiscriminate, and works as well on the clever as on the stupid. Isn't there something a little ersatz about every emotion it produces? Isn't there something a little empty about all the loud and extravagant claims made day after day after busy day to feed those bellies that have to laugh? And wasn't it Wolfe Henry who really taught us to laugh at other cultures we barely understand? Those mirabilia from countries whose televisual cultures cannot challenge the sophistication of our own – how they made us laugh and feel so much better about ourselves.

Once a philosopher lived in a tub, but now this great philosopher whose enlightened works excite jiffy bags and critics alike, has become one – filled to the brim with judgements on everyone from Montgomery to Elias Canetti, for whom he has great contempt, although I believe that this world would be poorer in very different ways if those two had not come into it. And can I get to know anything about them through a dab of tittle-tattle from Henry? But he does like politicians and how smoothly he flatters them. The autobiographer enjoys their autobiographies.

Now I am as mad as Don Quixote – mad eyes, mad mind filled with mad thoughts – and I tilt at politicians, because I think they are giants... But there is a difference: Quixote's windmills did a good job of milling the corn, especially on a windy day, and they never thought too much about whether they were giants or not. My targets, on the other hand, also think they are giants, and they always need other giants to reassure them that they really are giants too.

These political giants of ours are not like the ones in fairy tales who merely get on with the business of crunching the bones of lesser people, while endlessly repeating insane rhymes in a gruff voice. Yes, of course, our giants do this too, but they also keep a measuring tape attached to the wall of one of their very high rooms. Because our giants are sensitive souls. They have a terror that one day they will wake up and find that they are giants no longer. Their being giants resembles having to pump hard to keep inflated a balloon with a slow leak. And one day that microscopic hole – that tiny weakness or blemish – will rip and with what terrible result?

A tiny piece of crinkled rubber, a little like a used condom.

§   §   §

"This dialogue is unfair," Henry says quite justifiably. "No dialogue at all, in fact. You are in complete control and choose to caricature me. And I don't share your right to gloss this dialogue with erratic thoughts. If you were successful and mixed with politicians, you would like them too, I'm sure. You know they're very likeable and good company. It's a cliché to go on about politicians."

"You're right", I admitted. "I caricature you because for me you are a caricature of your own making. We rarely know our close friends that well; what can we possibly know about celebrities who are synthetic constructs mass-produced electronically in every home and no less artificial than the plastic wrappings that fill our overflowing bins. You – that is the individual you – are probably a very fine person. Most persons are. Whereas most crimes or mere acts of badness are committed in the family or, what concerns us here, professionally, because family and work are institutions in which we become inured by habit to our own badness or rather the badness expected of us. That is why writers should of course be skilled craftsmen and women, but never professionals. A professional must learn to be practical and place each human phenomenon in its correct professional box, while a writer must always observe the particular truth and magnify it in relation to the general one. A writer must retain a degree of wonderment, even in cynical old age.

"Yes, I'm sure you're a fine fellow," I effervesced. "And I'm sure that better writers than us are morally more reprehensible when they are not writing, but when they write – when they hurl their reckless souls into that wild current of fantasy, thoughts and troubling truths that speak with their own voices, then they are better people than we are."

"So you admit it. This is just a vile caricature – a personal attack from some no-hoper."

"I admit it, but do not feel a moment's guilt. I repay you with the same coin – but, forgive me, with a little more subtlety."

"The same coin? I've never heard of you. Why would I attack you? Why would I pay you such a compliment?"

"This is not personal. You have placed yourself up there and pass judgement in a manner that will never unsettle the powerful, who should club together and buy you a golden gargoyle blowing a raspberry."

"That is quite uncalled-for," says my reader firmly. "You invite yourself into this man's home and you insult him. Have you no manners?"

"I apologise, and anyway quite a few golden gargoyles would have to be handed out. You are not alone," I mutter contritely.

"Yes," says Wolfe Henry, who is hardly in need of being emboldened, "you take a lot on yourself. You really think you know it all."

"I don't even know what it is to know," I retort, emboldened in turn by the logic of argument. "I have no real sense of reality. I can only approach conviction by negation. Those who are convinced I distrust; those who believe in themselves strike me as lacking all credibility and those who show contempt come the closest to being contemptible."

"How very liberal!" he mutters wearily to underscore his complete faith in the power of sarcasm – his own above all others'.

"'Liberal' is no insult for me, whatever the tone it is pronounced in," I am now in full flow. "Of course I know that 'liberal' is a word that, like most political terminology, wriggles around as does a fish caught on a baited hook. It leaps and darts, and if the fisherman has no skill, it still has a chance of breaking free – of eluding all useful definition. We define something by what it is not, because in politics, too many people are motivated by what they detest and not by what they desire for the public thing. And yet all the other desired outcomes – even the opposites – have their part of the truth. Globalism, regionalism, localism – all have valid demands on us. Collectivism and individualism – who can deny the need to respect them both? Although we might disagree over the proper balance. Only with the racist one cannot talk, because by dividing humanity along mythical distinctions racists irredeemably cut themselves off from the humanity they wish to mutilate."

"You're all over the place. It's difficult to pin you down. Try talking a little sense for a change," he drawls.

"Yes, I am a chameleon – to some extent. Put me in a room with a nihilist and I will try to be understanding of his nihilism. My default position is indeed somewhat liberal and humanistic, but I can see why someone might despair of humanity and ultimately find our whole species a canker on the planet. It does not offend me that nihilists exist; in fact, I delight in them..."

"Oh God! I'm arguing with some 'peace and love' hippy," Henry leans forward, his eyes blazing. "Get this! Nihilists are narcissistic wankers who believe that the world has neglected their supreme talents. They project their paranoid sense of rejection onto the universality and affect a contemptuousness that fails to conceal their desire to be loved by those they reject. They are not cuddly fellows who have taken a slightly mistaken route for understandable reasons; they are monsters. I'm very much a liberal but if there's a depraved side to liberalism, then you've become its spokesperson."

"Yes, we disagree on the definition of most things; liberalism isn't the only one."

"So what else have you got up your sleeve?"

"Most of all I hate that old lie: that communism and Nazism are identical. One could forgive an ambitious young man in the sixties and seventies for repeating such drivel to secure a post in journalism or at the BBC, but now? – twenty years after the fall of the Soviet Union when we are meant to be so busy detesting Islamists of various hues. Of course, the innocents who went into the gas chambers and the innocents who were driven without their coats and boots in an open lorry in sub-zero temperatures to dig their own graves in some featureless Russian forest suffered the same fate. But the category of executed innocents – a torrent of blood that flushes out of that slaughterhouse called history – is no more informative than the category of famine victims or of war dead. Clearly these acts should be condemned by all civilised people – to use an adjective you like to use; I would prefer to say 'all human beings'."

"They seem clear enough categories to me."

"Yes, of course, but not proof of the equivalence of Nazism and communism, as the logic of this proof is that all regimes are the same – right-wing dictatorships, constitutional monarchies, autocracies, authoritarian regimes of the left including communist ones and democracies."

"Democracies?"

"Yes, even democracies – and that leads to the important distinction between these regimes. The relationship between the victims changes vastly between one kind of regime and another. If we look at the regimes that dominated the mid-twentieth century, we see an incredible difference. At one extreme, Nazism murdered the other – first the communists, then the socialists and trade-unionists and then the 'inferior' peoples as they perceived them, such as Jews, Gypsies but also all Slavs and thus nearly all peoples to the east. For Nazis, the category of Jew included German Jews, even German Jews who fought patriotically in the First World War. Nazism was a dictatorship not only of xenophobia, but also of perceived myths of a perfect self.

"The madness of communist slaughter was that it weighed most heavily on its own: communists, as Koestler makes clear in *Darkness at Noon*, were at risk in both communist and fascist states, even if they were orthodox, even if they themselves had been the purveyors of the most foul denunciations against other communist 'comrades' – that ill-used word worthy of a Newspeak dictionary. In Koestler's novel, the central character has already sacrificed his lover for a stay of his own execution, justified by a belief in the importance of his 'work'. In this communism was unique, although the Soviet Union did have a period of anti-Semitism too and Stalin was quite capable of punishing minority nations. As always, things are complicated."

"And democracies?"

"So you believe that democracies are above such things? Then you are no different from so many 'honest' communists and Nazis, who were often more sheltered from the truth and entirely immersed in their own regime's propaganda. Of course, democracies do not engage in wholesale slaughter of their electorates, but do export it either through proxies or, on occasions, directly. As they are usually the more powerful countries, they have economic interests to defend, even at the cost of other peoples' democracies or attempts at democracy. Democracies have to ensure that their electorates get their cheap commodities at whatever human cost."

The autobiographer looks bored. His expression mutters, "Bleeding hearts, how they drain your will to live," but he actually says, "There is no comparison between the crimes of Nazis and communists and those of democratic regimes. It is simply perverse and pig-headed to say anything else."

"There may be a difference of degree, but perhaps not if we examine the question within the historical cycle. There is a particular type of crime that unites both centrally planned economies and 'liberal' economic models, and that is the unnecessary famine. Paradoxically, right-wing authoritarian regimes are not usually guilty of these, as they use an interventionist capitalist model that is not resistant to a reorganisation of resources through state intervention, albeit in a manner that is least likely to harm vested interests. Forced collectivisation in Russia, the Great Leap Forward in China and the Potato Famine in Ireland are examples; the absolute figures were much higher in the first two cases, and the percentage figure higher in the last one; in all such cases, an unbending ideological rule prevents any kind of flexible and contingent reaction to the crisis."

"Again there is no comparison."

"You are the ideologue. Ireland continued to export foodstuffs in large quantities while its people starved. A similar famine in the Scottish Highlands was averted by the allocation of relatively small sums from the Church. In the Soviet Union and China, the folly of untested, large-scale economic experiments often meant that there was no real opportunity to reverse the situation in the short-term, given the perennial scarcity of those societies. And in Russia, America colluded with Yeltsin to fix the election and he introduced a Capitalist 'Great Leap Forward' that broke the country and left it standing still. They changed the wrong part of society. Russians wanted openness and democracy, and a chance to tentatively experiment with economic change – not necessarily in a capitalist direction. Our governments' concerns were never with democracy and human rights. Twice in the last century the Chechens suffered terrible injustice, and on both occasions the West remained silent for its own strategic reasons."

"So, having finished your scholastic analysis, what am I meant to think? That, after all, communism produces a charming society, and we should overlook the odd peccadillo."

"Not at all. The problem with arguing an unpopular position is that people are always ready to ascribe absurd arguments to you in an attempt to close down the whole debate – to prevent it going where the orthodox do not want it to go. Let me ask you a question: do you think that Catholicism should be condemned for eternity for the extermination of all the Arawak population of the main Caribbean islands or British free-market policies for the extinction of the indigenous population of Tasmania?"

"Of course not."

"So why should communism be condemned for all time because of the criminal acts of the Stalinist regime, condemned in part by the Soviet Union itself?"

"If you apply this argument, then Nazism too could be exonerated."

"You see where your lack of analysis leads you! The difference is in the intent. Nazism preached the mistreatment of 'non-Aryans'. It set about this task with determination to the detriment of all its other policies, including its own war aims. Sure, some Nazis may not have known about what was happening in the death camps, but they must have known about the endless petty humiliations, beatings, expropriations and the camps themselves. They must have known that fundamental injustices were being inflicted on one group of citizens, and this did not surprise them, because this was what they signed up for. Communism, on the other hand, propagated the ideas of equality and international solidarity. Like Christianity and Islam, it was universalist. This does not exonerate it – perhaps it makes it guiltier because of the mismatch between ideological intent and practical outcome, but it certainly means that it is something fundamentally different."

"So you're a communist then," he sneers.

"Call me what you like: communist, socialist, leftist. I am very ecumenical about these things, and if there is one thing I hate about the Left, it is its ability to split over matters of dogma. We should not be divided over whether or not we are Marxists; we should not be divided over matters of historical analysis; and, good God, we should not be divided over whether the Soviet Union was 'state capitalist' or a 'degenerated workers' state'. Some of these things are worthy of intellectual debate, but politics is the art of the possible, and more can be done through alliances."

"All one happy family."

"To talk about these things is impossible in these conformist times, and you represent for me an archetypal conformist – an establishment intellectual. Of course, we're not a happy family. We're not a family. And there are fundamental distinctions within our ranks, but only two of them: the first is the distinction between non-violent gradualism and the violent overthrow of society to be rebuilt from year zero, and the second is the distinction between liberals and authoritarians."

"They sound like the same distinction."

"They're not. They're not theoretically and they're not in practice, although I grant you that in practice they do converge, because the ranks of liberal revolutionaries are swelled by those who are revolutionaries for reasons of fashion or posture, and would run a thousand miles from any revolutionary situation with its uncertainties, disruptions, civil wars and economic misery – just as revolutions attract chancers, adventurers, thieves, sadists, idealists and tourists, who may not have had until the day before any sympathies for the Left."

"You're talking complete nonsense. How can you be liberal and communist?"

"Quite easily. At the Grunwick picket line, there was a bearded hippy who sold a newspaper called *The Anarchist*. I never bought it, as I considered the state to be an unfortunate necessity."

"Your closed mind."

"Possibly, or perhaps I just had too many newspapers. Anyway, he changed the name to *The Libertarian Communist*."

"And did you buy it?"

"Yes, I did."

"What was it like?"

"Not at all bad."

"What a relief! I suppose you are going to come to the point. This is not much of a conversation – more of a lecture."

"In Italy they had a liberal-socialist movement – and that is just as good a term. They were big in the anti-fascist movement, bigger than the communists perhaps, but when it came to the elections, they got a handful of votes, while the Communists and Christian Democrats leapt ahead. And that is another important point: it is democracy that creates ideology in the negative sense of the term, because only simple arguments can be successful in elections. To win them you need slogans not analysis, and flags and banners in place of books and magazines. And where did those liberal-socialists go when their Action Party was wound up? They went to join the communists, the socialists or the rabidly anti-communist social-democrats, the latter being men of principle you would have admired, and they never lacked a ministerial chair."

"Look, social-democracy won. No one in Europe argues against the need for free education and health care. Now the argument is just about how to deliver those services."

Now it's my turn to feel the pointlessness of our conversation. When you disagree about the big things, it is very difficult to find a fixed point on which to lever up an intelligent dialogue. "It seems to me that all politicians are in agreement: public services should be delivered through further privatisation by agencies that pay their staff less and keep them on temporary contracts. The link between the individual and the workplace community is dying."

"Enough of politics, it is a dull subject."

I don't agree in general, but here he is right. I decide to take a different tack. "Having read your book – a good book on the whole – I realise that you are not a political writer. You like Peter Mandelson, because he was polite when you interviewed him, but you must also like him because he allows the wealthier middle classes to feel completely relaxed and even virtuous about their wealth. He is a man entirely of his time; he can do that because he is a politician. You, a poet and essayist, cannot, particularly if you are concerned about posterity. You are right about Leni Riefenstahl, the film-maker who rose to prominence under Nazism. As with Gustav Gründgens, made famous by Klaus Mann's *Mephisto*, Riefenstahl's case is starker because of the criminal brutality of the regime, but her story is also instructive for those who live in more open societies. The most important thing for writers, reviewers and artists is not their careers because, if they believe that it is, then they are diminished as writers, reviewers and artists – activities that must all occur within society without being of that society. You have to avoid the slightest whiff of temporal provincialism – the tendency to interpret the world strictly within the methods and prejudices of one's own age."

"But I don't, and I don't have to agree with you or love communism."

"I'm not asking you to do either of those things. Nor would I expect that. People often shift from left to right as they get older, and become some of the more extreme exponents of their newly adopted views. Very rarely do people move from right to left as they get older, but in the few cases they do, they become the best exponents, retaining somehow an understanding for the territory they have abandoned. My plea is that people such as you should take nothing for granted and at least admit the validity of the opposing argument so that you have to argue against it, rather than dismiss it with a sneer. I am also saying that your thoughts have to come down on one side or other of the class divide, which has now been globalised. I am not a 'class warrior'; I don't hate anyone, and communism from its inception was unnecessarily contemptuous of others, I admit. This is a danger for all movements based on a moral precept. I am not defending just communism, but also socialism and any other movement that takes the side of the 'have-nots', which includes Tolstoyans, Gandhians and Liberation Theologians. The radical Italian priest, Don Milani, would say, 'the communists think they are classist; *I am* classist.' For a long time after his death the Catholic Church kept the priest they found contemptible at arm's length, but now it seems that they embrace him. Nothing changes. They will find a way to make him a posthumous champion of orthodoxy. But communists, who were they? Danilo Dolci, who recorded the real experiences of the disinherited, tells the story of a child who was sold by his parents to a criminal gang in Naples, which used him as a lookout. As a young man, he abandoned the relative prosperity of criminality to work in an even more dangerous field as a communist organiser during the Sicilian land battles. The mafia had engaged a bandit to assassinate the communist leaders, and when the land battles failed the bandit was shot by the police. He was no longer of any use to anyone except a few British intellectuals who wanted to lionise him.

"Those intellectuals missed the main story: they worshipped the Sicilian peasant turned gangster and not the nameless Neapolitan gangster who abjured his past and risked his life so that Sicilian peasants could own the land they worked. And that is why your claim that fascism and communism were two brands of totalitarianism and effectively identical is so disgraceful. Nazism never inspired anyone to a good act. There may have been and almost certainly were misguided but not entirely evil persons amongst the Nazi ranks, but it was not the Nazism that redeemed them, it was the part of them that had not been entirely Nazified. The fine ideals of communism inspired many to great acts of sacrifice: most of them, contrary to Marx's expectations, were peasants, like the ones described in Isaac Babel's short stories. Very possibly Marx was right, or rather the Marx of the Bernstein tradition was. The immense courage of the peasants who fought the revolutionary wars of the twentieth century could not make up for their pitiful lack of political savvy. They had no ownership of the victory they obtained in the name of a class that barely existed in the countries where they were successful. It may be that revolution itself requires terror because all regimes attract legitimacy of a kind, precisely because most people are provincial. It takes great effort to go beyond the boundaries imposed by our times and by our geographical location. If you had been brought up in the Soviet Union during the sixties, you – we – would have a different viewpoint, even if we were dissidents. Trifinov, who was published during that more open period, was always a communist, but in his major work, *The Old Man*, he is critical of the regime not under Stalin, which we might think of as the absolute limit for dissidence, but under Lenin, the regime's founder.

"Primo Levi, who you admire, would get angry at the idea of an equivalence between Nazism and communism even in the specific area of human rights abuse and the camps. I think he was wrong on that strictly legal point. Murder is murder, and mass murder is mass murder; it makes no difference who is doing it to whom. The crimes should be punished, and international law needs to develop so that such atrocities do not recur, but what do they tell us about the nature of regimes who were guilty of them? Do the British massacres in Kenya and India define the British political system and way of life? Does American connivance in the overthrow of democracy in Iran and Chile and with Suharto in the massacre of half a million Indonesian communists and the imprisonment of many others in camps mean that America should be reviled? I know that your answer is no. But there was a time when even the broadsheets worried about these things. I remember an interview with an Indonesian poet in a camp on an island where he had been rotting for twenty years.

192

Who knows how long he had to remain after that? I suppose you think the author of that article was part of what you call the perpetual dimwit left-consensus?"

"Did I say that?" Henry asks and stops drumming his fingers on the table.

"You did and you claim that it must eventually disgust every liberal."

"Look," Henry adopts the irritated expression of those who are misunderstood by the stupid. How do you explain it to the slow-witted? he appears to be thinking. "It is quite obvious that mistakes have been made. Big mistakes, no doubt. But no, they don't define us. I don't have time to explain these things, which should be obvious to anyone except a dimwit leftie. To some extent, we have to defend ourselves against a greater evil."

"The very argument – foul and illiberal argument – adopted by the Soviet Union."

"Give us a break. Western capitalism has its faults; I don't deny it and you have no right to imply that I do, and it may well be that it doesn't stand up too well against your abstract ideal of the perfect global system, but it is better than anything else. It has brought great wealth to most of the population in the West, and will eventually pull the rest of humanity out of the mire."

"No, Keynesian policies and the nationalised industries of Social Democracies rebuilt Europe after the war and provided growth rates unheard of before or since."

"Listen, you have lectured me for long enough. Allow me to speak. Capitalism in its various forms has provided for us very well. If you don't like it, you are welcome to go and live in Cuba. There are plenty who would change places with you." He gets to his feet and opens the study door to wave us down the stairs.

"How dare you?" says my reader as soon as the Filipino maid has closed the front door behind us, "You invited me along to an interview with an eminent writer and then just lectured him. I know no more about him now than I did beforehand. You blew it, and I am not happy about being used in this way."

She's right of course, and I am covered with confusion and embarrassment. Neither of us have, of course, paid any money to travel to the great man's door, but I have so far inflicted 6,692 words on her (ah, the wonders of modern technology; before Microsoft, I would have had to count the words one by one). I owe her an apology: "You are quite right, reader, but it was only when I started the conversation that I realised that I have no idea why he thinks what he thinks. He rails against the 'dimwit left-consensus', but nowhere in his book does he give us any idea of what that really is and why he detests it so much – apart from its dimwittedness, about which, he assumes, the reader is already convinced. And, in spite of his protestations, this can only mean that he believes himself to represent the current consensus. I don't represent the consensus, so I have to elaborate."

"That's all very well," my reader looks at me with an expression of mixed frustration and intelligent indulgence, "but does it always have to be about politics?"

"Of course not, literature is not just about politics, but it is also that. Literature is everything and says nothing definite, because its job is to spread doubts and not beliefs. When Jaan Kross wanted to speak about Stalin and the dominance of Russia, he wrote about the czar and his madman, and who is a writer if not someone fool enough to speak to power."

"But we live in a democracy," the reader inflects her voice to imply a question.

"We live in a freer society and we can say what we want, but there is still a price. Have you heard of Randall Swingler?"

"No," she replies.

"Nor had I. It seems he was a prominent writer in the thirties, but his membership of the Communist Party appeared to have put an end to that in the forties and fifties. This has recently been confirmed by a release of MI5's papers."

"So we're just half free?"

"I suppose so. But perhaps absolute freedom and justice can never exist anywhere – and if they could, I don't know that they would last for long. But the fact that we are corruptible does not mean writers should stop examining our corruptibility."

"So you're a bunch of sanctimonious prigs," she smiles.

"Indeed, and self-serving ones, but we have a function. And the reading and study of literature change society; they give it a heart and undermine consensus. Wolfe Henry makes fun of crime novels – whose familiar plots are designed to reassure, even if the explicit violence revolts. He's right about that. We human beings are not termites, which simply start to swarm and rebuild their mounds when crushed under someone's boot. Faced with cataclysmic events, of which we had many in the last century, we react both individually and socially, and we rebuild in pain, in hope and with imagination. Literature celebrates this even as it lays bare the horrors of which we are capable. Literature and particularly its now dominant form, the novel, are inherently humanistic, in the wider sense of the term. The demise of what is now called the literary novel will deprive society of its sensitivity."

"That's something I cannot deny. But I still don't see why we need all this politically explicit stuff."

"We don't. We need everything – all the great muddle of ideas. But when reviewers speak of dissidents biting the hands that feed them and writers are chummy with the powerful, you have to put up your hand and say that this is not what literary culture should be like. Would Shelley have liked a Castlereagh who interviewed nicely? Does a political cartoonist give a politician a kinder face just because the politician bought him a drink at the pub? Christ, our actors are now more politically active than our writers."

"You have a point," she admits, "but next time, get someone else to do your note-taking."

"Look," I say, "I'm sorry about the interview. He eluded me. I couldn't transfer him from his pages to mine, partly because the image of the television celebrity always got in the way. I hope I haven't put you off and I promise to get back to fiction on the next page."

"This has been fiction too, silly," she laughs and leaves for the Underground. She's right, of course, and, conceited fellow that I am, I fancy that my reader is more intelligent than Dan Brown's. "Pochi ma buoni," the Italians would say.

The Sad Passing of Chris Cary

Garry Lochrie has been drinking since the post came. He drinks and then he stares at a photo in a small magazine, and then he drinks some more. He laughs. But then the absurdity makes him angry too. The picture proves what he already knows: he is a defeated man, and worse, everything that he has held dear has been defeated too. It has been defeated by those whose sensitivities go little further than the sense of camaraderie that feeds off death – the death of the disinherited of this earth.

The Old Middletonian is a scrappily edited collection of nostalgia, glorified pasts, and prejudices so deep that they could bury a person in their heavy material of smugness and cruelty, a deadly combination. And indeed Lochrie has been buried alive ever since he went to Middleton Military College. Since then, life has been a struggle and his movements slowed by the weight of something he cannot and will not examine too deeply. He has, it is true, started to write a novelised version of this story, but that too has turned out to be painfully slow.

He based the story around his main persecutor, Chris Kray, whom he intended to make more interesting and more intelligent than he really was. The fictional character he created has, or had until now that he starts to fade, a conscience – a stunted one, but a conscience nonetheless. This fictional Kray, whom he has renamed Chris Cary with only a slight adjustment, is an ambitious man capable of cruelty and indeed incapable of compassion, but one who does not hide his evil from himself. He is driven more by ambition than by the real Kray's emptiness which Lochrie has never been able to understand. An emptiness totally unsuited to fiction which has its own logic, precisely because emptiness is so inexplicable, so utterly terrifying in its banality. Now that Kray's photo is before him, Lochrie's vague memory of his unremarkable features becomes more real: Kray and Cary separate, and never again will they come back together. Cary has become a fictional character deprived of a story in which to pulse with the bare minimum of imaginative potency. Kray lacks the necessary intricacy to take Cary's place in the novel. The real character is more two-dimensional than the fictional one.

Torturers are perhaps thought of as fat men with bad teeth, bad breath and a drink problem – or in other words, men who actually resemble Lochrie himself. The real Kray, as Lochrie now recalls, was a tall, athletic man whose weak expression stopped him short of handsome, in spite of the blue eyes and blond hair of which he was so proud. He wore the expression of someone who has no soul – or that is how Lochrie likes to describe Kray's emptiness.

Lochrie pours himself another whisky and walks to the window that looks out across Glasgow's violated cityscape, whose destruction in the sixties had accompanied his own. He enjoys a sweet moment of melancholy, as he remembers his childhood holidays in the city before he was sent off to a military school by his father, an ex-army doctor who had set up a practice in the city's West End, not far from the squalid high-rises where Lochrie now lives, but socially half a planet away. Destruction removes an object to a part of the memory that is like a shrine, a place where inaccessibility becomes a kind of mystic yearning. These are the pleasures of passing years, the only compensations for our defeats, and he sips the agreeable bitterness of his whisky. Tomorrow, he knows, depression will set in, but for now the whisky and the photograph are setting his mind buzzing.

Lochrie chortles – he isn't quite sure why. His wryness feels a little forced, but there is indeed a humorous side to all this. Why does he care? It feels as though the anger of his youth is also being removed to that shrine of mystic loss and eventual oblivion. Once he could not accept oblivion, but now oblivion holds few fears. To lose his sense of compassion and outrage would once have been to lose his humanity and thus himself. Perhaps he chortles because he is still here and that makes him feel good. Lochrie knows how to enjoy being in this world precisely because he is clever enough to understand what happened to him, and therefore to keep it to himself. But then, with his unending mental restlessness, he sometimes feels that keeping it all to himself may have damaged him – particularly in a generation in which everyone talks so freely of their woes.

His life has taken such a different turn from that of Kray's. Thank God. Lochrie lived in a Florentine dormitory with Arab guest-workers; Kray went to Oman to fight Arab insurgents. Lochrie loved the generosity of Arab culture; Kray would only have acknowledged its existence to stress its inferiority, its backward "medieval" nature. Lochrie and his Arab friends would have shared their last meal with each other; Kray wanted to kill them – not them in particular but them in general. As the rich go shooting grouse in Scotland, so Kray went to Oman – to a war Lochrie read about at the time, and whose cruelty he can remember. Of course, where else could Kray's callousness have been given such a free rein? On secondment to a regime that was inherently brutal, as so many of the other British officers have admitted in their memoirs. Underneath the photo, the interviewed Kray is quoted as boasting, "We did what we had to do and were able to report back that the job was done and done well." The British burned villages, poisoned wells, killed livestock and cut off food supplies, while also resorting to Churchill's tactic in Iraq, the bombing of the civilian population, who were forced to live in deep caves. Knowing Kray, Lochrie is certain that the non-specific and euphemistic nature of "what we had to do" hid brutality, torture and summary death. It meant the exercise of massive military superiority over those who did not submit to imperial diktat. The opportunities for cruelty would have been limitless, and the risk slight. Those who fell into Kray's hands would have had little chance, while there had been limits to his treatment of Lochrie.

They used to march him in for punishment two or three times a week, and Kray had ceased even to bother with presenting a charge: "You'll have put your hands in your pockets some time today, even if I haven't seen you; so you're on hook." "Hook" was the informal punishment handed out by "cadet officers", the senior boys or prefects in the pretence world of a military school. For an hour, the cadet officers would take it in turns to shout at Lochrie, and then they would cane him. Initially these punishments were due to Lochrie's forgetfulness and inability to dress smartly, but then something odd started to happen: he lost control of his own body when it was put on display before the panel. First his hands would shake, then his legs and terrifyingly even his whole body. It was as though an engine had started to run and was shaking his flesh, while he desperately tried to steady it. This was the real punishment, because it made him look a coward. He simply could not control that involuntary movement of his body. After this, of course, he was far too entertaining not to punish on a very frequent basis. Kray became more vicious, and started to take a run with the cane, drawing blood on most occasions. The first thing Lochrie did when he got back to his dormitory was to see if there were any red lines in his pants and then he would count them. He wasn't particularly bothered either way; he was used to being hurt physically. He had been selected for the boxing team "because he had guts and knew how to take punishment". He had been at boarding school since the age of six, so he understood only too well what it is to be punished. What he could not bear was having his body out of control for others to laugh at. On the night before he ran away from school, he had returned to the door of the "mess-room" where the punishment was administered, so that he could listen to them. Chief Cadet Captain Kray never said a word, because Kray was empty of all things, most particularly words and ideas. Cadet Leader Hill was sniggering at the way Lochrie trembled from head to foot, and asked what they should have Lochrie back for, the following week. No one answered that question; they dwelt on different aspects of the night's entertainment. There would be time enough to make that decision.

On one occasion, Kray exposed himself to his only defeat in all the time he persecuted Lochrie. He liked to call the offender a worm, and in order to extract a further humiliation, he shouted, "Lochrie, you're a worm. What are you?" When there was no reply, his white, white skin turned red with genuine emotion, which proved that for Kray, at least, this was never a game, but a way of life – a way of being. "I said, 'Lochrie, you're a worm.' Lochrie, what are you?"

If it had ever come to an all-out verbal conflict, Lochrie would have won, as he did in this little skirmish. "You can cane me, if you want – even if I haven't done anything. You can shout at me, and call me anything you like," and he felt a little pompous but they were vying for the pompous high ground. And he lied, "but you will never affect the way I think of myself."

Kray was furious. His face was now deeply flushed; only his expressionless blue eyes remained cool. "Lochrie, you creep, tell me what you are. Tell me you're a worm." When nothing happened, he turned to the panel of cadet officers and encountered their embarrassment. Their expressions told him not to push the point any further, so he started to prattle about self-discipline and how he was punishing Lochrie for his own good. From then on, the punishment followed its usual course.

Lochrie studies the photo, and sees many interesting clues carelessly left behind in what was clearly meant to be a monument to camaraderie. The men in the photo are smiling with varying degrees of self-consciousness, with the exception of the Arab driver who is sullenly and dutifully holding the wheel, presumably to emphasise his role, because he could not have been driving the car in that moment. Apart from the fact that the photographer must have been directly in front of the car, all four men are sitting on the jeep's front seat, so the third man is sharing the space of the driving wheel with the driver. Kray is in the middle of the three British officers and has his arms loosely around his two companions. On Kray's other side, another old Middletonian sits with studied insouciance. Kray himself is recognisable because, even on this happy occasion, his face has no expression. In front of them, these boys have placed an automatic rifle as an emblem of their hunting expedition. Of course, it must have been a temporary position, because it could not have stayed on the bonnet once the jeep moved off. The published photo, whose width is far greater than its height, must have been cropped just under the gun, and Lochrie could not help wondering about what had been excised and for what reason – whether there had been captives or even dead bodies piled against the radiator as trophies in an original unpublished version. Surely something has been removed from their favourite picture. Surely such a posed photograph had a purpose – surely it was a souvenir of "what they had to do".

Lochrie tries to grasp onto the fading vision of Cary, his fictional Kray who became a New Labour politician much later in life. He always thought that Kray would never have had a chance to indulge his cruelty more fully in adult life. The imagination never learns; it holds to a belief in humanity that has no justification. Lochrie likes to complicate things, but this article speaks only of a dull simplicity – that always wins. He felt that New Labour had gone over to the mindset of Middleton School and the mediocrity of its hopeless imperial yearnings – that it had stooped to the basest jingoism in its treatment of immigrants and asylum-seekers. He was, of course, right, but the guilt of New Labour is not in the sullied work of these psychopaths – it is in their ability to avert their eyes and ignore what such men do in the name of our country. And not just New Labour: the Secret War in which Kray participated was "fought" during Wilson's prime-ministership – the government that so honourably refused to get involved in Vietnam.

A few days ago, Lochrie read in the newspaper of a former SAS soldier who was denouncing the illegal tactics adopted in Iraq. He was not the first in this Iraqi war, but such things would have been unthinkable at the time of the Secret War. Indeed it appears that generals and soldiers are now more concerned about human rights than Labour backbenchers. Perhaps Governments got a little worse, and armies a little better over the thirty-year interval. Their policing roles have perhaps slightly increased their humanity. Indeed, behind the dramatic changes of that generation lies only a measured shift in cultural attitudes: an improvement here and a deterioration there. Of course, the difference in the scale of the war then and the war now is enormous; what was a spark is now a conflagration. Then Lochrie believed in a better future, and Kray was busy organising a worse one. And now we live with the outcomes of Kray's victory, which will be of little interest to him, because he has had his chance "to show off his professional skills" and can now bask in the company of equerries, brokers and landowners who will marvel at his stories of how he took on the *adoo* with much derring-do.

For Chris Kray has told the school magazine that Dhofar "was an opportunity to prove one's mettle against the common enemy, communism," and Lochrie was then a communist. He read *The Communist Manifesto* during the period in which he was being persecuted by Kray. It gave him hope and a means to interpret a complex and brutal world although, always a sceptic, he had never applied that interpretation rigidly, which is why, he thinks, he has been able to keep faith with socialism, albeit a socialism now weighed down with pessimism that only whisky can cure. Drinking himself to death seems an entirely rational choice: most other medicines also shorten your life.

When Lochrie was a communist, Kray had been a slayer of Dhofari communists, who also fought for their autonomy from Oman and, no doubt, for a host of local and international issues, of which Kray could never have had any understanding. According to the article, the insouciant man with a soft smug smile, sitting to his left, was at least a frontline man, an adrenaline junkie. He proudly displays his professional cynicism by stating, "We were fighting for oil and we knew it." Kray would have been "fighting" for something else: proving himself and impressing others, while enjoying the cries of a beaten man. Lochrie remembers Kray's vanity well: he used to return to his old prep school in his uniform for the kick of being mobbed by the kids. Lochrie heard later that Kray flew a military helicopter to Middleton and landed it just next to the parade ground at a time when he knew that it would be in use. The cadets abandoned their parade and mobbed him, while teachers and officers happily looked on at an acceptable chaos.

Chris Cary is physically different from Chris Kray. He is thin and of medium build, and his sharp features and shifting eyes display a keen intelligence. He is capable of cruelty, but not particularly interested in it for its own sake. "Cary, you bastard, you're fucked," says Lochrie assertively, and then more quietly, almost with a sigh, "you're fucked, and perhaps I'll regret your passing. You were my companion while I tried to work you out."

And in Lochrie's mind, Cary seems to say, "It's your loss, my friend. With my cunning and self-awareness, I could have taken you very far indeed. I had the makings of a superb character, the sort that people hate to love because, although I break the rules, I do so with disarming honesty about my aims. These cardboard characters who inhabit the real world wrap up their evil deeds in cant. They crudely apply their declared ends to justify their means, when really they want 'to prove themselves' and play with guns against the poorly armed who have no air cover. They call the rebels *adoo* and cannot hide their racist contempt, but at the same time they grovel to the violent despot of the same race who makes war against his own people. My inconsistencies were to be altogether more elegant and literary. Your loss, my friend, you're letting your emotions get the better of you."

Lochrie wanted Cary for a novel on the Christian ethic of forgiveness: Cary beats a fictional version of Lochrie, but this fictional version is a better man than the real Lochrie just as Cary is more intelligent than the real Kray. Fictional Lochrie forgives Cary, who needs to be forgiven because he has acted out of calculation rather than instinct. Cary incessantly plots and follows with some success the impelling force of his ambitions until an entirely random event – a car crash – ends his life and all his carefully constructed plans which have been so costly to others, whilst the fictional Lochrie, who is totally inept, somehow averts the danger of his every fall and ends up if not living in an idyll, at least in an entirely tolerable and pleasant situation for his later years. The book, to be called *The Success of Failure*, was supposed to be a satire on the obsessions and self-obsessions of our consumer society, but now this photo and this article have destroyed all possibility of the novel being completed. The reality of Kray is too powerful. You can only forgive a "man", by which Lochrie means a moral agent. A "non-man" is no more responsible for his actions than is an animal trained to react in manners calculated and instilled by others. Kray was an instrument, not an agent. Cary would have become a self-conscious and autonomous agent of power.

The photo tells him something else – something unconnected to Kray's empty expression and the Secret War in Oman. It is that memory is imprecise – not over facts, although that is surely possible too. The most common imprecision of memory consists in the way it isolates incidents. His life had already taken a turn away from acceptance of the norm. Security and the numbing kind of supposed happiness it creates are overrated: those who have lived without them have heightened senses; they feel moments of supreme and fleeting rapture engendered by the nuances of light, sound, smell, taste and touch, and the pleasures of ideas, discovery and paradox. Drab staple foods taste delicious to the half-starved and overworked, while for the affluent no food quite manages to set the taste buds dancing: the dish could have always been cooked a little more – less salt, I think – were the ingredients fresh? – are you sure you beat the eggs hard enough? Happiness requires consummation, which simply triggers further desire. The unhappy are free from ambition and desire, and therefore enjoy the greatest freedom of all – the freedom of being honest with themselves.

Unhappiness attracts the vacuous and the vicious, who circle round like wolves whose bellies have been emptied by a protracted winter, but unlike wolves their hunger is unnatural. The prey can sense the danger but is unable to avert it.

Because of the power of this memory, Lochrie has mainly thought about its effects but almost never its causes. For many years afterwards fits of trembling would recur, often for no apparent reason, although the presence of a crowd would sometimes appear to be the cause.

But what can differentiate more than loneliness and freedom? The first requires the subject to invent highly individualistic patterns of behaviour, and the second encourages the individual to implement them almost unthinkingly. Unthinking is the foundation of courage.

The photo did not just bring back the unpleasant reality of Kray, it brought back those years of stubborn resistance – a schooling in independent thought. In that context, Kray was just an accident that was no accident – and as such should not be afforded greater importance than it deserved, simply because of its abnormal nature. Lochrie's suffering was a series of public events he could never adequately explain and of which for many years he was intensely ashamed, solely because of the immense and misplaced importance he attached to it. If Kray's photo told him anything, it was that the time had come to reduce this memory in size and push it to one side. The world is full of Krays who have done much worse, and Kray would have done much worse in Oman.

Well, you always emulate a little of your enemy and wrap up your justifications in a few of their values: it is undignified and unmanly to seek other people's compassion or, worse, their pity. And the shame. To tremble, no more able to control your flesh than a tree can stay its quivering leaves against a gentle breeze, is a shaming thing indeed. At the time, he would often wish for a further punishment, not out of any masochistic oddness, but to prove himself. This time, he used to tell himself, he would control his body. His will would prevail. The next punishment was never long in coming and the outcome was disappointingly predictable. All his mind concentrated on not shaking, and for a minute or two it seemed to work. Then a finger trembled. It was probably imperceptible to his panel of persecutors, but he felt its enlarged reality, just as the tongue misjudges the size of a dental cavity. All the time he had to stand still and straight and unable to see his rebellious body. The twitch of a finger seemed to fill the room with monstrous, shameful weakness. From that moment to the one in which his whole body was convulsed was short indeed, and his will had to renounce all further effort. He wished to prove himself primarily to himself, and never could, and this only made him want to prove himself elsewhere: in the ring where his body followed commands, and he could apply the technique he had been taught. Every time he hit a face he hardly knew, he really aimed his fist at Kray's empty, sullen look that haunted him, even though its lack of character or distinctive features made it a hard one to recall. The system, as usual, trained through violence, and taught its hunting dogs to shift violence received in another direction. In this way you produce a body of empty men whose taut springs of violence can be activated like the levers of a machine. Only after leaving school did he start to understand fully that all violence humiliates the victim and demeans the perpetrator. "Proving yourself" by taking violence is almost as foolish as "proving yourself" by inflicting it.

The thing he despised – the thing he had learnt to despise in Kray was his unassailable arrogance. And he was indebted to Kray for that lesson for the rest of his life. He had observed with the passing years that people on the whole accept other people's own evaluations of themselves. This is why politicians must never communicate anything but total self-belief. This is why military heroes are not the courageous, but those who tell everyone about their courage. This is why saints are never the good, but only the sanctimonious. If nothing else, Lochrie's persecution had taught him never to give credence to other people's self-definitions. Every evil teaches us something, whereas every good relaxes us into false securities we should properly call delusions.

Lochrie has always felt that it would make no sense to write about the real events of his life: autobiography distorts and besides he always believed, at least until his mid-thirties, that he had survived intact. What happened was only a tiny drop in the great flood of human oppression, while only a few islands of peace survive, like so many brightly-painted Noah's Arks, inward-looking as they bob along merrily on the miseries of others.

But then the incidents began to prey on him, proving that his victory was only relative and not complete, probably like every other victory there ever was, small or great, heroic or mundane: something had broken in him all those years ago. And he could hear the sound of running footsteps on a wooden floor as a young man gathered speed with the sole intention of hitting him as hard as he could with a cane and for no other reason than the pleasure of inflicting pain. Sadism was accompanied by athleticism, which perhaps explains why Lochrie has little time for sport and the modern cult of the human body. The pain is something he cannot remember with any great clarity, but the humiliation and sense of injustice is written deep into his soul. In his moments of greatest joy, they are still there and both extend that joy and diminish it, and in his moments of greatest depression, they both deepen it and mitigate it, because he rejoices in belonging to the *submerged*, to those who are constantly struggling in the floodwaters and cannot, by some strange function of our dreamlike existences, drown quite yet. Although modern capitalism's unacceptable face has launched a thousand Noah's Arks, it has also deepened the floodwaters, where the *submerged*, unseen and ignored, live out their aquatic existences and can never communicate with the floating zoos that sail above them.

There is a knocking at the door, and Lochrie slowly manoeuvres across the room. It is Mrs Haggerty from the flat next door. "I thought I would pop by," she declares solicitously; "I just thought I would see how you were getting on. You know how it is." She nods her head as though she has said something weighty, but actually she is just expressing her difficulty in talking to the strange man who has too many books and a drink problem, and with whom she has developed a friendship of sorts based on her kindness and his neediness.

"Ah, Susan," he mutters, "nice of you to come," and then a bit louder he repeats, "nice of you to come," as though the statement has emptied his supply of conversation.

"Are you needing anything from the shops?"

"From the shops? No, I don't think so. I don't think I need anything from the shops just at the moment," he says slowly as though struggling with an immensely complex question, and as he does so, he also fumbles around for his glasses as though he needs them, which he doesn't.

"You look full of life today."

"I got some mail," he replies making an obscure connection.

"Oh good. Are they going to publish your book after all?"

"No," he is irritated by this reminder of a persistent problem. "It was not a good thing. It was something that made me think."

"Really?" she says with what appears to be genuine interest.

Encouraged, he replies, "Yes, there was a war in Oman..." but he has already lost her attention. "Have you got any washing? I'll put it in with my own. I haven't got enough for a wash." She smiles fondly, almost maternally, but does not hide her hurry to get on with her day. He marvels at his own stupidity; he has forgotten small talk, or perhaps small talk has become something worse than tiresome – something that drains the real substance of existence.

He edges over to the window, once more sipping a whisky. He looks down on the city: he very rarely leaves the heights of his flat to visit it, so this is how he perceives it –

as something out there, toiling incessantly while he slothfully pursues the slothful meanders of his own erratic and unfettered thoughts. What does he know of the city except its integers of traffic darting busily along its roads, the occasional car horn and other miscellaneous noises? How do you know what is going on outside your brain? How do you know what is going on in this world? He has become very good at finding ways to avoid opening the flat door and descending the filthy concrete staircase, the only reliable way down the ten floors that divide him from the formless formality of the geometry of concrete and grass that divides one block of flats from another. But if he were to go down and walk past the overflowing refuse containers and the patches of muddied green to the boarded-up houses ready for demolition where the most desperate hide their broken lives and beyond that circle of hell in any direction, would he understand any more about this cityful of passions, wants and dashed hopes? Or has he learned all he will ever learn from his random and fairly passive trajectory through life? He certainly feels that to engage makes little sense now.

He swings around the room, and sees his books stuffed into the bookshelves at all angles or in piles on the floor. Books he has read and books he has not. Books he has loved and books he has forgotten. Books that once seemed crucial and now seem mediocre. Books that you can read three or four times and still they yield up more of themselves. All are stuffed with people, real and fictitious. Each one has more density than a crowded street. Because of their static and artificial nature, they cannot fully express the thinness of existence which floats on every passing gust of wind and finds no point as firm as a writer's momentary beliefs set in print. Lochrie's tower may not be made of ivory, but it is a tower of reclusion nevertheless.

The last time Lochrie went past those boarded-up buildings, it was to go to a Chinese restaurant, which was in fact an old-fashioned British greasy spoon. True enough, it augmented its menu of fried food with a few oriental dishes, and it was always full of time-heavy customers who contrasted with the two overworked Chinese waitresses. An old man sat down heavily close to Lochrie and eyed him up warily. One of his nostrils was dribbling clear liquid onto a reddish upper lip stubbled with a few days of deathly grey growth. He wore slippers and was incongruously over-dressed for one of Glasgow's warmer days, but showing no sign of wanting to remove his heavy jacket. He greeted the arrival of his fried-egg roll with a cup of tea like a man settling down to a solitary banquet. Behind this extra-vagant event, Lochrie felt sure there were a few days of waiting and anticipation.

A fat middle-aged woman blew in like an overworked manager into her office. She sat down and, immediately flipping open a conspicuously neat mobile phone, she started to shout in a theatrical voice that filled the small restaurant. Lochrie did not feel that he was eavesdropping but rather that he was listening to a carefully constructed script which he could examine with professional interest. Following a tortured conversation with someone called Aiden, she rang someone called Angus. "Aiden's at home, Angus, and I want you to go there straightaway. D'ye hear me?" So Aiden was the son and Angus the husband or lover. "Angus, are you drunk?" the woman cried, as though this were an unusual occurrence but Lochrie thought it probably wasn't. "Angus, I'm leaving you. I'm telling you, I'm leaving."

Having completed his meal, the old man was now trying to stand up, but it was not easy. He started swinging backwards and forwards in his chair in an attempt to build up sufficient momentum.

"Angus, if you're no home when I am, you'll find the door locked," she said while showing no signs of panic herself and ordering an abundant meal. "And the lock'll be changed," she continued before the waitress had finished scribbling the order down. "Are you listening, Angus? You'd better be bloody listening." By now, Lochrie had created Angus's character in his brain, and Angus, he felt sure, did not list listening amongst his greatest achievements.

The old man was still swinging in his chair and Lochrie had not made a move to help him, while he concentrated on the fascinating phone call. The other waitress moved forward and helped the old man to his feet. He rewarded her with a smile of such gratitude that Lochrie felt ashamed, but he thought the gratitude was not only for a helping hand; it was also for a yearned-for female touch – something Lochrie, who, like the old man, is portly and short of breath, would not have been able to provide. The overworked waitress helped the exultant old man to the door.

Silent and loud poverty had thus recited their parts. The old and the new. And it was for the new that Lochrie felt most sorry. The woman, a child of the television age, could only feel alive by publicising herself. The old man, lonely no doubt, knew how to draw pleasure from the smallest things while living out a private existence.

Communism was the "common enemy" – but whose? Lochrie wonders. Now we are led to believe that communism was the movement of a few misguided European intellectuals who hung around the universities and had nothing better to do. Kray was presumably talking of the communism that overthrew an empire and fought off at least a couple of others within a few years – and could only rely on the fragile bodies of badly armed men and women who believed in what they fought for. It is undeniable that almost from the very beginning injustices were committed on both sides – on the side of those who promised the peasants the "peace, land and bread" they never got, and on the side of those who promised to return them to a state of total subjugation to the Tsar, the landowner and the priest – a promise they would have undoubtedly fulfilled with bloody zeal had they won. The survivors of the civil war and then many of their persecutors were ground down and killed by a political machine that appeared to make no sense.

Like so many movements of the twentieth century, communism tended towards dogma – although it did embrace a range of ideas. Because it believed in the perfectibility of mankind and its need to be homogenised under the aegis of a pseudo-scientific credo, it committed crimes against humanity. All the other movements, including liberal democracy, committed crimes against humanity, but only communism had a vision that had humanity and grandeur. That was its power, and everything else was a reaction against it – an attempt to overcome it in part by adopting its methods and ways of being, even some of its demands. Lochrie feels that communism lacked one important element: religion. And by religion, he means not any particular religion or dogma of the afterlife, but humility and bewilderment in the face of humanity's complexity, creativity, diversity, kindness and, yes, immense brutality. Communists did not deserve to be shot like dogs by the Krays of this world and they fought not for themselves, their nation or for somebody else's oil – they fought for a universal ideal of equality. And their dead go unremembered: the half a million killed in Indonesia by Suharto have no memorial. The millions of Soviet dead, who did not all fight for communism, but rather to rid their land of the Nazi hordes, have their memorials removed from the lands they freed. When they are not thought of as intellectuals, Communists are usually thought of as workers, but globally they were more likely to be peasants, always susceptible to a utopian idea that promises release from their millennial oppression. Their generosity and ability to suffer turned them into formidable soldiers; their victories exposed their lack of political judgement and formal education.

The rebels of Dhofar were just such peasant communists. In the 1950s the people of the Sultanate of Oman had risen against their brutal Sultan to follow their Iman (who had the backing of the American oil company Aramco), but the power of the Royal Air Force initially seemed to have made short work of them. Then they counterattacked, this time equipped with American mines, which were to cause casualties on the imperial side. When a British soldier was killed by a mine near Muti, his officer had the village destroyed: "We set fire to one house after another, using paraffin. When we left, there was nothing but smouldering ruins." In the long run, the rebels had no hope against the Venom jets and Shackleton heavy bombers which, according to an Air Chief Marshal, "carried out a heavy programme of attacks on cultivation and water supplies. So effective was this form of harassment that cultivation and movement by daylight in the villages under attack came virtually to a standstill." But the peasant army was not lacking in bravery against this technological behemoth, and it took artillery, night-time bombing and the SAS to finally break their will.

There was almost unanimity amongst the British warriors that Sultan Said was a vicious tyrant, although many seemed to justify him as a medieval tyrant for a medieval country, which was a disservice to the Middle Ages. Unsurprisingly he was more typical of neo-colonial puppet dictators of the second half of the twentieth century, and his military advisors could be quite explicit: "The evidence of my own eyes suggested the British were bolstering a corrupt regime where the Sultan and his chosen few lived sumptuously, enjoying the first fruits of oil wealth whilst the mass of Omanis lived out their lives in squalor and illness benefiting not at all from the culling of their country's riches. And here I was volunteering my services to the military machine that upheld the old man in denying eight hundred thousand Omanis their rightful inheritance: the benefits of human progress, hospitals and schools," wrote a famous British military man and no one on the Left could have put it better.

The "old man" had said, "If you are out walking and meet a Dhofari and a snake, crush the Dhofari." So it should not come as any surprise that the peasants of Dhofar were the next to rebel against him. Equally it should come as no shock that, in the following decade of internationalism and anti-colonial breakthrough, these new rebels started to identify with communism, although in practice their guerrilla war differed little from the previous one. This novelty, however, came as a great relief to the imperial warriors, who now dressed themselves up in the cant of the Cold War. Or at least it was a great relief when they later decided to write their memoirs. Even though one of the most common criticisms of communism is its supposed use of "ends to justify the means", a British commander declared that the *adoo*'s conversion to communism was a "comfort to an uneasy conscience" – a conscience, it has to be said, that had been lying dormant up to time of this comfort's convenient arrival. This was the self-righteous drivel that Kray is still mouthing over thirty years later. The communist guerrillas, on the other hand, were fighting for their own land against a contemptuous Omani sultan, British advisors with all the military equipment, and two Iranian battalions. Although forced into war out of oppression and misery, and not to prove their mettle, these men and women surely fought with the greatest courage and tenacity, and suffered the miseries of losing their fellow fighters and their families on a scale that their enemy would not have been able to sustain. The Cold

War warriors expressed their surprise on finding dead women fighters, for a British officer never wanders too far away from his prejudices and this scene did not fit with their stereotype of Islamic society.

But communism did bring changes – far-reaching changes in tactics. With a dazzling display of British common sense and pragmatism that forgets each word as soon as it is said or written, one warrior explains the problems with the Dhofari rebellion, "However daft or outrageous the restrictions the Sultan imposed upon his people might appear to us, he was not an inhumane man, and he always had his reasons. ... He was monumentally ill-equipped to lead his country in a modern war against Communist-inspired guerrillas. ... Moreover, there had increasingly been concern that Britain was supporting a regime which was imprisoning its people in disease, squalor, hunger and ignorance." It all ended with British officers running around the palace exchanging fire with the Sultan and his few remaining supporters, and during this exchange, the callous autocrat inexplicably and quite literally shot himself in the foot. The British replaced him with his son, the British-educated Qaboos who had served in their own army. After this imperial farce, the total war against civilians would continue, but now the villages that switched sides would be rewarded with funds and new facilities. The carrot joined the stick, and it was communism that brought about this change of heart.

Throughout the history of communism, exceptional men and women filled the prisons of the world and were hounded by anti-communist and communist regimes alike. Communism, the ultimate stage in the process of rationalist humanism, was not so much an extreme idea as the generator of extreme reactions – for which its aggressive rhetoric was in part to blame. "A spectre is haunting Europe" is a dramatic opening line, but it hardly reflected the resources of the two eccentric, bearded authors – an odd couple whose differences were as instructive as their similarities. Communists, supporters of collaborative communities, were likely to die penniless and alone with only a stubborn idea to sustain their last moments of lucidity. To be a communist meant to suffer and be rejected, even in countries where communism was victorious. When they remained loyal to the idea of communism, communists ended up in labour camps or exile communities in the West where they became either pariahs or, worse, anti-communists – the righteous tormentors and persecutors of their former selves.

Lochrie remembers an elderly Romanian couple who in the mid-sixties lived permanently in a rundown hotel on the west coast of Scotland. He was a child full of his parents' prejudices and in the cramped hotel foyer said something dismissive about communism. The old man broke into the conversation in his laboured English, "To say that, you must first know the ideals of communism. The ideals of communism are great, but maybe humanity is not ready for them yet." And then perhaps a little angrily, suggesting that he felt Lochrie had not understood him, he added even more firmly, "First you must understand what communism stands for. Then you can criticise the bad things communists have done – have certainly done."

The child Lochrie was stunned. He had never come across anyone who defended communism, and was both delighted and perturbed to discover such people exist. He started to utter a few confused words, and then the old woman came to his rescue. "But what are you saying to this child?" she raged.

"I think he should know," replied the man sullenly. "They don't teach the children anything; they just fill them with hate."

"What is he doing?" she seemed to plead with the gods who had struck her so low, "Now he is trying to convert the children. Come on. Stand up." The tired old man stood up and meekly left after a meaningful half-smile to Lochrie, which intimated that in any case he had said all he wanted to say. They crossed the room as she berated him in Romanian. Lochrie now feels he can reconstruct those events: the man was an exiled communist official, while his long-suffering wife had probably lost almost everything because of his loyalty to ideas instead of himself and his family, and did not want to lose what little dignity had been left her. But Lochrie has always felt that the wife was wrong: if anyone sowed the seed, it was her. Would he not have forgotten the whole episode of the eccentric old man, if the man had not been martyred by his wife? Initially Lochrie felt liberated by her intervention, but then empathy took over. Besides it was her behaviour and her hidden fears that most aroused his curiosity.

The history of communism is the history of an ideal that has died. And that tragic death, which has brought great wealth for the few and great misery for the many, has at least freed us to pursue a different kind of egalitarianism in which difference is allowed. The task ahead of us is once again immense and the possibilities of more brutal repressions innumerable. We must think as pessimists and act as optimists – but Lochrie knows that optimism will never be for him, because his only act will be to write, and that's the act of chloroforming thoughts and pinning them in the display case we call a book. His life was once one of movement and hope. Now his physical confines have been reduced to a small flat, while his intellectual confines have all been removed, so his agitated thoughts wander the planet unable to find interlocutors. What else could he do but chase after them lethargically and place them in some kind of order, however tired and dead. The pain he felt in Middleton Military School was one of physical containment; the pain he now feels is one of intellectual dispersal – a kind of loneliness of the mind he no longer wants to cure.

Cary is still in Lochrie's mind, getting at him with that rasping voice and weasel expression, "Just my luck to be chosen by a loser like yourself. Look at you sitting there feeling sorry for yourself and drinking your whisky! Have you ever thought what a pathetic figure you cut?"

"You wouldn't understand. I don't feel sorry for myself. Not at all. If anything I feel sorry for mankind," says Lochrie.

"You take a lot on yourself. Do you think mankind cares whether you, holed up in a shabby little flat in one of the wettest and most windblown parts of a wet and windblown island off the north-west coast of a continent whose greatest times are now in the past, feel sorry for it or not? Who are you and what have you done? You publish a few third-rate novels and think that gives you the right to go around with your heart on your sleeve."

"I don't go around anywhere. I stay here, remember."

"Yes indeed, fine behaviour for a writer. You should be out there observing, feeling, responding and getting it all down. Writing is about living, not moping about here and reflecting on politics of all things – who takes that seriously these days? Where's the fun in that? Listen, if you want to criticise the powerful, then go ahead, but once you've rattled them, you have to switch to their side. The literary world is full of those who have gone over to the other side, and the powerful love such people more than their favoured sons.

"But come to think of it, you do not have enough talent. That system is strictly for the most brilliant. If you really must persist with this left-wing silliness, write for the powerful until you are at least partially established and then switch to your real self. They will leave you a little place for partial success as a symbol of their supposed liberalism. But I'm not sure you have even the mediocre talent for that second solution. Have you ever thought of churning out a series of hack articles in which it looks like you're going to say something very radical and then in the last few lines, you twist it all around and end up projecting the status quo as the least worst option. It looks very intelligent, and is the surest route for a political writer of limited talents."

"Chris Cary, you really are a mean bastard. I almost hate to throw you on the reject pile."

"Damn it, Lochrie, what's this with the reject pile? I have energy, I have personality and, above all, I have a great desire to be. You're not going to get any decent characters out of namby-pamby do-gooders. Christ, you should know; you went to Middleton, and surely that must have taught you that 'mankind' or ever-so politically correct 'humanity' is almost entirely made up of shysters and all the rest are just a bunch of suckers. The guys who get to the top are the guys who know how to kick everyone else in the teeth. Come on, don't you get it: writing is about the truth. It doesn't matter if you come at it from the left or the right, or from the top or the bottom, it has to be the truth. Not the big truth – you should leave that to the philosophers and those political ideologues you're so fond of," he waves his hand in contempt. "No, it's the little truths that count – the things you can nibble at. Go get them; don't waddle about this moth-eaten flat of yours in a state of eternal angst – a flat that a fucking tramp wouldn't stay in. Sit down, take a deep breath and then go after them – those little truths. Yes, yes, and I know you want to do something about power, and you think that a supposedly amoral shit like myself is the appropriate vehicle for your high-minded ideas. Am I correct?"

"Yes."

"Well, okay, then I'm your man. I've got no problem with that. I'm absolutely up for it."

A knock at the door announces Kevin's weekly visit. Garry Lochrie opens the door and waves him to a chair in the understated manner that befits a regular and ritual meeting. "Have a seat," Garry says as he goes to pour him a whisky, but Kevin is already seated.

"Fine, I've had a good week actually. We clinched the deal for building the new housing scheme. It's very exciting," Kevin loves to talk about his packed week, and possibly thinks it gives Garry some vicarious pleasure.

"You mean it's going to make you rich."

"That too. It was easy. Increase the units and everything looks better. So we have made each house as thin as a piece of string. You can sit down on one side of the room and bump your nose on the other," he laughs at his own brilliance, and then remembers who he is talking to. The moralist. The man who shuts himself up with his impractical ideas that take no account of human nature – of human weakness.

"That must be good for families that want to talk to each other. But presumably there is room for the television?"

Kevin only half understands the jibe and wearily replies, "Of course there is. I exaggerate. They are actually very well-designed and comfortable homes for *our people*. Energy-efficient too, so we're protecting the planet. I don't want to sound pompous, but I really am very proud of our homes."

Houses have become homes, and Lochrie winces at "our people". He hates it when New Labour slips in a token fragment of "Old Labour" values, but with an even greater portion of patriarchal worthiness.

"So what have you been up to today?" says Kevin forcing himself to sound interested while fully expecting that nothing of any possible interest could have happened in Garry's life.

"I think I am about to kill off a character."

"Really?"

"Actually, he was a bit like you."

"Me? I'm flattered. You have based a character on me? So he's energetic, good-looking, and fatally attractive to women?"

"He's a bit of that, but he isn't based on you."

"Really," Kevin repeated, this time with a trace of irritation, rather than a pretence of interest. "So who was he based on?"

"No one. He came from my imagination and events of long ago. But the imagination often wanders too far from the truth. He was not believable."

"Am I not believable then?"

Garry understands that Kevin is not in any way a bad man – he is simply incapable of standing up to the idiocies of his own times, even though he is at one level quite aware that they are idiocies. This is why he finds political discussion so difficult: it is an exercise in evasion. And in this he exudes normality and the self-confidence of normality. He survives and is damaged by doing so. The poison of this self-deception is crueller than the excessive alcohol Garry Lochrie pours down his throat. Garry's defeat brings rewards that Kevin could never understand.

Superficially there were parallels between Kevin's life and Garry's. When they met casually in the eighties at one of Kevin's parties, Kevin was a secret socialist or perhaps a socialist taking a well-earned rest from politics. He was concentrating on his career as a chemist in a large corporation, and his Labour Party membership had lapsed mainly because it did not seem to be leading anywhere.

"So you're an ex-Trotskyist!" were Lochrie's first words.

"How did you know?" said Kevin, taken aback.

"Deutscher's trilogy on Trotsky's life and the total absence of any other books of the left. Where are they? In the attic?"

"They are!" Kevin was astounded and amused, and from such encounters great friendships can be formed, even between people who have little in common.

"Which means you have not yet cut yourself free from youth's ideals – you have merely shifted them to the back of your mind."

Kevin appeared hurt by that "yet", and replied defensively, "Not at all. I am just as much of a Marxist as I ever was. Perhaps more so. It's just that I see no point in riling people and ruining my career. How is that going to help socialism? We don't live in a free society where you can say and do as you please. We have to get wise and leave all that childish seventies stuff in the past."

Garry noted that at that time Kevin defined himself as a Marxist rather than a socialist, and that very probably marked him out as someone persuaded by political science and not the great injustices of this world. Of course these great nineteenth-century thinkers are an excellent starting point. Lochrie has always thought that the difference between Marx and Nietzsche was that Nietzsche was wrong about the big things and right about the small, while Marx was wrong about the small things and right about the big.

Although Kevin had once enjoyed political debate with Garry, he now only comes to endure it. Garry is soon off on one of his favourite subjects: "Intellectuals are drawn to revolutions, because they are theatres of ideas, in which for relatively short periods of time, great speeches are made, fantastic utopias are constructed out of words of fire, and, it seems, the great thirst for justice is finally going to be slaked. But they are wrong; they should stay with the past revolutions that live in books, and shun the real thing with its lack of nuance, the cruel settling of real and imagined scores, the rule of rhetoric and, worst of all, the necessary repositioning of corrupted and disloyal souls who shamelessly use a small and costless act of contrition to justify a fearful and unswerving crusade against their former selves or rather their former friends, in order to establish a dictatorship of the converted. And as we know, the converted can never really understand their new faith and usually reinterpret it in terms of the one they have just reneged.

"But it is not only the lack of revolutionary 'masses' that makes revolution impossible, at least in the West; it is also that revolution is flawed for many reasons: violent revolutions are the product not of an evolving society but of a society that has resisted change for far too long; revolutions do not change their own societies as much as they do the societies that surround them, and those external changes move in two diametrically opposed directions; revolutions polarise; revolutions use violence;   violence corrodes even the fighters for the best ideals; and above all revolutions create new types of conformism and the dreaded 'finger-pointers'. Only non-violent revolution can create the degree of change that balances continuity with discontinuity – that accepts that parts of every regime are functional or in any case cannot be improved simply by central decree. Non-violent revolution is the only one that can work because the technology of power has become so sophisticated and so pervasive. Power cannot be challenged with cyclostyled leaflets and soapboxes, or indeed the invisible ink so beloved of the conspiratorial. Power can only be defeated by acting in accordance with a genuine morality which is itself the end and not the means – a morality that is primarily founded on the truth. Power cannot be defeated by those who become a mirror image of itself in the exultant moment of their success."

Kevin wearily lets Lochrie's speech wash over him like a jumble of words. His protégé has a habit of doing this, and he has long since learnt that any objection merely leads to a tiresome argument and other lengthy diatribes from the man he really wants to help. "So we're agreed for once: socialist revolutions are a bad thing, and all we need to keep alive our socialist values is to enact them through the free market."

"Did I say anything as trite and as stupid as that?" retorts Lochrie while dramatically slamming his glass down on the side table and splashing orange-brown liquid over the already ruined surfaces of ring stains and cracked veneer. Alcohol is transforming into aggression his exasperation at not being able to present a mildly complex political argument in our new land of certitude and unprecedented – some might say superfluous – affluence of the many rather than the few. It is an affluence of trash.

Kevin often wonders why he bothers to come. He carved out the time for this meeting with a useless drunk from a busy schedule. He has just come from a difficult meeting in which he rescinded a contract with a small central heating firm. He had good reason, because they were clearly in breach of contract, but it was very convenient that they were, as this opened the way to a much more price-efficient deal with a massive concern, which is likely, moreover, to invite him onto their board some time in the not-too-distant future. And in an hour's time, he will lie in the youthful arms of one of his lovers, a true soulmate whose ambitions first opened his way to her vigorous, tanned and reasonably athletic body. He helped her on her way to success, and she lowered her white, white pants with just a hint of feminine frill, down over her light brown, flexing thighs. The primitive economy of barter never dies and is the foundation for all the greater things. But what he loves about her is her lack of hypocrisy. She never demands that he play the tiresome role of the misunderstood husband. There is no pretence at unhappiness: neither his with his wife nor hers with her partner, a computer expert and health fanatic who suffered a nervous breakdown a year ago. He only heard of this through a colleague and he slightly wondered at her loyalty to someone he would define as a loser; it suggested something in her he had

never imagined or wanted. He loves her for her uncomplic-
ated sex, but is happy that this happy state is maintained
when afterwards they each rush back into their busy lives
with little more acknowledgement between their now re-
clothed bodies than a squeeze of the hand or a peck on the
cheek.

The visit to Lochrie is therefore an act of extreme
charity, but although Kevin never consciously admits it to
himself, he does feel better about himself when, having
completed this weekly ritual, he finally gets out of the dingy
flat heavy with the smell of sweat and alcohol. The Lochrie
project is the one indisputably selfless act in his life, and
he leaves as a Catholic leaves his church after mass and a
particularly severe sermon from the priest. Something
niggles, but he feels purified by the spiritual exercise of
self-discipline. He can now return to the business of life
with renewed vigour.

Of course, Lochrie is entirely unaware of Kevin's
sacrifice; indeed he believes that his own tolerance of a
friend fallen into a corrupt life is itself a good act. And he
knows that all he can get from Kevin is company, the
occasional bottle of whisky and a certain amount of mild
irritation. In fact, he often finds these regular dialogues of
the deaf somewhat noxious, and he broods in silence. He
despises the crass, and as he gets older, this nausea
becomes more pungent. Kevin is the kind of man who
would once have tripped out that old cliché about revolutions being the "locomotives of history". But history, like
everything else, is the sum of its parts. Who can tell which
are its vital organs and which are not? Revolutions are
imperfect and inefficient ways of bringing about change,
which in a perfect world should be gradual, but there is
nothing gradualist about human nature – a volatile mix of
greed, altruism, fury, love, fashion, an hysterical herd
instinct and a little common sense. Communism is rightly
criticised because within its love it carried great oceans of

hate that kept flooding the fertile terrain of its rational redistribution. But shouldn't we judge Christianity just as harshly? – the persecuted religion became the persecutor once it was the established religion of the Roman Empire. The Christian crowds stole, plundered and killed until no trace of the ancient religion was left. The ruthless and ambitious then controlled the new religion just as they had the past ones, and we might reasonably ask what had changed, except perhaps a few underlying ideas. Did martyrs die for that? And die again as the new powers depicted them as lifeless, characterless figures in a Christian-realist art? And yet who can deny that again and again the primitive wonders of the Christian ethic are rekindled in new forms not by the powerful, but by the humble and the poor for whom it was intended. And of all the Churches, the Catholic one most expresses the divergent spirits of real existing Christianity. And so it was with communism. The persecuted became the persecutors, thereby losing their souls and then their reason, but the socialist ethic is destined to reappear precisely when it appears to have been completely obliterated. Given the behaviour of Christians in power, Julian the Apostate may have been one of the more honest emperors, and the pain he inflicted on Christianity may have done it some good, although not for long. Socialism will learn from this bleak period, but whether it will be capable of retaining those lessons when things move in its favour again is an entirely different question. Most probably in this as in everything else, human beings are destined to repeat the errors of the past, not because they are inherently evil but simply because they are incapable of sustaining good political practice; the power-hungry minority will always find a way to corrupt and render void the best and most wisely constructed laws. The rule of law is the third utopia after socialism and democracy. It should be sought after and something approximate to it can be achieved, but it will never last. Nothing ever does, and particularly not the good, the useful and the beautiful. The dyke can be built, and it is hard work to maintain, but one day, hopefully in the distant future and not the near one, it will break and the waters of violence and confusion will flood through the breach.

"God, you can be superior, Garry! Just listen to yourself. Trite, stupid. So damn superior. You think that I have given up on all my ideals, but what about yourself? What do you believe in now? Nothing at all. At least I believe in humanity."

As always Garry is irritated and disappointed with the direction of the conversation – with the way Kevin never analyses anything but always trumpets his "I believes", and when he comes up with "I still believe in socialism", Garry knows he is in for an extravagant display of repulsive sophistry. In Garry's somewhat puritanical mindset, a man who has betrayed himself is sick in his soul, because now he only has the present. What he doesn't understand is that Kevin is very happy with the present. The present makes him feel good.

Garry has no choice but to let himself be guided by the logic of a dialogue in which each participant interprets the key words in an entirely different manner. "Of course, I believe in humanity, but I also know the power of evil and the evil of power. The powerful fear the 'mass' because they believe them to be very similar to themselves, which is a partial truth, as we humans are made up of the same things and differ only in their proportions. The powerful want to believe that the powerless are depraved and dangerous, that their souls are as ragged as their clothes. They do everything they can to make this prejudice become a reality by depriving them of good diet and good education. They scoff at the awkwardness of the beaten and the troubled, and consider their own advantages innate, rather than products of an unfair society. In spite of this, the human spirit is such that the powerless prevail and gain a kind of superiority."

"Very classist," says Kevin, unable to conceal his distaste. "And I suppose we are to believe that the only thing innate about the rich and powerful is their greed and their cruelty."

"Not at all. It is often the case that the greediest and cruellest people are the powerless who have just become powerful."

"Oh. So it's the turn of the nouveau riche to get it in the neck. I might take this personally – but I *know* that I do much good with my wealth. Your ideas are all a little formulaic – so dated, so blind to what we now know. The right has won the economic arguments."

"Well, please don't take it personally. It was not intended as such," Garry does not want to offend his friend, although most Sundays he manages to do exactly that. "Everything is, I agree, a great deal more complex. Look, it is often said that nothing breeds success like success, and this is perfectly true but success breeds many things besides: cruelty and greed there is no doubt, also self-obsession and a crippling fear of losing that success, and perhaps worst of all an inability to be oneself in this world – in relationships with others. Total failure is equally crippling, but only in the extreme does it undermine our humanity in a similar manner."

"I see. Sackcloth and ashes. Have another whisky, Garry, and pour me one too. You're ruining my Sunday afternoon. Remind why I come here to listen to your drivel?"

"Because it's good for you."

"And why would that be," says Kevin more irritably.

"Because we all enjoy dipping into other people's lives, and besides no one with a brain wants to have everyone around them agreeing with them all the time."

"Oh, so I do have my uses, then," Kevin laughs, but Garry ignores him and simply passes him his whisky. Now Kevin feels uncomfortable and attacks on what he believes to be his strongest ground. "I noticed that you didn't object, when I said the right has won all the economic arguments."

"The reason was simply that I know it to be pointless to discuss such things with a man of fashion like yourself. And the dismal science always was the most fashion-conscious of the social sciences. You know that there aren't just economic cycles; there are cycles of greed and folly, of intolerance and war, of collectivism and hard work with a variable degree of unpleasant Puritanism."

"So basically, we're fucked."

"In a word."

"You talk such shite," says Kevin, quickly finishing his drink. "I've had my fill for today and I'm off."

"Quite right, and as ever, it was nice to see you, Kevin."

"Yeah, yeah! See you next... if I'm feeling suitably masochistic."

Garry laughs, and the door closes behind Kevin.

Just as he feels the same sense of relief that Kevin feels as he swiftly moves down the stairs towards more entertaining ends – relief mixed with an acknowledgement of the friendship that always grows from regular acquaintance and familiarity – Garry Lochrie hears once more the nagging persistence of Chris Cary. "I'm still here and have a right to some answers," the voice insinuates itself as though it came from a source of moral integrity, and maintains a tone that is both flattering and threatening. "You wish to spurn me, your wonderful fictional character, the creation of your awkward, scattered imagination, to make way for the real, the petty preening Chris Kray who is settled in his emptiness. I am your son, the echo of your brain. Why do you do this? So that you can become just another misery memoirist?"

"No, Cary," says Lochrie, now tired beyond measure. "You are more real to me than the fading, diaphanous phantom of my past. You are made of rational and emotive arguments that settle in the brain and fertile blossom there in tangled chaos. These things are real enough, even though you cannot feel their surface – rough or smooth – or squeeze the juices of their tender life.

"I cannot write of those events, and thus of you I have no more to say, but that you were here," and Lochrie taps his head, "and kept me company."

"How very sweet..." Cary purposefully pauses and wanly smiles, "you spineless shit."

"I'm sorry, Cary, what can I say?"

"What can you say? You bastard with a head so full of words you never stop. You let that arsehole dictate your life, forty years after the event? Stand up and shout it out, and do it not with him, who has no conscience and no conscious self, but use me! A devious bastard whose cruelty is tempered by a cunning and inexplicably erratic mode of thought that reflects a tortured soul – this is the stuff of which stories are made."

"Of course, all this makes you more culpable, more interesting and perhaps less real. I've told you: I will not write of him, nor of you, now that I can see his role – what he has done and could still do. He has not provided literary material, but he has made me, sure enough, and now he's made me see how the human spirit struggles ceaselessly in its Manichaean strife against a few empty souls that are scattered in our midst. Kray represents all that I despise, but if I were to hate him, denounce him and take some revenge, then I would turn into him, become an echo of his distasteful self. I walk away from all these thoughts – from him and you."

"You cripple."

"A crippled consciousness is consciousness indeed."

"I'll give you that, but only if you have the will to overcome your infirmity – and fight. Goddam it, what is it with this passivity, this endless attentiveness to the purity of the soul. You accuse him of preening, but look at yourself. In your different way, you too seek an image of yourself, and don't think of what hurt you cause when you go off in search of it."

"I know. You have a point. At our age, we look back upon the devastation of our lives: the shattered dreams and, worse, the dreams that did not shatter but became half true. What you can never understand and I can never explain in words – not in words, you hear – is how he changed me, made me who I am. That cowardly youth put me through a process that removes the self and did it with so little – just banal and senseless acts of cruelty that merely raised a smile and sat within their days with other trivial pursuits like games of cards or drinking illicit booze. On the victim, such events leave an unstable sediment within the geology of life, and as the other layers build up, they start to shift under the pressure and make their presence felt by buckling into passive will-lessness."

"You say that Kray made you who you are, but Kray never made anything; he was made. Empty activism has no creativity, just as conscious passivity changes and animates all that surrounds it; I'll give you that." Lochrie smiles at Cary as a teacher acknowledges a good student. "He justifies his war," Cary continues, "by the word 'communism'; yet he has no idea what that word means."

"Of course not. It simply means 'bad thing that challenges my world'. He did not consciously make me – that was done unconsciously by his idea of sadistic kicks. He could never have thought about the outcome of his actions – he would not have consciously set about making communists, just as the war the British fought in Dhofar was not with the conscious intent of turning the rebellion from a secessionist one into a communist one. Once it did, they changed their tactics – demonstrating that the collective imperialist is more intelligent than the individual one. That's what I wanted you for, Cary – I wanted you to represent the intelligent and unscrupulous imperialist, who manipulates even the best values in his pursuit of this aim. But after all, I think they are right when they say that literature should not be political – should not be committed to anything."

"Bullshit. What happened to your much-vaunted honesty? I know you, and I know that you couldn't write anything that wasn't political. You're being evasive. You're trying to fob me off."

"I am, and in your case, it was foolish. I am tired of this conversation. I want to forget about Kray and ..."

"Come on, get over it," Cary snorts. "You're becoming obsessed with this alter ego of mine."

"Of yours?"

"And he is only a shadow of myself. An altogether lesser creature."

"I am not obsessed with him," Lochrie counters with complete confidence, "but I am struck by the words of this wordless man. The Krays of this world are everywhere: in Russia they took the oppositionists off to the firing squad by the hundreds of thousands, they battered their victims to death in short-lived Kampuchea, and they tortured and killed insurgents in 1950s Kenya. Most of these Krays were even worse than Kray and these soulless beasts will always be with us, like famine, plague and pestilence. They are an ill we must learn to control, and they are the justification for having a state.

"As I say, I am obsessed with his words: he the dapper sadist and his idea of himself as the crusader against communism, 'the common enemy'. Every age has its witches – the people condemned by their very existence. Then it was 'communist' on one side and 'counter-revolutionary' on the other. Today, in a particularly bizarre war against shadows, it is 'terrorist' or 'Islamist' and 'decadent Westerner'. In almost all cases, the victim is nothing like the official stereotype."

"Really, you are enough to drive a man to drink," says Cary lightly and jokingly affecting an expression of exasperation. "All that stuff is gone. Wakey wakey! Revolutionary communism is dead."

"Of course it is," retorts Lochrie, "for many reasons. Firstly, where are the peasant masses willing to fight? You could no more fight a revolution and the inevitable war that follows than you could fight another First World War. The young no longer have that sense of sacrifice, and that is a very good thing. Lenin might have sold revolution as a 'festival of the oppressed', but he was wrong: revolutions are acts of desperation, anguish and hope, always teetering on the point of falling back into themselves. Now sixty-eight was a festival all right but not of the oppressed; it was the festival of a pampered generation – my generation, our generation."

"Thanks for counting me in," says Cary grumpily.

"Well, a revolution with slogans such as 'it is forbidden to forbid' or 'we are realists, we demand the impossible' was not a revolution but a holiday from reality with no intention of taking the difficult decisions that revolutions involve. That too was probably a blessing."

"Fine revolutionary you are. Is there anything you know how to do properly?" Cary restates his exasperation. Lochrie remembers the day his friend Pino took him to see a mad revolutionary. The man was a violent hothead, but what has he now become? Impossible to say, the conceivable outcomes of such mental instability are infinite.

"Lochrie, can you not see that you have been just a mirror image of this Kray, to whom you feel so morally superior," says Cary with his mischievous grin. "You rebelled against the discipline at Middleton, but then went off to find an organisation that imposed a similar discipline."

"But it was my choice," protested Lochrie.

"Now that is just silly. What is ever just our choice? We act out of necessity – out of a response to certain needs. You had been trained to discipline and you needed discipline to keep yourself together. Subconsciously you knew that. And look at you now you don't have any structure in your life. Are you happy?"

"Happy, what is that?"

"Happy. You know what happy is: it is getting what you want, and what you want is discipline, which you are incapable of generating within yourself. So you go off in search of political justifications for your failings."

"Please. Don't make me laugh," Lochrie laughs.

"Seriously, the harder you fight against something, the more you turn into it. That's what happened with your revolutions. An eye for an eye, and no one remembers whose eye was first. And to make a nation, you need the existing human material, and who made the existing human material? The *ancien régime* of course. That is why your revolutions will never work – can never work. It is much better – much more enlightened – to simply follow your own selfish interests and see what happens. Enjoy the chase, and forget everything else!"

"I am not Middleton's mirror image. That is absurd. My life has been about absenting myself from power."

"Hah! The self-delusion of the liberal – particularly the failed liberal. You hate power because you were never good at it. And therefore dream of getting rid of it," Cary shouts triumphantly.

"No. There is one thing worse than power: the complete absence of power called anarchy. That is what they have had in Iraq over the last few years: an absence of the state. And an absolute dictator, however evil, is better than that. But that surely is not going to be our yardstick. The state is necessary, so how do we tame the state? Not by diminishing its benign functions, privatising everything and handing over sovereign rule to corporations, but by hemming it in with legislations, constitutional checks and an educational system that encourages freedom of thought."

"Well, well, well, you have got it bad! But there is some truth in what you say," Cary admits. "The bit about anarchy, not the rest. The individual always has to strike out for himself, and change of regime merely means a change of rules. In the end, it is all about power, and without it you can never do what you want."

"True, but nor can you when you have it. You are still a puppet of those rules."

"You don't understand. The fun is in getting your own way, even if you don't really care that much what your own way is," Cary smiles as he explains. "Once you have made up your mind, you must, if you have any balls, follow through and do everything that logic demands in order to get that way of yours. You'll probably say with your usual miserabilist obsession with the 'bigger picture' that someone who gets their own way has probably not guessed the outcomes correctly and what seems important in one moment proves to be rather insignificant in another, particularly after it has been successfully obtained. So what? You focus on another aim and carry on. People are not in power primarily to obtain ends but for the pleasure of exercising power itself. That is what I want you to give me: a chance to seek power. I really don't mind if you kill me off in a car crash. No one lives forever, and no one holds power forever. Power's the thing, and obtaining power by building each little success on the previous one. You just don't get it, do you? No wonder you've been unable to write this book."

"Cary, what do you take me for, you foulmouthed fucking bastard! With your blasphemous cult of power!

You take me for a sucker. I'm telling you that you simply will not do, because no one is quite so self-aware as you. You're just too damn honest for your own good."

"What do I take you for, Lochrie? I take you for a weak fool and a pathetic liberal, which are the same thing. You remember that character in a Trifonov novel you read recently – the one who looked at a soldier in the war against the Whites and said, 'that man is one quarter Bolshevik, one half Socialist-Revolutionary, and one quarter Tolstoyan romantic.' Well, I would describe you as 'ten per cent communist, twenty-five per cent romantic socialist, fifteen per cent peacenik hippy from the sixties, forty per cent pathetic liberal and ten per cent crabbit old fool.'"

"I have no problem with that, although I might toy with the percentages."

"Which says it all."

Cary is right: all states do the same things, only they do them differently and wrap them up in different terminology that often suggests the opposite of what it really is. A state does not become socialist by calling itself socialist; its emphasis on socialist rhetoric may mean that it wishes to jettison elements of its socialism. Now there is much talk of freedom and democracy, but civil liberties are being torn up in the name of the "war against terrorism", and bizarre and often unreported reforms to electoral laws are changing the nature of our already flawed democracies. Then there is the rule of law. Lochrie remembers the day two policemen propelled themselves into his home in the late seventies. His wife told him the story when he returned from work. They pushed her aside without showing her their identification and simply announced that they were Special Branch. After finding the kitchen empty, one stopped to question his wife, and the other went off to inspect the rest of the flat. Almost immediately he reappeared slightly flustered. "Out of here," he said, "there's a baby asleep in the back room." His wife reported that one almost apologised as they rushed out, and from the exchange between the two she inferred that they were unhappy with those who had sent them off on a false errand. But isn't that the problem: intelligence is so rarely intelligent. Without barging into the house, a cursory investigation would have shown that Lochrie could not have been a member of the IRA, the Angry Brigade or the Baader-Meinhof Group. Instead he was at that time a shop-steward with communist leanings who worked as a labourer for a miserable sum that hardly fed his family and could not paper the crumbling plaster walls. But what if they had not found this slightly tattered domestic bliss? How would they have acted then? Very differently, it is quite clear, as their initially forceful behaviour showed that they thought they were going to be tangling with a potentially difficult situation. Had they found Lochrie at home while his wife and child were at the supermarket, things could have taken a very different course.

All states have their fears and suspicions. Did the KGB agents who went to arrest innocents in the night do this out of sheer badness, or did they honestly believe that they were defending their socialist homeland? The latter must often have been the case, although cynicism would have crept in with the passing years. All states do indeed have their fears and suspicions, but they dismiss those of other states as paranoia, a convenient modern word that turns an understandable phenomenon into a clinical condition. The state's overreaction often exacerbates terrorism, and terrorism make states more repressive. This has been so since People's Will, a tiny clandestine organisation with about sixty members and no more than three hundred fellow-travellers, murdered a Tsar. From then on, states with a repressive vocation and no justification for it have seen fit to provide the terrorist acts themselves – to create disorder so that they can re-establish order in ways more congenial to those in power. In this environment of fears and counter-fears that obscure the issues, Lochrie feels that only non-violent actions that are entirely transparent can bring about positive changes. Their aim should be not to take power, but to curb it.

"But we must act as optimists," Lochrie says aloud.

"As optimists?" Cary objects, "that's insane. Optimism is not just a repudiation of the intellect; it is a dereliction of duty – our duty to live our lives intelligently in the real world, which frankly leaves little room for anything as asinine as optimism."

"I did not say we should think as optimists. You know my views on this. We must act as optimists because, if we cannot believe in our future, then our future is lost forever."

"So? Let the future look after itself; the present is much more fun. We need to experience life, and to experience life, you have to live in the present. You cannot feel anything in the future; you can look forward to a pleasure but you can't actually experience it. Even that pleasant feeling of anticipation is actually experienced in the now, not at the time when the future pleasure is or is not experienced. Life is to be lived, and the winner takes all. Everything else is just froth."

"You, my friend," says Lochrie cruelly, "are not going to experience anything – not even in the imaginative world of my mind. You are finished."

"Don't rub it in," says Cary in a voice full of mock hurt, "but you won't find me weeping into my whisky. To hell with it, go ahead and write whatever shit you want. They've written enough about lovers who go clink when they meet and then quarrel over whose self-obsession is more meritorious. They've written enough about quirky police-men and heaps of bodies murdered by the least important characters. They've written enough about which dull politician quarrelled with another and slept with a third, and where they left the contraceptive equipment. Write your leftie stuff. No one cares any more but it's another taste. Everyone wants this year's flavour – and yours might be it! Old-Labour humbugs have suddenly been found to be good for our cholesterol levels – that would sell it."

"You're a child of your times, Cary. What I like about this age is that it doesn't believe in anything too much and what I hate about it is that it believes in nothing with such a passion."

"And I sure do believe in nothing. I'm your man, I tell you. I am your foil – your cunning weasel who steals off with your egalitarian values like the bandit who kidnaps the virgin. Let's be honest though, nobody'll read your shite. Take me on and it'll give me a new lease of life. We could have fun together."

"You're finished, Cary. You simply won't do. A story postponed is a story that will never be completed, and a character who hangs around too long is just an irritation."

The new generation of writers and intellectuals, comfortably looking down from the lofty heights of their own urbane moral superiority, cannot understand why anyone in another generation would have wanted to be a communist. This is in part because, being so inured to the miseries of this world, they find it difficult to understand why anyone should care so much that they would reach out for radical solutions to impose justice, and in part because hyper-capitalism's wear and tear of the planet's fragile fabric makes it look futile to make any attempt to reverse and even halt the machinery of greed. The first reason merely shows the provincialism of the Western enclave of affluence, but the second is terrifyingly unanswerable. Humanity may have passed the "tipping-point" that tips the entire species into oblivion. If you believe this, then a broken humanity is as incapable of avoiding self-destruction through over-consumption as poor broken Lochrie is incapable in the very short term of preventing his internal organs from rotting through over-consumption of alcohol.

The copy of *The Old Middletonian* that Lochrie has received is clearly a message. One day Lochrie might write a short story rather than a novel to narrate the meagre and squalid realities behind the photo that comes from the past. And in the meantime, Chris Cary quietly dies as Lochrie's drunken sleep rearranges the information his brain has gathered during another solitary and formless day.

AFTERWORD

Author's Afterword

"Non ha l'ottimo artista alcun concetto
c'un marmo solo in sé non circonscriva"
Michelangelo, *Rime*, 151

In my first short story, which is in fact part story and part introduction to this collection, the Narrative Voice asserts, "Society moves an inch and they [intellectuals] think it has moved a mile. To my mind, there was only ever a trickle of compassion, and if it's changed, it hasn't changed that much." This caution has to be justified, because it is so difficult to assess something as elusive as compassion, which is by its very nature hidden. What we do have are words, which are still pretty opaque, because the motivation behind words is often mediated by self-interest, although our experience of their tone and content can give us some guidance in interpreting them.

Next to compassion and not unrelated to it, I develop the theme of passivity, which is represented by the obsessive metaphor of the leaf blown by the wind (I have always been influenced by Borgese in this, whose masterpiece, *Rubé*, establishes a compelling link between water and death). Passivity is not an absolute (little is) and in "No Such Thing as a Free Lunch", that inability to react has fatal consequences, but the "activism" of Western thought is an irrational intensification of rationalism that exaggerates our ability to make things happen.

The idea that something in our lifestyle is already damaging our psyche has become a recurring theme in recent years, and this possibility was foretold long ago in such works as Yevgeny Zamyatin's *We* or perhaps even in sixteenth-century utopias starting with Thomas More's original one. However, the inspiration for "The Difficulty Snails Encounter in Mating" came from a radio interview with a former curator of Roslyn Chapel who complained about the increasing numbers of visitors there, following the publishing success of *The Da Vinci Code*. He was

245

concerned about their footsteps, their breath and, most particularly, their touch. The poor builders of the chapel could never have imagined the fragility of their workmanship or the corrosive power of the human body. Here are the wondrous banality and heroic absurdity of the dreams, fears and fixations that fill our lives. Here is the modern obsession with conserving everything, which is perhaps a reaction against the speed with which our human environment changes. Some Bolsheviks spoke of "permanent revolution" – a doubtful concept, but modern capitalism is the economic form that brings constant disruption and change which undermines our human achievements. Too little change stultifies; too much leaves no room for the solid human relationships that make life bearable and are much more important than affluence.

Just as this book is going to press, events are drawing our attention to the quality of words used in political discourse. First there is the explicit case of the attempted assassination of Congresswoman Gabrielle Giffords, which focuses our attention on the aggressive and puerile level of political debate in America, but we should not delude ourselves that ours is that much better. Second there is the more complex and equally disturbing case of the secret policeman Mark Kennedy, an *agent provocateur* who was affecting the way in which legitimate debate was being developed in our society, presumably with the aim of making protesters appear dangerous and erratic, and thus making their repression more palatable to the public. Of course, secret policemen have always existed and their noxious behaviour produces similar results under very different regimes. The ex-Stasi officer in "No Such Thing as a Free Lunch" typifies the psychopathic detachment that necessarily lacks all compassion. The secret policeman undercover is somewhat different – more loquacious, more extrovert and perhaps even more devious: he becomes a caricature of the people he is trying to destroy but never fully understands because his mindset is so different from that of his prey. And yet, quite absurdly, he does become a mirror image of his quarry, rather like the daemon in "Escaping the Self", a story primarily inspired by the idea that only by getting away from the tyranny of our own needs and desires can we obtain a few crumbs of happiness – an idea as ancient as writing itself.

The degradation of political discourse is not as new as some people think. In the past, the demonisation of the left or of minorities has often been crude and has incited violence, but what is unusual in America is that it characterises discourse between two mainstream parties whose political policies are not very different. The congress-woman became the tragic victim of a gun culture she on the whole supports, although her comments on political discourse were to prove distressingly prophetic. It is that mix of vicious quarrelling over an increasingly limited political spectrum and the ready availability of firearms that makes the United States such a tinderbox, but the infantilisation of political debate is also a problem here.

It appears (we can say no more than that) that our language is becoming less nuanced, less varied and less respectful of others. Manners – once considered an insincere and artificial barrier to discourse, which to some extent they were – have now been partly replaced by an etiquette of unmannerliness or a cult of the brusque, epitomised by the television programme *The Apprentice*. Many believe that the demise of literary culture is not a matter for concern and has played no part in this, because they do not understand what its function has been over the last five hundred years since printing was invented. We are the stories we tell ourselves, and we are also the way we tell our stories. Even those who in another age would never have read a literary novel or opened a collection of poetry would have been affected by the literature of the day.

247

Allan Cameron

Literature puts ideas out into society where they circulate in different forms. Tolstoy, not only a great writer but also a most "political" one, affected people far beyond his readership and also those amongst his readers who found him and his lifestyle vaguely ridiculous. Much less exalted figures also instruct far beyond their time and their place. Two highly political examples amongst the many from the immediate post-war period are Hans Fallada's masterly examination of the morality of subversion and the relationship between the individual and an oppressive political ideology, *Alone in Berlin* (in a brilliant translation only available to the Anglophone reader since 2009) and Gwyn Thomas's recently republished *The Dark Philosophers*, in which the brutality of his highly political writing sometimes shocks and its stylistic cleverness surprises. And literature brings to political debate the ability to increase the diversity of opinions rather than reduce them, because each literary work is interpreted by the reader in the light of what the reader has thought and read in the past. The reader of fiction has more control than the reader of non-fiction. The novel in particular is or should be an exercise in empathy, albeit for non-existent people. It is an exercise in "escaping the self" and ultimately changes people's behaviour. It can increase compassion. It can also increase vocabulary and exercise the mind in more nuanced language. Could it also lead to a more mannerly approach to conversation and even political discourse?

Alongside the growth of the cult of unmannerliness, there is the related growth of the cult of success. The last story in this collection should be dedicated to Victor Serge, a man whose failure should be his greatest boast, because there are times when no decent man can succeed. His courage and his stamina had no limits, and his isolation was almost total. When French intellectuals finally secured his release from Stalin's gulag, the Soviet authorities destroyed three of his manuscripts. Few writers could survive and keep writing in the conditions he suffered not only in Russia but previously in France where he had been arrested by a slightly apologetic policeman for publishing an anarchist newspaper. His years in prison there are described in *Men in Prison*. Only in very recent times has an English version of his *Unforgiving Years* been published, some sixty-one years after he wrote it shortly before his death in 1947 (by New York Review Books, which is possibly the most effective organisation in maintaining the range of contemporary literary novels available to the reader of English). It stands alongside *The Case of Comrade Tulayev*, a masterpiece and a monument to a man who shames us with his steadfast loyalty to the idea of humanity.

"The reactionaries," Victor Serge wrote, "have an obvious interest in confusing Stalinist totalitarianism – exterminator of the Bolsheviks – with Bolshevism itself; their aim is to strike at the working class, at Socialism, at Marxism, and even at Liberalism. ... I have found that the writer cannot even exist in our decomposing modern societies without accommodating himself to interests that forcibly limit his horizons and mutilate his sincerity." Those words seem very relevant once more, and we should remember that, long before other dissidents, he denounced not only Stalin's crimes but also those committed earlier in the Soviet Union. He was not listened to, because he held firm to his belief in socialism.

I started this afterword with the first two lines of Michelangelo's famous sonnet: "The best artist cannot come up with any idea that is not already encompassed in a block of marble." As I reread these short stories before publication, my principal emotion was one of disappoint-ment at their inability to live up to the original idea. I had not been able to chisel out of the English language what I thought was the full glory of my original concept. The reasons for this failure probably lie in that original concept itself and in my limitations as a writer. It also reminds me of an episode in the very short story, "This", which is entirely written in an iambic/ trochaic metre. It was an unplanned story, and actually started as an introduction to "Outlook", the only story not written for this collection. Its style and rhythm were entirely different from the earlier piece and it took off in its own direction. When it came to the creative aspect of life, I was guided by a television programme on Peter Howson in which the artist attacks his own painting with a brush loaded with black paint. My similar attitude to these stories now is one of wishing they more faithfully portrayed the complexity of some thoughts I sometimes fail to control. I lack, however, that brilliant artist's boldness and lack of vanity. I cannot say that I would like to these stories to be destroyed. I want them published, and I am vain enough to want them flattered, while being only too aware of their shortcomings.

In his *Hold Everything Dear*, John Berger discusses despair as opposed to mere misery, from which it is distinguished by a sense of betrayal, as in the case of the poverty suffered during the Civil War that followed the Russian Revolution. He mentions Platanov's use of the term *dushevny bednyak*, "which means literally 'poor souls'. It referred to those from whom everything had been taken so that the emptiness within them was immense and in that immensity only their soul was left – that's to say their ability to feel and suffer" (pp. 94-95). In Scotland we also have a frequent but less profound and calamitous use of the expression "poor soul" as well as the very slightly condemnatory "poor soul, really". Whatever connotations, good or bad, may be contained in this expression, it ultimately emphasises that the person referred to is a sentient and deserving entity, and perhaps something more, depending on your religious beliefs or lack of them. It has at least a modicum of compassion, the essential attribute we may be losing; some might say that it is what makes a soul a soul. Then we have another word, its American "synonym", which has achieved success in southern England and will, no doubt, colonise all of our island (in my brain I hear the word with an Estuary accent and not an American one). The word is "loser". It is shorter but carries even more baggage (the amorality of dismissiveness and its implications is heavier, I think, than the subtlety of *dushevny bednyak* or "poor soul"). Not only is it entirely bereft of compassion and indeed denies the existence of such a useless commodity; it also condemns the subject outright for his or her inability to engage in the fierce and supposedly wonderful struggle for riches, fame and a home in a gated community.

Words are made of infinite shades that bring their own intense pleasures, but they have no worth in the age of the market and numbers. Indeed, they are subversive and must be destroyed. Our age of supposed freedom and democracy has found a more effective way of destroying words than the Ministry of Truth in Orwell's *1984*.

Have you seen him shuffle by? His whitened flesh and sickly eye?
He brought it on himself. Old man he is, and old before his time;
for who could credit what he did? He did so little but what he did
was stubborn foolish, a folly fixed upon a whim, a childish thing.
He said all men are equal, when it was still the modish way
to play with all these grand ideas that no one really holds for true
within their soul, within the inner order of their ordered minds.
He did, and then continued to believe when all around had meekly
admitted to the error of their ways, and their fond youth
was little more than youthful go and get up to another place,
more comfortable to our increasing needs. And yet he fell apart,
and headstrong held to that one truth, while falling and parting
for his way, his lonely way of wanting justice for the damned.

"The Loser", *Presbyopia*

Allan Cameron, Isle of Lewis, January 2011

Allan Cameron's *In Praise of the Garrulous*

About the book

This first work of non-fiction by the author of *The Golden Menagerie* and *The Berlusconi Bonus*, has an accessible and conversational tone, which perhaps disguises its ambition. The writer examines the history of language and how it has been affected by technology, primarily writing and printing. This leads to some important questions concerning the "ecology" of language, and how any degradation it suffers might affect "not only our competence in organising ourselves socially and politically, but also our inner selves."

Comments

"A deeply reflective, extraordinarily wide-ranging meditation on the nature of language, infused in its every phrase by a passionate humanism" – Terry Eagleton

"This is a brilliant tour de force, in space and in time, into the origins of language, speech and the word. From the past to the present you are left with strong doubts about the idea of Progress and the superiority as a modern, indeed at times post-modern, society over the previous generations. Such a journey into the world of the word needs an articulate and eloquent guide: Allan Cameron is both and much more than that." – Ilan Pappé

I like *In Praise of the Garrulous* very much indeed, not only because it says a good many interesting and true things, but because of its *tone* and style. Its combination of personal passion, observation, stories, poetic bits and serious expert argument, expressed as it is in the prose of an intelligent conversation: all this is ideal for holding and persuading intelligent but non-expert readers. In my opinion he has done nothing better." – Eric Hobsbawm.

Price: £8.00   ISBN: 978-0-9560560-0-9   pp. 184

www.vagabondvoices.co.uk

Allan Cameron's **Presbyopia**

About the book

Cameron's collection of bilingual poetry is introduced by an essay on the distinction between myopic and presbyopic poetry: the former focuses on the self, its emotions and its immediate vicinity, while the latter focuses on what is distant in space and time. Poetic myopia is not as negative as the name might imply, nor presbyopia the only desirable form of poetry, but now that two centuries have passed since Wordsworth, whom Heaney has described as the "an indispensable figure in the evolution of modern writing, a finder and keeper of the self-as-subject", the time has perhaps come to put aside our prejudices against the presbyopic. In reality, all poetry reflects a mixture of the two, and Cameron's poetry is no exception. He writes on politics and philosophy, but always with the passion that comes from a humanist sensitivity.

Comment

"Cameron confesses to a weariness with poetry's old forms and old concerns, particularly the perennial Romantic subjects of love and exploration of the self. As a corrective he steers clear of personal topics, turning his presbyopic gaze outward in a sequence of poems that takes in eco-vandalism, press barons, George W. Bush and death. One admires this determination to reject ... pretension and obscurantism ..." *The Sunday Herald*

Price: £10.00   ISBN: 978-0-9560560-3-0   pp. 112

Five Vagabond Five Vagabond Five Vagabond Five

www.vagabondvoices.co.uk

Allan Massie's *Klaus and Other Stories*

About the book

Allan Massie, the prolific novelist and non-fiction writer, is here revealed as a consummate master of the short story. This should not surprise, given his dense and highly effective style. Some of the short stories come from his early career, and some are the product of a recent return to the genre.

Klaus, the novella that opens and, to some extent, dominates this collection, tells the story of Klaus Mann, son of Thomas, and in spite of the long shadow of so famous a father, an important novelist and political activist in his own right. His struggle against Nazism gave him a focus, but its demise and what he perceived as Germany's inability to change led to depression and an early death.

Massie succeeds in evoking that period of courage and hypocrisy, intellectual fidelity and clever changeability, sacrifice and impunity, personified by the tragic Klaus and the mercurial and indestructible Gustaf Gründgens, his former brother-in-law and ex-lover. Between these two lie not only those broken relationships but also a novel – Klaus's novel Mephisto, a thinly disguised attack on Gründgens that for many years could not be published in West Germany. Massie's subtle prose merely suggests some intriguing aspects of this network of relationships and the self-destructive nature of literary inspiration.

Comments

"Allan Massie is a master storyteller, with a particular gift for evoking the vanishing world of the European man of letters. His poignant novella about Klaus Mann bears comparison with his subject's best work." Daniel Johnson, editor of Standpoint

"The tale of Klaus Mann's final days is, however, tremendously interesting, a warning and an example. Aspiring authors should read it. They'd do worse than study Massie's craftsmanship." – Colin Waters, *Scottish Review of Books*

Price: £10.00   ISBN: 978-0-9560560-6-1   pp. 208

www.vagabondvoices.co.uk

Allan Cameron's *Berlusconi Bonus*

About the book

"Allan Cameron's intriguing novel is set in a near future where the predictions of the US theorist Francis Fukuyama have been taken to their logial conclusions. Fukuyama declared that, with the collapse of the USSR and the hegemony of neoliberal capitalism, history has come to an end. In Cameron's book, history has indeed been halted by decree and the citizens live in a permanent present of spurious consumer choice and endless material consumption, their bovine lives ruled by the embedding of Rational Consumer Implant Cards in their brains. A cardless underclass exists in the Fukuyama Theme Parks, vast squallid concentration camps on the outskirts of cities. At the pinnacle of this society sit those lucky individuals who, because of their dedicated pursuit of stupendous wealth, are awarded the Plutocratic Social Gratitude Award, popularly nicknamed the Berlusconi Bonus as it effectively puts the recipient beyond the law.

"The book take the form of a confession by Adolphus Hibbert, a recent recipient of the Berlusconi Bonus, who is recruited by the sinister police officer Captain Younce to spy on dissident elements. Adolphus embarks on a dizzying journey among the clandestine opposition, in which he finds love, betrayal and violence; discovering terrifying truths about himself and his society." – *New Internationalist*

Comments

"… a profound, intelligent novel that asks serious, adult questions about what it means to be alive." – *The Herald*

"The *Berlusconi Bonus* is an adroit and satisfying satire on the iniquities of present-day life from insane consumerism to political mendacity, globalisation to the War on Terror. It is both very funny and an extremely astute analysis of the evil results of a philosophy that which sings the victory song of extreme free-market economics." – *New Internationalist*

"It makes you think." – *The New Humanist*

Price: £10.00   ISBN: 978-0-9560560-9-2   pp. 208

www.vagabondvoices.co.uk

Renzo Llorente's **Beyond the Pale**

About the book

Whence the condemnation of loitering? Why this aversion to what is, after all, the definitive metaphor for "the human condition"? To loiter: to remain in an area for no obvious reason (Merriam-Webster)

And this is a book for loitering and loiterers. You can ramble through, or simply dip in at will. It says something about our times that the aphorism has almost but not quite disappeared from contemporary English literature, and the reason must, at least in part, be our attitude to time:

It may seem remarkable that those who have the least time – old people, the elderly – have the most patience, but this is no doubt the true hallmark of their wisdom. Having grasped that it makes no difference in the long run whether they do one thing or another, they are indifferent to the delays that prove such a torment for the rest of us.

Renzo Llorente's aphorisms challenge the accepted faith in the free market without adopting another form of blind dogmatism:

We demand cheaper goods, knowing full well that lower wages are usually the key to lower prices; members of oppressed groups compete against one another for opportunities and benefits (...and by demanding cheaper goods); radical groups find themselves obliged to use violence in order to combat injustice and oppression: in capitalist society, moral entrapment is the order of the day.

He challenges our religious conceits in a similar manner:

Theology is the pious form of sophistry.

Like many writers of aphorisms, Llorente does not provide absolutes but encourages readers to think for themselves:

It is little wonder that people are happy to grant that so-and-so – usually a writer, thinker, political activist or the like – is the "conscience of our time": it relieves them of the responsibility of having a conscience of their own.

Price: £8.00   ISBN: 978-0-9560560-8-5   pp. 112